Also by
Sandhya Menon

When Dimple Met Rishi

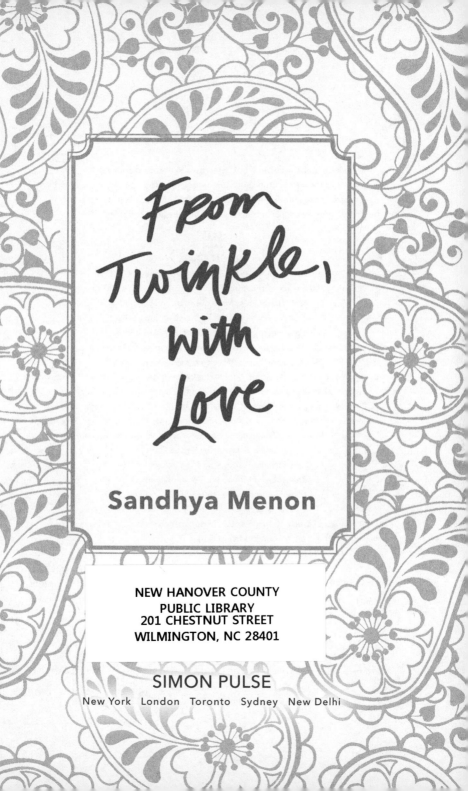

From Twinkle, with Love

Sandhya Menon

SIMON PULSE

New York London Toronto Sydney New Delhi

SIMON PULSE

An imprint of Simon & Schuster Children's Publishing Division
1230 Avenue of the Americas, New York, New York 10020
First Simon Pulse hardcover edition May 2018
Text copyright © 2018 by Sandhya Kutty Falls
Jacket photographs copyright © 2018 by Jacob Pritchard
For information about special discounts for bulk purchases, please contact Simon & Schuster
Special Sales at 1-866-506-1949 or business@simonandschuster.com.
The Simon & Schuster Speakers Bureau can bring authors to your live event.
For more information or to book an event contact the Simon & Schuster Speakers Bureau
at 1-866-248-3049 or visit our website at www.simonspeakers.com.
Jacket designed by Regina Flath
Interior designed by Mike Rosamilia
The text of this book was set in Chaparral Pro.
Manufactured in the United States of America
2 4 6 8 10 9 7 5 3 1
Library of Congress Cataloging-in-Publication Data
Names: Menon, Sandhya, author.
Title: From Twinkle, with love / Sandhya Menon.
Description: First Simon Pulse hardcover edition. | New York : Simon Pulse, 2018. |
Summary: Told through letters, aspiring filmmaker and wallflower Twinkle Mehra learns
a lesson about love while directing a movie for the Midsummer Night arts festival,
in which her longtime crush and his twin brother are also participating.
Identifiers: LCCN 2017048138 |
ISBN 9781481495400 (hc) | ISBN 9781481495424 (eBook)
Subjects: | CYAC: Producers and directors—Fiction. | Dating (Social customs)—Fiction. |
Brothers—Fiction. | Twins—Fiction. | East Indian Americans—Fiction. | Letters.
Classification: LCC PZ7.1.M473 Fro 2018 | DDC [Fic]—dc23
LC record available at https://lccn.loc.gov/2017048138

For t, n, and m.
Who else?

One

Homeroom

Hello, *namaste*, *buenos dias*, and *bonjour*, Mira Nair!

The basics.

Name: Twinkle Mehra

Age: Sixteen

Occupation: Sadly, a junior at Pikes Peak Charter in Colorado Springs. And ugh, the only one who's still sixteen. Mummy and Papa obviously thought they'd birthed a prodigy when they stuck me in kindergarten a whole year early . . . ha. But that doesn't matter. If you learn only one thing about me, it's that I think I have a filmmaker's soul. Like you, Mira. There are so many universes I want to explore with my camera.

BFF: Maddie Tanaka. Well, used to be, anyway. Now it's . . . complicated.

Crush: Duh. Neil Roy. Since *forever*.

So, now that we're acquainted, can I just say that I'm a huuuuge fan? Like, the biggest. I mean, okay, I'm not deluded. I know you're never going to read this in a million years. But somehow, writing to you in here feels like you're listening.

This diary was a birthday present from Dadi, by the way. She was all, "Take this, Twinkle. Put the words of your heart in the pages as you put the images of your heart in your movies." As far as grandmothers go, she's pretty cool (and pretty kooky, but that's a story for another day). Anyway, it sat in my desk drawer for about nine months, but then I thought, *Why not? What's it going to hurt to try to journal?* I thought writing to my fave female filmmakers would be way more fun than writing to myself. Or to one of Dadi's "soul bearers from beyond the veil." (Too long of a story to go into right now.)

Some might call people like me losers. I myself prefer the term "groundlings." See, in Shakespearean times, these were the poor people who would have to stand in the front of the stage and got called out (unfairly, IMO) for being rowdy and smelly and having the mange or whatnot. And then there were the snooty people in the back, who got to sit in, like, covered areas and look down at the groundlings and feel all superior in their silk feathered hats. But Shakespeare would never have gotten famous if he hadn't appealed to the groundlings.

Here's a little secret, though: I wouldn't *completely* mind if I were something other than a groundling. It's not like I'm silk feathered hat material or anything, but still. To be even one social status level above the one I am right now would change my life because I'm pretty sure it would give me my best friend—who is now definitely one of the silk feathered hats—back. And bonus: It would help transform me from Invisible Twinkle to someone people recognize, maybe even someone who tells stories others want to hear.

So now I'm sitting here in homeroom and Hannah Macintosh just took off her six-hundred-dollar shoes (I know because she told the entire class that's how much they cost in Milan) to show Victoria Lyons her pedicure. If I were a teeny bit braver, I'd go over there and ask, "Hey, Hannah, did you steal those shoes? I only ask because it seems you like taking things that don't belong to you, like my best friend." Maybe I'll ask Dadi if she knows any incantations that'll grow me a courage gland.

Oops, there's the bell. More soon.

Love,

Twinkle

Still Monday, June 1
AP Bio

Hey-o, Sofia Coppola.

I'm sitting here trying not to expire of *totalicus boredumus* while Mrs. Mears explains the life cycle of the royal walnut moth, aka *Citheronia regalis*, aka kill me now. And you wanna know what Maddie's doing?

Drawing a six-color diagram of said life cycle. With gel pens. I guess she doesn't make mistakes? Even Mrs. Mears, the *biologist*, didn't draw us a diagram. But Maddie probably wants to be thorough. Oh, and she's written her name at the top of the page with her new markers (she gets new stationery and school supplies as often as regular people get new . . . Um, actually, I don't know where I was going with that. She just gets them a *lot*), along with the date, and underlined everything three times.

Maddie wants to be a physician-scientist. Yeah, that's really a thing. Being a plain old doctor or a plain old scientist isn't challenging enough, so she decided she wants to combine them. But I'm thankful. Because if I ever get a rare disease that causes my butt to break out in fluorescent hives or something totally rando like that, I know Maddie's the only one who could save me. She's sort of a genius.

It must run in the family. Her dad, James Tanaka, is a world-famous artist who regularly challenges ideas of the mundane with his mixed-media pieces and has gallery showings in the United States, Tokyo, Paris, and London (literally what it says on his website in the "about" section). Plus, Maddie's ultra-rich. She lives in one of those old neighborhoods in Broadmoor in a giant mansion.

That's one thing that hasn't changed even after Maddie gave up her groundling membership and became one of the silk feathered hat people. She's still super ambitious. I haven't been to her house in months, but I bet she still has that poster board she made of her five-year plan. It has pictures of the Johns Hopkins campus, where she wants to go to college and med school, places she wants to travel (Shanghai, Tokyo, Mumbai, Edinburgh, London), and pictures of the type of boy she wants to date (Japanese-American like her, with tattoos and not taller than 5'10"; she says she wants to meet him in the second year of medical school).

Meanwhile, I'm like, maybe I'll waitress/travel after high school? Or go to film school at USC if I can get a scholarship? Or live in my parents' house forever, decrying the death of the arts?

Maybe that's why our friendship is as doomed as the Globe Theatre. Maybe I'm not ambitious enough for Maddie. Or cool enough. Or confident enough. Or, or, or.

A lot of your films were about being on the outside looking in, Sofia. I wonder what advice you'd give me. How do I step over the threshold and join my best friend again?

Oh, crap. Mrs. Mears is giving me the *evilicus eyeicus*. I better go.

Still later on Monday, June 1
My room

Hi again, Sofia!

You'll never believe who I saw today at Perk (full name: Perk Me Up Before I Go Go, but who has the time to say all of that?) drinking coffee and lounging like the half-Indian, half-white god he is.

Neil. Freaking. Roy.

It's a travesty, but the only class we share right now is AP English. He's pretty bad at it, for someone who's definitely headed to Harvard. He once asked Ms. Langford why Hester in *The Scarlet Letter* didn't run away from her town in basically a big F U to society. He implied she was being dumb. And I was like, *Neil*. How do you not get that Hester wants to stay there and find out what the scarlet A means to *her*? She clearly wants to try to determine her own identity in an agentic manner versus accepting one that's forced upon her by a patriarchal society.

I even opened my mouth to say that. But then I closed it. Being a human belonging to the wallflower genus, I'm kinda used to swallowing my words instead of speaking them. (Dadi says it's because my *aatma* is made of gauze and feathers, whatever that means.) And anyway, this was Neil.

So when I saw him at Perk, I almost walked right into the display by the door, but I stopped myself just in time. He was sitting there, his legs splayed like he owned the place. Patrick O'Cleary and some of the other guys from the swim team were with him, too, all of them talking about the upcoming season and how Neil wouldn't be at school because he was going to some pre-Olympic training camp for the rest of the month.

I love swim season. Neil, in swim trunks. Broad male shoulders glistening with water. The smell of chlorine. Neil, in swim trunks.

Okay. Here's something I've never told anyone: My crush isn't just because of Neil's looks or his hypnotizing athleticism or the fact that he's a future physicist genius. It's because if someone like Neil Roy went out with me, the other silk feathered hat people would want to hang out with me too. Like Maddie. Maybe I'd come out of my shell, bringing my camera with me, and people would *finally* listen to the stories I have inside me. I've always felt like I was meant to be more than an invisible wallflower. This could be my ticket to an alternate life, Sofia, a way to become one of the insiders.

I walked up to the counter, overly aware that Neil was behind me now. Was my back sweaty? Was my T-shirt sticking to me? Could he see my cringesome ratty beige bra through it? Curse you, eighty-degree summer days, when I have to walk everywhere and live in a house with no AC. I casually loosened my braid so my hair could cover what my T-shirt might not. Then I tossed a strand over my shoulder and hazarded a look at his table.

Huh. He hadn't even noticed me.

I deflated a little. I was *that* overlookable? I glanced around the café at the other silk feathered hats. None of them had noticed me, either. I deflated even more, until I was about half my original size.

My gaze passed over Neil's identical twin brother, Sahil Roy, who apparently *had* noticed me and was now smiling, his face bright and happy. He sat at a table with his best friends, Skid (white, short, and wiry) and Aaron (the only black and openly gay person in our class; seriously, diversity, PPC. Look it up). They were being quieter—and geekier—than Neil's group while discussing that new alien movie, which goes without saying. They're total groundlings too. I smiled back.

"Can I *help* you?"

The thirtysomething mustachioed barista behind the counter was staring at me in a way that meant he'd probably had to ask that more than once. His name badge read STAN.

"Hi, Stan," I said. "Can I get a small iced mocha? I have this." Rummaging in my pocket, I fished out the coupon I'd gotten for winning an essay contest before winter break and handed it over.

He barely looked at it before handing it back. "It's expired."

"No, no, it's not." I pointed to the fine print, my palms getting sweaty even at this tiny amount of confrontation. "See? It says June first is the last day to claim this. And it's June first."

Stan's mustache twitched spitefully as he pointed to the *finer* fine print. "See that? It says June first at five p.m. And it is now"—he checked his wristwatch—"five twenty-four p.m."

Twenty-four minutes. He was denying me for a lousy twenty-four minutes. "Okay, Stalin," I muttered as I stuffed the coupon back into my pocket.

He leaned toward me. "What did you say?" Oh God. His mustache quivered indignantly, almost independent of his face.

"Uh . . . nothing. I said, um, thanks, Sta-an." I stretched his name into two syllables to make the lie more believable and smiled weakly.

"So, are you gonna get anything or not?" he asked, eyeing me like I was a bug he'd found swimming in his perfect coffee.

I looked at the menu and sighed. It was almost five dollars for the coffee, which was my lunch allowance for the week. If I bought it, I'd have to do without at school, and hungry Twinkle was hangry Twinkle. "No, that's okay," I said, my cheeks hot. In that instant, I was kind of glad about my invisibility powers. At least none of the silk feathered hats had heard how Twinkle Mehra couldn't even afford an iced mocha.

In my hurry to escape, I almost smacked face-first into a muscled chest. *OHMYGOD,* my brain shouted as I tipped my head back and took in those light-brown eyes, that thick lacy fringe of eyelashes. *IT'S HIM IT'S NEIL OHMYGO—oh, wait.* My brain registered more details, like the red skull on the black T-shirt. The smile that was half shy, half awkward, not at all like Neil's full-on, sear-your-retinas-with-its-strength-but-you-won't-even-notice-the-pain-because-it's-so-glorious smile.

"Oh, hey, Sahil," I said, trying to go around him. "'Scuse me."

"Wait. I could buy you that coffee?" he said, pivoting to see me. "Um, if you want?"

I stopped and looked at him, feeling that cringy-hot feeling I always get when people call attention to money. Specifically, how they have it and I don't. "That's . . . nice, but you don't have to do that."

"No, no, I want to," he said, putting his hands in his pockets and then taking them out again. "Um, heat wave."

Huh? Was that supposed to make sense? "You . . . what?"

"I . . . just meant there's a heat wave outside. You definitely need an iced coffee." Then he grinned suddenly, this thing that set all his teeth on display, and leaned back. It all had a very rehearsed vibe.

I opened my mouth to (a) tell him eighty degrees and a light breeze hardly qualified as a heat wave and (b) point out that he was edging dangerously close to the napkin holder. Sadly, I was too late delivering point (b).

Sahil sent it flying to the floor, and the napkins went *everywhere*. He stared at the mess for a minute in silence. And then we both ducked down to clean up the mess, knocking heads (of course; how else would two groundlings clean up a mess?) and groaning.

"Oh God, I'm so sorry," Sahil said as I rubbed my forehead.

"That's okay." I stuffed the remaining napkins back into the holder and then stood up to face mustachioed Stan, who was watching this unfold with unadulterated glee beaming off his annoying, dictatorial face. "Um, yeah. I'll have that iced mocha after all." I figured it was easier to just accept than risk another mini disaster. I smiled at Sahil. "Thanks."

He waved me off. "Ah, no, no worries." And then I'm pretty sure he asked me a question, which I didn't hear because it was then that *Neil Roy began to walk toward me.*

No kidding.

His eyes were locked on mine and everything.

At least, that's what I thought at first. But then he got closer and I saw he was looking at his brother, Sahil. *Just* Sahil.

"Yo, I'm heading over to Patrick's," he said. "Can you catch a ride with someone?"

"Sure," Sahil said, turning back to me.

And then Neil Roy winked at me. Winked. At me. "Hey," he said, all casually, running a hand through his soft (it looks soft anyway), thick black hair. "How's it going?"

Neil Roy asked me a freaking question. And I responded by gawking at him. What should I say? Something cool and casual and maybe even a little bit funny?

The seconds ticked by. I realized I was still standing there with this idiotic, glazed smile on my face. OH MY GOD, TWINKLE, JUST SAY SOMETHING. ANYTHING.

But by the time I'd decided to rejoinder with a perfectly acceptable, "Pretty good, and you?" his back was already to me. And those bulging calf muscles were taking him to the door.

"Uh, Twinkle?"

I blinked Sahil back into focus, trying to ignore the thudding disappointment at my own geekiness. "Yeah?"

Neil smoothly tossed a balled-up paper napkin into the trash from across the room, and then he and his friends walked outside together. *His* back wasn't sweaty. And the other guys had their heads swiveled toward him, constantly watching him, listening to what he had to say. See? *That* was the sort of guy shiny, future Twinkle Mehra should date.

" . . . business card."

Crap. I'd missed what Sahil was saying—*again*—because I was ogling his brother. Anyway, context. Come on. Look around. Look at his face. What might he have said? Oh, right. He was holding out a business card. I took it, frowning slightly.

Sahil Roy, Film Critic, it said. There was a phone number below it.

"You're into films, aren't you?" he asked, tugging at his T-shirt.

Am I into films? Ha. Ha ha ha. Only like Bill Nye is into science. "Mm-hmm," I said. "Definitely."

Sahil smiled his shy/awkward smile. "Cool. I am too. You should think about joining the film club sometime." He rubbed the top of his ear. "And that's, uh, my cell number there." He cleared his throat and then coughed violently, choking on his own spit. I patted him on the back while he stared at me, his eyes wide.

"Do you need some water?" I was starting to get worried about the color his face was turning.

He shook his head and walked back to his table, where his friend Skid, sighing, handed him his cup of water. Aaron tossed me a smile and I nodded back.

"Coffee."

I found Stan holding out my cup and I took it. "Thanks." I

walked up to Sahil's table. "Hey, uh, thanks again for the coffee. I gotta go, but it was nice seeing you guys."

Aaron and Skid held up a hand and Sahil cleared his throat. "Sure, no problem," he said, all hoarse and funny-sounding. "Take care."

I giggled. How could two brothers be so different, honestly? "You too."

I looked for Neil once I was back outside, but he was long gone. Ah, well. Our Bollywood romance would have to wait.

One day, though. One day I'll be the Alia Bhatt to his Shahid Kapoor.

Two

Tuesday, June 2

AP Economics

I was ambushed today.

Okay, so maybe "ambushed" is too strong a word. But I was definitely, in no uncertain terms, reminded of my groundling status.

I walked into the girls' bathroom with Maddie at lunch, expecting to have a quiet chat. I'm not exactly sure why we walk together anymore. We don't sit together at lunch since she left Camp Groundling. She sits with Hannah and Victoria and Francesca and all the other girls who aren't on the lunch program. I sit in the back by myself. Well, maybe I do know why we still walk together. Maybe if we spend enough time together, I'll figure out why she feels like I'm not BFF material anymore. And if I figure it out, maybe I can fix it.

Anyway, it's not so bad, sitting in the back by myself. The only slight drawback is that I'm one table over from Brij Nath and Matthew Weir, both of whom slurp cafeteria chili and gargle it in the back of their throats as a joke. It's just as horrifying (and oddly hypnotic) as it sounds.

They're also computer geniuses who like to brag that they could "hack into this pathetic excuse for a secure network" anytime to change their grades. Except they don't need to because their grades are already beyond an A. I think PPC had to invent a new grading system for them and Maddie. Oh, and there's a rumor that Brij had to leave his last (expensive private boys') school because he felt they were mismanaging their fundraiser money by putting in a third tennis court. So he hacked into their database and rerouted all the money to the Worldwide Fund for Nature. Which, naturally, earned him an expulsion.

Maddie and I pushed open the door to the girls' bathroom on the third floor, and inside, instead of it being all quiet like it usually is, I found Hannah Macintosh and Francesca Roberts leaning over the sink, putting on mascara. My heart dropped to the floor.

"Heya!" Hannah said, running over to give Maddie a big hug without even glancing at me. She smelled like ripe plums, which suited her. Seriously, what dark arts do I have to do to smell and look good in everything? "Did you know this bathroom is always empty at lunch? Apparently people are too lazy to hike up here from the cafeteria!"

"I know! It's, like, the best." Maddie laughed and walked to the third—and last—sink and pulled out her makeup bag from her backpack.

I lounged against the wall and checked my fingernails. Mainly I did this because I'm too poor for my parents to get me a phone and I didn't want to stare at them while they did their makeup.

Also, I don't wear makeup. I don't have anything against it. I just don't get it.

After a minute of Maddie, Francesca, and Hannah chattering about Hannah's upcoming seventeenth birthday party and how she wanted a diamond bracelet (a conversation to which I could contribute nothing because, hello? Just imagining my parents' faces if I asked for a diamond bracelet makes me want to burst out into maniacal laughter), Maddie caught my eye in the mirror. Recapping her mascara, she said, "Oh, hey. Twinkle saw this thing about diamonds on the History Channel." Seeing my confused face, she continued. "Remember? Weren't you telling me about that a couple weeks ago? I can't recall exactly what you said, but . . ."

Oh. I got it. Maddie was trying to give me a conversational in. I straightened, ready for the challenge. "Oh, yeah. So, conflict diamonds are a real thing. The diamond industry estimates they make up to fifteen percent of the diamond trade and children are forced to work in extremely horrifying conditions to mine them. The toll on local communities is enormous. Not to mention the environmental devastation because of soil erosion . . ."

I trailed off when I saw Francesca and Hannah staring at me blankly, like I was speaking in Elvish. Maddie was sorta wince-smiling, like, *Great. Good effort, Twinkle. A+. Now please stop talking.*

After a slight pause, Francesca smiled and said, "Cool," and then they went back to their conversation. I slumped against the wall, wishing I at least had to pee so I'd have something to do.

You know what? Scratch that. Hannah would probably just judge me on my pee splatter patterns or something.

After Hannah and Francesca hugged and air-kissed Maddie a million times (and invited her to walk with them instead, an invitation she dodged while darting nervous glances my way; YES, I HEARD THEM, MADDIE), we made our way to classes with about five minutes left.

I felt myself unwind as we walked, until my shoulders were shoulders again and not ear barricades. We rounded the corner and passed Patrick O'Cleary and Callum Truesdale (he of the Caveman Callum fame—more on that in a minute) who were saying:

> **Patrick:** Dude, Midsummer Night's on the twenty-seventh. We should definitely do that one idea we had last weekend.
>
> **Caveman Callum (CC):** Oh, you mean how each of us could chop a different fruit onstage? Showcase our strength as swim-team studs?
>
> **Patrick:** Yep. I'm gonna do a pineapple. Unpeeled.
>
> **CC:** Dude. Epic. *fist bump and grunting follow*

Okay, Callum doesn't grunt. And he isn't a caveman (not technically, anyway). But he got his nickname because one time, in third grade, Maddie and I were playing on the jungle gym at recess when Callum came over and began to taunt us. He was saying stuff like how Maddie and I weren't *real* Americans and how my parents were fresh off the boat.

And then he accidentally-on-purpose hit me with a basketball.

Maddie and I looked at each other, and in one coordinated move, we hopped off the jungle gym and walked over to Callum like we were in a music video. Maddie pinned his arms behind his back (he was pretty scrawny back then) and I kicked him in the shins until he howled. Guess what? He never bothered us again.

That was all cool. But my favorite part was when Maddie and I began to call each other sisters after that. And ever since, Callum's been Caveman Callum. (To me, anyway. Maddie stopped calling him that when she stopped being a groundling. I hold grudges a lot longer. What can I say? I'm like a cat. They can hold grudges for ten years.)

I was staring at Maddie, wondering if she was thinking about the good old days like I was, when she grabbed my elbow and speed-walked me around the corner.

We passed by Sahil Roy, also apparently on his way to class. Huh. He was taller than I remembered, in a good way. And . . . better built, too. I briefly wondered how *he* looked in swim trunks.

"Ow," I said when Maddie finally stopped rushing around like the Road Runner. "What are you *doing*?"

"Did you hear what Callum and Patrick were talking about?"

"You mean Caveman Callum?" I asked, and she rolled her eyes. "Um, what? Something about making fruit salad?" I waggled my fingers at Sahil, who was still looking at me.

And then he tripped over nothing that I could see. I looked away and pretended I hadn't noticed. We groundlings have to watch out for each other.

Maddie sighed in this overexaggerated way. She forgets sometimes that we mere mortals don't automatically assess a situation and then arrive at a conclusion at the speed of computers. "Maybe if you were less focused on calling him Caveman Callum and imagining him grunting, you'd hear the more important stuff. I'm talking about Midsummer Night being on the twenty-seventh."

Principal Harris had reminded us about the Midsummer Night festival during morning announcements too. "Oh, yeah. What about it?"

"I have this genius idea." Maddie's eyes sparkled, and that's when I knew I was in trouble. Not that she doesn't have good ideas. Just that when she relies on me for execution, things generally don't go as planned. Like when we tried to throw her dad, Mr. Tanaka, a black-tie forty-fifth birthday party two years ago. I was supposed to get a cake shaped like the Eiffel Tower, one of his favorite places in the world. Only I somehow picked up a cake meant for a bachelorette party and . . . well. Let's just say the tower inside was not of the Eiffel variety. Mr. Tanaka nearly choked on his whiskey in front of eighty-five guests while I couldn't stop staring at the cake and, in my shock, asked loudly, "Well, are we still going to eat it?" Total disaster.

I rallied my courage. "What's your idea?"

"You should make a movie for Midsummer Night!"

I stared at her. "Are you serious?" Midsummer Night was the biggest event of the year at PPC, before we got our measly one-month-long summer break.

She raised her eyebrow, like, *Duh*.

"Maddie, *no*. I can't do that. Everybody would be *watching* it and stuff."

"Um, yeah. That's basically the point? Plus, you could use it in your college apps!"

I felt a pinprick of cringy-hotness again. Like my parents could afford college. "I'm still thinking no. I mean, I've only ever made videos on YouTube before. You know how many subscribers I have on my YouTube channel, Maddie? Seven. Three are Dadi, who keeps forgetting she made an account and making more, one is you, and the rest are porn bots. That's a little different from airing a movie for the *entire* school to watch *on-screen* in an *auditorium*."

Maddie sighed so hard I felt my hair move a little. "Twinkle, what's your number one goal in life?"

"To change lives with my films and show the world what a *Desi* girl can do," I said proudly. It was sort of my mission statement. (Mission statements were Maddie's idea from three years ago. Hers is "To become the premier physician-scientist working in the realm of gender-based medicine and, specifically, takotsubo cardiomyopathy as it affects women.")

She nodded. "Okay. So, do you have any other ideas to get the world to notice you?" Maddie crossed her arms, and all her charm bracelets clinked together.

Not to be nitpicky, but she used to hate bracelets. She said they made it super annoying to type and lowered her words per minute to under one hundred and thirty. But then Hannah, Francesca, Victoria, and she went to this little boutique in Denver, and now they all wear the same matching charm bracelets.

"No," I mumbled, scuffing the floor with the toe of my Converse. How am I supposed to begin changing lives if said lives don't even know I exist?

Someone cleared their throat behind me. I turned to see Sahil Roy looking down at me from his six-foot vantage. "Hey, guys.

Sorry for eavesdropping, but, um, I might have an idea. About how to get noticed?" he said.

We both stared at him. Me because I was confused and Maddie probably because she was wondering why on earth Sahil Roy was talking to her at all.

"About a film you could make for a big audience, I mean," Sahil continued hastily when he saw our blank faces. "Instead of making one by yourself, what do you think about making one with me?" Seeing my "meh" face, he continued. "Pretty much the entire student body shows up for Midsummer Night."

My "meh" face transformed into my terrified face. "I've never directed a movie before. Not on this scale."

Sahil kept going. "I know it sounds scary. But I think I could really help as a producer and general sounding board. I get the analysis side of movies." He paused, as if deciding whether to share something before continuing. "Um, my film criticisms have been published on Film FANatic, if that helps."

Whoa. "Are you kidding?" To Maddie, I said, "Film FANatic is the biggest film website out there. They usually only publish reviews from professional critics. There are rumors that Roger Ebert got his start there." Even Maddie looked impressed.

Sahil waved his hand, looking embarrassed. "Ah, I don't know. . . . I think that might just be a rumor. But my point is, if you want exposure, if you want to make a career at this thing . . . this might be the way to do it. You direct, I produce. I'm good, Twinkle. I can help."

Despite my debilitating shyness, a spark of excitement began to fizz and pop inside me. How long had I dreamed of someone besides Dadi and xxlovebotxx watching my videos? How long had I wanted to get my stories out there, have my voice heard? "It might be cool," I said, a small smile at my lips. "A bunch of media peeps from the paper and stuff come, too. Now that I think about it, it could be huge." What if my movie made it into thousands of people's houses on local TV channels? What if they began to trickle over to my YouTube channel, to see if I had more? My heart raced. This could be it, the beginning of using my art to change the world. Of people *seeing* me.

"Yes!" Sahil grinned, seeming relieved, and held out his fist for a fist bump. Only by the time I reacted and went to bump it, he had switched to a high five and we ended up with his hand wrapped awkwardly around my fist. I could see Maddie watching us groundlings, her lips clamped together like she was trying hard not to laugh. Sahil cleared his throat and dropped his hand. "Uh . . . anyway. I have zero interest in making movies. But you . . ." He shrugged. "If you think you might wanna do this, we could talk more?"

Maddie looked from him to me and back again.

Since she wasn't weighing in, I made an executive decision. "Yes, okay," I said, nodding firmly. "Let's meet up tomorrow at lunch."

"Cool," Sahil said, smiling a slightly mischievous smile. "Maybe on the green outside the caf? I think it's supposed to be nice."

I smiled too, excitement bubbling inside me. "Sounds totally grab!"

He stared at me. And blinked.

My excitement dribbled away, my face going purple. I did *not* just say that. *Smooth, Twinkle. You're off to a great start as an aspiring director.* "Um, great. And, um, fab. I kinda . . . combined . . . Anyway. See you then."

He laughed a little and then loped off quickly, awkwardly dodging a trash can in the hallway at the last minute.

At least I wasn't alone on Planet Doofus.

I shook my head, actual goose bumps sprouting on my arms and legs as it sank in. "Oh. My. God. I might be directing a movie for Midsummer freaking Night."

Maddie's pearly pink lips had gone all pouty. "But *Sahil*?" Her expression made it clear she definitely didn't think Sahil Roy was my ticket to greatness and discovery. "I don't know if people will take him seriously. He's . . . geektastic."

I looked at her, this sinking feeling in my chest. Because to her being a geek was a bad thing now. Was that why she wasn't my friend any longer? "Geeks are smart and talented and passionate," I mumbled, not even looking at her. "I don't think that's a bad thing." *And you never used to, either*, I wanted to add. But didn't, because I am a total coward.

Maddie half shrugged. "Maybe not." She paused for a moment, thinking. "And, you know, working with Sahil might be your in to hanging out with Neil. And more." She winked lasciviously.

I wished she wouldn't broadcast my crush on Maddie FM. "Shh!" I leaped forward and put my hand on her mouth. And then immediately pulled it back. My palm was covered with her lip gloss. "Oops, sorry."

"S'okay," she said, pulling out a tube of lip gloss from the side pocket of her backpack and reapplying it. She snapped the lid on and slipped it back.

"Besides," I continued, "Neil's at that pre-Olympic swim training thingy. I heard them talking about it at Perk yesterday. He won't even be back in school until the end of the month."

"I know, but he goes home at night and on the weekends. Maybe you'll go over to Sahil's house once or twice for movie stuff and he'll be there. Voilà!"

I laughed, happy that things seemed better between us, at least for right now. "Maybe."

"Meet you at your locker after school like usual?"

"Okay."

Maddie nodded and then planted two air kisses on each of my cheeks. She smelled like her Poppy perfume, warm and sunny. Hooking a hand around each of the straps of her pink plaid backpack, she spun with a swirl of her skirt and walked off to class.

I stood there for a moment, feeling suddenly insecure. Was making this movie and showcasing it for the *entire* school a giant mistake? I mean, this was going to essentially be a message from my *soul*, on display for all the silk feathered hats to gawk at. Besides, I'd never, ever made a movie with someone else before. Making art was intimate. Was I ready to share that with a boy I barely knew?

But Maddie was goals for me when it came to following her passion. I had no doubt she was going to become the premier physician-scientist of whatchamacallit. And I wanted what she had. I wanted people to *see* me, to like me for who I was and what I had to offer. I wanted to use my talent to transform people's lives and how they saw the world. So I nodded (to myself) and walked off to class, trying for the same swagger Maddie had.

Except I wasn't wearing a skirt. And my shoelaces were untied. But, you know. Same difference.

Love,

Twinkle

Three

<Text message 2:02 p.m.>
From: Sahil
To: Skid, Aaron
I did it. She's meeting me tomorrow about the movie idea

<Text message 2:02 p.m.>
From: Skid
To: Sahil, Aaron
don't forget deodorant. i speak from experience

<Text message 2:03 p.m.>
From: Aaron
To: Sahil, Skid
Good luck man. Hope your Twinkle crush finally becomes
a real thing

<Text message 2:04 p.m.>
From: Skid

To: Sahil, Aaron

yeah then maybe you can drop the Twinkle drama. she doesn't know I exist guys! no wait! she talked to me at perk! that means we're gonna get marrieddddddddddd

<Text message 2:04 p.m.>
From: Sahil
To: Skid, Aaron
HAHA. Very funny. I can't stop laughing. Oh wait yes I can and in fact I never started at all

<Text message 2:05 p.m.>
From: Skid
To: Sahil, Aaron
srsly tho. you just gotta be honest with her bro. like look twinkle I like you baby girl. let's go out for a burger

<Text message 2:05 p.m.>
From: Aaron
To: Sahil, Skid
DO NOT DO THAT

<Text message 2:06 p.m.>
From: Sahil
To: Skid, Aaron
Skid man I'm not gonna take dating advice from you. your last gf dumped you because you laughed at her great-uncle's funeral

<Text message 2:06 p.m.>
From: Skid
To: Sahil, Aaron
dude next to me farted! it was a 6-second symphony; a one-of-a-kind auditory experience

<Text message 2:07 p.m.>
From: Sahil
To: Skid, Aaron
Sure man just keep telling yourself that. I better go before Rotten Staunton takes my phone for his collection

Tuesday, June 2
School bus

Dear Nora Ephron,

Maddie didn't meet me at my locker. I wish I could say I'm used to it and I don't feel bad, but I'm softer inside than I look on the outside. Like a slightly stale jelly bean.

So I was standing by my locker like a total loser well after the last bell had rung, in case Maddie showed up late, when Brij Nath came by. Brij is Indian too, so I've always felt a little bit of solidarity with him even though most of the time when he talks I can't understand what he's saying because he functions on a completely different level from my own. I mean, it's sweet that he thinks I can keep up with his thoughts on the approaching technological singularity and human-machine interfacing, but yeah.

Anyway, today, out of nowhere, he gave me these notes he'd taken in econ (to be more precise, they were photocopies of his notes. And they were bound together in a little folder. And they came with a cover letter, which I'm pasting below).

"I noticed you were writing in your journal and not exactly paying attention," he said, smiling a little.

"Wow," I said, taking the folder and flipping through quickly. "These are really detailed. Thanks!" I put the notes into my locker and rummaged around for my umbrella.

"Uh, no problem," Brij said to my back. "Some of that stuff is complicated and I remember you saying you hate econ." Huh. I had said that, but I was pretty sure I'd been muttering to myself during a test. "So, if you want to get together to study or if you want me to explain anything, let me know."

I turned back around with my umbrella, a little confused. "Oh, no, thanks. That's okay." Then I laughed. "I mean, the less time I spend on econ the better."

Brij laughed really quickly before getting serious again. "Right. If you want to study something else, I can help too. How's your grade in calculus?"

He wanted to know my calculus grade? What was he, Principal Harris's spy? "Um, it's, you know, fine, as far as calc grades go . . . ," I said vaguely, edging forward. "But it's getting late and I've gotta go or my *dadi* begins to troll the Missing People's hotline. Talk to you later! And thanks again!"

"Yo, Nath!" It was Matthew, Brij's friend, waving to him from the computer lab.

With one last look at me, Brij walked way.

What was that about? Was he just trying to be friendly? Nora, you always said boy/girl friendships were complicated pits of madness, and if that was an example, I was beginning to understand why.

But maybe Brij was scoping out the competition? Indian people could get pretty intense about grades, and maybe his parents were putting the pressure on. Ha. As if I were even anywhere near Brij's GPA league. He needed to spy on Maddie if he was worried about his future valedictorian status.

Thinking about Maddie made me feel pathetic and unwanted all over again. Why was I so desperate for her friendship when she obviously didn't value mine even a little? Ugh. My excitement about making a movie for Midsummer Night felt damp and wilty. If I had a cell phone, I'd angry text her right now.

Brij Nath's Economics Notes, Cover Letter

Dear Twinkle,

Economics isn't easy, but these notes are.

They're guaranteed to cut your studying time in half (I timed it). Some of these terms are pretty complicated, though, so if you have problems, just text me. Here's my number: 555-555-0128.

Sincerely,

Brij Nath

01111001 01101111 01110101 00100000

01100001 01110010 01100101 00100000

01100011 01110101 01110100 01100101

The one thing I can't figure out is his weird signature at the bottom—is that a special code? Okay, Brij, maybe you don't know this, but my IQ is not higher than 1,890 and therefore, like 99.9 percent of the population, I do not speak binary.

Tuesday, June 2
My room

Dear Ava DuVernay,

I walked up our cracked sidewalk and in the front door to find Dadi sitting there in her white cotton sari on the couch, with her hands on Oso's cheeks. Oso is our little black Pomeranian. Also, Dadi thinks he's the reincarnated form of my *dada*, my grandfather and her late husband, Chandrashekhar.

I told you, as grandmothers go, Dadi's pretty out there.

"Twinkle, *tum aa gayi*," she said in this mystical voice. Oso's beady black eyes rolled toward me, like, *Help. She's doing it again.* "Dada told me you would be arriving soon."

I kissed her on the cheek and crossed the tiny living room to the kitchen to wash my hands and grab a banana. "Right, Dadi. *Dada* told you."

When I flopped down beside her, Dadi sighed and put her arm around me. Oso, sensing her distraction, made a hasty escape. "Such a skeptic. Perhaps one day you will understand, Twinkle. Perhaps one day you will accept this gift." She cupped her bony brown hands to her chest and then held them out to me, but I gestured with my hands full of one whole banana, to show Dadi why I wasn't accepting her socially unacceptable gift of *aatma*. That's what she wanted to give me: a piece of her soul.

So we're clear, this isn't Hinduism that Dadi's practicing. When she immigrated to the United States with my parents before I was born, she enthusiastically embraced American New Age culture like a long-lost friend. She still practices her own version of spirituality, which she cobbled together from too many Deepak Chopra-esque books and TV shows. The rest of us mostly put up with it because, well, Dadi's just Dadi, and so what if we have a few dozen crystals on our windowsills and we'll probably never get the smell of sage out of the couch and we're on a first-name basis with the county firefighters because of the number of times her "scrying" experiments have gone awry? If Dadi wasn't all hippie-dippie, she wouldn't be Dadi.

"Are Mummy and Papa working?" I asked, biting off a chunk of banana.

"Yes," Dadi said. "So it's a Twinkle and Dadi night." She grinned, genuinely happy, even though we had "Twinkle and Dadi nights" all the time because my parents are workaholics. I try not to take it personally, but it's hard when your dad would rather spend his time with kids who aren't his own and your mom pretty much pretends like you don't exist because, through no fault of your own, you happened to be born in a different country than the one where she wants to be.

Fidgeting with the edge of a couch pillow, I thought about making that movie with Sahil Roy. "Dadi . . . how do you know if a decision is the right one to make? Like, what if you could opt to keep the status quo *or* you could make a scary decision and shake things up? Which one would you pick?"

"Hmmm." Dadi nodded and closed her eyes for so long, I thought she had fallen asleep. Then she snapped her eyes open and looked at me, her irises like shiny brown stones. "First you must ask, am I happy with the status quo?"

I took another bite of my banana and thought about it. "Not exactly," I said finally, thinking about how, if things didn't change, I'd never be able to share my stories with the world. And what if there was another girl coming up behind me? What if I could be her Ava DuVernay or her Mira Nair? "But . . . change is scary. What if I fail at what I'm trying to do?" What if no one likes the movie I make? I've never directed anything before. Making YouTube videos about Dadi or Maddie is totally different from managing an entire cast.

"You might fail, *munni*," Dadi said, cupping my chin. "But when you're off in college, will you wish you *hadn't* taken this chance? Or that you had?"

I stared at Dadi, easily the wisest person I knew, just thinking of how many lives I could change if my movies went mainstream. You might say, *Okay, but when has a working-class Indian-American girl with a kooky dadi and ripped jeans ever become a famous filmmaker?* And you'd be right. It's never happened. But there are people out there, people exactly like me, who *need* someone to come along and tell their stories. To explore all those different universes for them. So why can't I be the one to do it?

Maybe Dadi's not the only kooky one, eh?

That's when I knew: I *had* to take this shot. I had to go talk to Sahil Roy tomorrow and then, unless he wanted to make a movie about people hurting baby pandas, I had to do it. Just carpe the freaking diem by its hairy chest.

Somehow, I think, Ava, that you would approve.

Love,

Twinkle

June 3

The Reel Deal Blog

Posted by: Rolls ROYce

My friends, Slide and A-man (names changed to protect the not-so-innocent), are constantly on me to seize the moment. Grow a pair. Grab life by the horns.

Quit being such a chump baby, essentially.

Well, I did it. Yesterday I walked right up to . . . um, Sparkle, and told her how I felt.

Okay, that's a lie. But I asked her to work with me on something. And I think that's a big step. I mean, I've pretty much had a crush on her since girls stopped having cooties. Dudes, I'm tired of my own basicness. This project? It'll take us almost a month of working together. And even I, the supreme god of awkward, can make this happen in three and a half weeks.

Besides the whole Sparkle angle, I'm psyched to do something outside of the shadow of my superstar brother. Movies have always felt like my thing. This is one area where maybe I won't be sized up against him. Maybe Sparkle and everyone else will see me for who *I* am and for once I won't feel like this is some competition I'm losing before I've even begun playing.

Maybe?

In any case, if you guys pray or chant or speak in tongues, now would be a great time to do it.

(Okay, anyone who knows me would be able to break my code and figure out who I am instantly, but since Google Analytics tells me I had exactly 0,000 visitors this month, I think I'll be all right.)

Wednesday, June 3
Homeroom

Dear Jane Campion,

If life is a fairy tale, I'm pretty sure I've been cast as the princess. *Huh?* you might be asking yourself. *What's she blathering on about now?* Well, let me tell you, my friend.

I got to school early because I was super excited about the movie thing, but also because Dadi kept asking if she could cleanse my essence, and there is not enough caffeine in the world for *that* ritual. So I was getting a few books out of my locker in the empty hallway when someone grabbed me around the waist.

I spun around, ready to karate chop the crap out of whoever it was, and found Maddie grinning at me. "Nice reflexes," she said, nodding appreciatively.

I let my hands fall and stared at her for a long moment, waiting.

"What?"

An apology. That's all I wanted. We were supposed to meet at my locker. *You stood me up*, I wanted to say. *Do you honestly have nothing to say about that?*

I shook my head, too much of a groundling to speak up. "Nothing. What are you doing here so early?"

She held up her AP calc textbook. "I have a test, so I thought I'd get an extra hour of studying in before school starts."

"And you call *me* a nerd."

Before she could respond, we heard footsteps behind us and turned.

That's when I died.

Okay, not really, but almost. It was definitely an out-of-body experience. Because walking up to us, smiling, was Neil freaking Roy.

I don't know what I did to deserve two close encounters of the Neil kind in less than a week, but I wasn't about to question my good fortune. I gazed dumbly at him as he stopped a few lockers down from mine. "Hey, ladies," he called breezily.

I shot Maddie a panicked look. Just like before, I locked up and couldn't think of a single thing to say. She shook her head at me and said, "Oh, hey, Neil. Aren't you supposed to be at pre-Olympic training?" She looked and sounded casual, but she couldn't fool me. Her voice was higher and squeakier than normal. Even Maddie was slightly starstruck, and her social stratus was adjacent to Neil's. So what hope did I, a mere groundling, have?

He got a few books out of his locker, slammed it shut, and sauntered over to us. I stopped breathing. "I still have to keep up with my homework and tests and stuff." He made a face and ran a hand through his perfectly spiked black hair. I kept darting surreptitious glances at him while also looking straight ahead, as if I had no business gazing directly at this perfect likeness of an Indo-Greek god, high school edition.

"So," he continued, "who's your pretty friend? It's Rinkle, right?"

My eyes widening, I stared at him, full-on this time. Did he just say PRETTY?

"Um, it's *Twinkle*," Maddie said, coming to my rescue. "Twinkle Mehra." She accidentally-on-purpose jabbed me in the kidney with her fingers.

"Right," I said, thankful for the pain that broke my paralysis. "Twinkle." Oh, great. What a genius thing to say. Just repeat your name like some half-brained parrot.

Neil snapped his fingers. "Twinkle, right. Anyway, I better get going. They make us do twenty extra laps if we're late."

"Ouch," Maddie said, laughing freely. How did she *do* that? I, meanwhile, croaked out a laugh that sounded like a rhinoceros in heat.

Neil waved at us, spun on his shiny Nike-clad heel, and was gone.

"Oh my God," I whispered at his retreating back.

Maddie grinned in my peripheral vision. "Did you hear that? He called you 'pretty.'" She paused, frowning a bit. "And 'Rinkle,' which is slightly annoying."

I turned unsteadily toward her. "Um, was that whole interaction real?"

Her grin returned, wider this time. "Oh, it was real. And you know what this means?"

I shook my head silently, but inside I was thinking, *Look, it's already happening. Maddie stood me up yesterday, but one small encounter with Neil and we're bonding again. Imagine if shiny, future Twinkle was Neil's girlfriend?* I wasn't worried about that Twinkle being struck silent in his presence. Once I was her, I wouldn't be intimidated by someone like Neil. By then I'd fit seamlessly into Maddie's circle. And then it would be like this *all* the time.

"This movie you're doing with Sahil?" Maddie continued. "Like I said before, the bonus is it'll get you closer to the hotter brother. The one you've had a crush on forever?"

I felt a tug of discomfort. It wasn't about "hot" versus "not hot." It was about taking a hammer to my life and completely rehauling it. It was about breaking apart Invisible Twinkle and putting her together again, only as a shinier, impossible-to-miss version this time. "They're twins, Maddie. They look the exact same, so Neil can't possibly be the hotter brother."

She waved a hand. "You know what I mean. Come on, Twinkle. This is your chance. Neil knows who you are now, *and* he thinks you're pretty." She shrugged. "You just need a chance to get in his vicinity, which you can one hundred percent do once you and Sahil become friends doing this whole movie thing."

I felt a slow grin spreading across my face. "You're right."

This movie could be the answer to all my dreams. It could be how I *finally* shed that cloak of invisibility. God, I'm so ready.

Love,

Twinkle

Wednesday, June 3
Lunchtime, on the green

Dear Ava DuVernay,

One.

    Two.

    Three.

    Four.

    Five.

Five measly minutes and Sahil will be here. How do I know? you ask. Well, because I ran into him in the hallway and he said so. Apparently, he had to go update his blog. This might be the beginning of incredible things. The chance to show the world all the stories I have crammed inside me, just waiting to get out. Like in *Supernatural*, when those Leviathan things were in Castiel's tummy and you could see them stretching the skin and stuff. I mean, ew, but also an illustrative way to show you what I mean.

    Oh, crap, there he is. Sahil, I mean. Not Castiel (though how cool would that be?).

Wednesday, June 3
AP English

Dear Jane Campion,

Ms. Langford is showing us that movie *The Crucible*. It's super cool because Arthur Miller adapted his own play into the screenplay for this movie. (Patrick O'Cleary and Caveman Callum don't seem to care. They sit right in front of me and are doodling pictures of different kinds of boobs. They think they're being all sneaky, BUT I HAVE EYES.) Imagine if I did that one day. Not the drawing boobs thing, but the writing plays thing. I could be a playwright *and* a director. Jane, your films were about sticking it to the man, snapping back at the patriarchy by showing strong female protagonists who didn't conform to gender roles. I could be one of those protagonists. They'd call me Twinkle the Glass Ceiling Smasher, and the world would be engulfed in a veritable tsunami of movies and plays and stories by women.

That reminds me:

I'm going to be directing a real movie for Midsummer Night! Sahil and I made it official at lunch.

I was sitting on the picnic tabletop when he came up to me and, grabbing my hand to shake it enthusiastically (even though I hadn't offered it), said, "I like your T-shirt."

It was my female filmmakers shirt, with a picture of you, Ava DuVernay, Sofia Coppola, and Haifaa al-Mansour. "Oh, yeah." I looked up at him and smiled. "It's my favorite. I like yours, too."

He was wearing a vintage *Night of the Living Dead* T-shirt. When people love something so much it fuses with what they wear, I feel this instant connection to them. The melding of passion and fashion is the song of my people. Sahil pulled at the front of his shirt and turned pink. "Hey, thanks. So, um, you want to talk about the movie?"

"Sure." I patted the tabletop beside me. "Hop on up."

After the slightest pause, Sahil dropped his backpack on the ground and climbed up to sit beside me. You'd think close proximity to a boy would make me nervous, but I was way, way too excited to care. Pulling my notebook and pencil out, I scooted closer to him. "So, I'm super psyched about this. I think it could be great!" I was flinging my hands around (I like to talk with them), and the pencil flew out of my grasp and landed on Sahil's lap.

"Oops, sorry," I said, and without thinking about it, I reached over and grabbed the pencil. My hand brushed his thigh through the thin fabric of his shorts. His *upper* thigh.

We both froze.

"Um, so s-sorry," I said, jerking my hand back like I'd accidentally touched the surface of the sun. "I just, um, the wood of the pencil . . ." I trailed off, horrified. Why was I talking about wood?? "I mean, um, it was slippery and—" Aaaahhh. Now his face looked all pink and sweaty, which I'm sure complemented my purple, sweaty one. *TWINKLE. Stop talking.* "Anyway. Um, movie?" I finished, apparently no longer able to speak in complete sentences.

"Yes," Sahil agreed, sounding relieved.

I squinted up at him in the sun. You know, I'd never noticed before, but his black hair has glints of red in it. It's gorgeous. I wonder if he gets that from his mom (she's white). I wonder if Neil has that too. Anytime I'm in his vicinity, though, my senses go completely dead from shock, so I haven't noticed. "So, do you have an idea of what genre of film we should make?"

His face, which was still stupefied-looking, suddenly became animated. "YEAH! Yes. So, I was thinking we could do a remake of *Dracula*. Like, the really old, classic version from 1931?"

I stared at him, nerves back once again, internal panic building. I was supposed to be the film expert here. The only acceptable answer to that question would be, *Why, yes, Sahil, I know exactly what you're talking about.* But I totally didn't. I'm more of a documentary and modern movies kind of girl. I mean, I've watched some Alfred Hitchcock, but that's about it.

Okay, Twinkle, I told myself. *Time to fake it till you make it. You can't sink this now. Especially not after your pencil disaster.* "Oh, right, *Dracula*," I said, nodding intelligently.

"Right." Sahil returned my nod, only his was super enthusiastic. *He* was clearly pumped (as I'd been before I realized I was about to be exposed as a charlatan). *He* had clearly watched the stupid movie. "So, I have my own ideas of what scenes we should shoot, but what are your faves?"

Crap. Okay, what do all vampire movies have in common? "Um . . ." I tapped my pencil on my notebook, trying to buy time. "Well, I liked the one with the . . . ah, bat? And the, ah, castle? It was such a great castle."

Sahil studied me. The corner of his mouth twitched. "You . . . haven't seen *Dracula*, have you?"

I hung my head, feeling pathetic. What sort of film expert has never watched *Dracula*? "No, sorry," I mumbled.

Laughing, he said, "Totally okay. This gives me a chance to convert another unsuspecting human to becoming a Bela Lugosi nerd, which is my mission in life anyway. I'll bring you the DVD tomorrow."

I grinned. My (as yet nonexistent) street cred as a director didn't seem to be damaged. It was pretty cool how Sahil accepted my shortcoming without judgment. Maybe it wasn't that big a deal to anyone but me. "Wait. Did you say DVD?"

He nodded.

"Wow," I said. "That's pretty old-school."

Sahil raised an eyebrow. "It's kind of my thing."

I snorted. "Okay, but if you want to capture people's attention at Midsummer Night, you have to go all out. You can't have a plain retelling. We need to put a spin on it that no one's done before."

Sahil frowned. "So, what are you thinking?"

I gnawed on my pencil eraser. "Ooh." I sat up straighter, an idea growing. "What about this? Dracula, but gender-swapped. Like, a Dracu-lass!"

Sahil beamed. "Bella instead of Bela! I love it!"

"Excellent." I hopped off the table and began to pace in the grass, energized now. "So, we could have our Dracu-lass be a total man-charmer like Dracula was a lady-charmer. All the roles in the film could be gender-swapped." I glanced at Sahil, realizing fully how important this idea was to me. Changing lives could start right here, right now. "Are you okay with most of the cast being female? Because I think probably a movie made in 1931 had mostly male leads?"

Sahil nodded immediately. "It did. And I'm on board. It's about time someone shook up *Dracula*."

I grinned, my heart all warm and happy. It was all . . . clicking. We were on the same page about everything. Maybe making a movie with Sahil wouldn't be as hard as I thought. "Precisely what I was thinking."

"So, we're going to need to get costumes and props. Maybe we could go this weekend."

I pursed my lips, feeling that bite of tension I always felt when the people of PPC, who seemingly had limitless pockets from Narnia, talked about money. I'd love to easily say, "Sure! Let's do it!" But my family doesn't have random spending money. Every dollar I use is taken from someone's lunch or clothes allowance or Support Group for Reincarnated Individuals and Those Who Love Them fees. "Um . . . I don't know if I can afford too much. . . ."

Sahil waved a hand. "Don't even worry about it. I'm bankrolling this operation."

Was it charity? I didn't want charity. I studied Sahil's expression closely. "Um, are you sure? Because that can get expensive."

His face was pity-free. "I'm sure. I'm the producer. All I want you to worry about is making the most kick-ass movie you can make."

I smiled at him, relief making me slightly giddy. "Now, *that* I can do."

I'm trying to be calm and casual about this, but inside I keep screaming, *I'M OFFICIALLY A DIRECTOR! LOOK OUT, WORLD, HERE I COME!*

How the heck do you have so much chill, Jane?

Love,

Twinkle

Four

Honors Calculus

Dear Sofia Coppola,

I just witnessed the weirdest thing in the history of PPC.

I was waiting by my locker for Maddie (we always walk to Honors Calculus (me) and AP Chem (her) together because they're right next to each other) when Brij came up to me. "Are you ready for that econ paper?" he asked, pulling a gigantic binder from his backpack. I wasn't sure how he'd fit that in there. It was like watching one of those clown cars, where people keep coming out of this tiny space.

Oh God, I thought. *Not this weird obsession with my studies again.* "Um . . . no." I eyed the binder warily. It had color-coded little flag things sticking out the side.

"I've got all the class notes in here," Brij said, patting the binder. "Plus old tests I got Mr. Newton to give me. This is the definitive study guide you need if you've ever spent a sleepless night wondering about the theory of rational self-interest or the three factors of production."

I stood there, trying to figure out how to tell Brij that I have literally never had a sleepless night about school, period, let alone about . . . all the stuff he said, when Maddie walked up.

"Hey," she said to me, and then, seeing the binder in Brij's hand, "Ohmygod. Are those *econ notes*?"

Brij smiled smugly and opened the binder. There was a laminated index at the front. "And so much more. This is the only study guide you'll ever need."

"And you used the RealNotes five-color assorted page dividers, Tuff-Enuff limited edition," Maddie said faintly, swooning as she ran her hand over them.

"Mm-hmm. Everything's organized by topic, subtopic, and how likely it is to be on the test."

I couldn't believe it. They were *bonding*. Brij Nath and Maddie Tanaka, the most groundliest groundling and the most silky feathered hat person in the entire school. Over sticky tabs and econ notes.

I cleared my throat, and Maddie jerked her head up at me, abashed. "Oh, right. Wake up, Tanaka. Um, you ready to go to class?"

I raised an eyebrow and nodded, and Maddie reluctantly came with me.

"I can give you a copy," Brij said to our retreating backs.

I looked over my shoulder and smiled. "Um, thanks, but no, thanks. I'm good." Hadn't we been over this already?

"No, I meant her." He nodded toward Maddie.

Her eyes shone like he was offering her the key to the biorhythm lab at Johns Hopkins. "Oh, but I couldn't ask you to make a duplicate. That would take too long."

"I've already done it," he said, and his eyes flitted to me and then away superfast. "But I don't think I'll need that second copy after all."

"Wow. Thank you," Maddie breathed as he handed the binder over.

Brij nodded, looking a little embarrassed.

"Nath, you coming or what?" Matthew called from his locker. "We're going to be late."

"Yeah." He lifted a hand to us and then plodded off.

I stared at Maddie. "What?" she asked, her eyes all big and innocent. Yeah, right. She wasn't fooling me. "I just liked his notes."

"Yeah." I snorted. "His *notes*. Is that what you kids are calling it nowadays?"

Maddie jostled me with her shoulder. "Shut *up*. I'm holding out for my Japanese-American tattooed artist, remember?"

"Sure, Maddie." I grinned, enjoying teasing her way too much. It felt like the old days again, just for those few moments. "Keep telling yourself that."

I didn't even have a chance to tell her about the movie stuff. Which was fine, because she told me to *call her later*. We haven't talked on the phone in forever. Wanna know a secret? I am ridiculously excited.

Love,

Twinkle

Yep, still hump day, June 3
My room

Dear Mira Nair,

I called Maddie tonight to tell her about the movie, but she didn't answer. Actually, her cell rang twice and then went to voice mail, which means she looked at the screen, saw who it was, and then hit reject. I may not have a cell phone, but I'm not stupid.

I guess that connection I thought we had at school, where we were back to being Twinkle and Maddie, was just in my head.

I didn't leave a message.

Love,

Twinkle

Thursday, June 4
School bus

Dear Jane Campion,

I found Dadi naked on the lawn today.

At least, I *thought* she was naked. It turned out she was wearing a brown housedress the exact color of her skin, and mistakes are easy to make at six a.m. when the sun is barely a blip in the sky.

After Papa poured me a glass of warm milk to steady my nerves, I went outside to see what she was up to. (My parents declined to go, muttering tiredly, *Woh Dadi toh aisi hai, na?* Which, okay, they have a point. This *is* just the way Dadi is, but still. My curiosity got the better of me. Besides, Dadi and I always check on each other.)

She was standing in the middle of our tiny patch of grass with this giant tub of water in front of her, her praying mantis arms waving around like she was conducting the world's hardest-to-hear orchestra. Oso was at the fence, sniffing at our canine neighbor, Maggie, this little white creature that's more fur than dog. (They have an epic romance that will never be requited because neither of them have opposable thumbs and therefore will always be thwarted by the gate. Legendary.)

I walked up to Dadi, stepping around the tub of water and wrapping my arms around my waist. My pajamas were cotton, and it was chilly enough that I had immediate goose bumps. Dadi, meanwhile, looked like she may as well have been sipping a sloe gin fizz in the Bahamas. (I don't know what a sloe gin fizz is, but it sounds like something you'd drink on a beach in the Bahamas.) "What are you doing, Dadi?" I asked. "Do you want me to get you a sweater?"

"Great things are coming your way, Twinkle," she said, like that was any kind of answer to my two very sensible questions. Her eyes glinted in the dim light. I was awed for a second, goose bumps rippling down my skin. Her words sounded . . . fortuitous. Like she knew something the rest of us didn't. I was captivated, struck silent.

Until I saw the fortune cookie wrapper. She crumpled up the fortune she'd been reading and slipped it into her pocket.

I sighed. "Dadi . . ."

Dadi grabbed my arm and yanked me closer to the tub. "*Dekho*. Look. And stop making your skeptical face. Don't you see them? *Hamaare poorvaj.*"

Hamaare poorvaj. Our ancestors. I raised an eyebrow and watched my reflection doing the same. Huh. Dadi was right; my skeptical face was very skeptical. "Our ancestors are . . . floating in the water?"

Dadi sighed. "Twinkle. The water is a conductor of the heavens. I'm listening for messages."

I tried to smooth my eyebrow down and only partly succeeded. "Right. Messages." Dadi was afraid of the voice mail feature on our landline, but sure, messages coming through *water* from our *ancestors* she had no problem with.

She grabbed my face with her cold hands. Her soft, iron-gray hair undulated in waves. Dadi was very pretty, even if she was around sixty-five. I bet she was a total babe when she was my age. "The decision you were asking me about yesterday? It will change your life. *Our* lives. They have spoken."

Okay, so I knew this was all nonsense. I knew better than to put stock in what Dadi said after one of her "sessions." I was a girl with a modern education, with parents who were both thinkers and readers, and a best friend who was the next Marie Curie. But I couldn't help it. I was immediately sucked in. "Really?" I breathed. "They said that?"

Dadi nodded sagely. "Indeed they did. But you must be unafraid, Twinkle. You must live life as if you cannot get hurt."

"I will, Dadi," I said, feeling a ripple of excitement pass through me. "I will."

And I wasn't only saying that, either. I am director, hear me roar.

Love,
Twinkle

Thursday, June 4
Library

Dear Haifaa al-Mansour,

Mrs. Mears sent me and Brij to the library. You know why?

Because we're the only two people in class who haven't completely lost our sense of humanity.

Mrs. Mears and the school board are evil. They want us to dissect *fetal pigs*.

I tried telling Mrs. Mears that pigs are social, intelligent creatures. Some scientists think they're even more intelligent than dogs. I mean, there's a reason I don't eat bacon. Then Brij said, "And also? They're gross. My family is Brahmin, and therefore vegetarian."

So she told us that we could both be excused. Brij on the grounds of religious tolerance and me on account of I'm a conscientious objector. We're supposed to do a report on germ line cell mutations in fruit flies instead. To which I say, fine, school board and Mrs. Mears. You can take away my will to live, but you can never take away my conscience.

Brij keeps looking at me over his computer. He-he. Let me see if I can get a rise out of him about Maddie.

Ten minutes later, still the library . . .

Brij Nath is so into Maddie. This was how our conversation went:

Me, sitting in the empty chair next to Brij's: "Hey. How are ya?"

Him, looking at me with big eyes: "Um . . . good?"

I smiled. "So, I liked your econ binder. Maddie, too."

He continued staring at me. (Probably overcome with the mention of Maddie.)

Me: "So . . . do you organize all kinds of stuff? Or only econ notes?"

He actually gulped. Like in the cartoons. "N-no, I organize

everything. Math notes, computer science notes, bio notes. Oh, and my MTG cards."

Okay, I had no idea what MTG cards were. But I rallied. "So notes of every kind, then." He and Maddie have so much in common. "Do you have, say, special markers?"

He was still staring at me like he couldn't believe we were having this conversation. It was cute. You know, in a completely fraternal way. "I do," he said faintly.

"And how many different kinds of Post-it notes do you have?" If it was beginning to sound like an interview, that's because it was. I was hatching this genius plan while we talked. It had started out fun and games, but imagine if Maddie and Brij did go out? She'd be forced to spend more time with the groundlings. And maybe the Twinkle-Maddie unit would even make a comeback. And what if Neil and I start to go out? What if the groundlings and the silk feathered hats start mixing because of Maddie going out with Brij and me going out with Neil? The entire social structure at PPC would collapse and chaos would reign! (but in a good way). Like how much healthy chaos you caused by becoming the first female Saudi director, Haifaa. Disruption can be really good, right? I could get my best friend back. This *had* to happen. I was going to make it happen. I mean, sure, Brij was no tattooed Japanese-American artist, but love did weird things to people.

"Thirty-six kinds of Post-it notes," Brij said, still staring at me in wonder. Just wait till I told him what I had planned. I felt like a modern-day fairy godmother from *Cinderella*, only without that silly outfit. "And I have four different kinds of flags. And this." He reached into his backpack and pulled out an actual personalized memo pad with *NATH* written across the top in this cursive font.

Perfect! I was planning their first date in my head already. It would be at Staples, naturally. Maybe in the office furniture section? Lots of comfortable seating available.

I wasn't able to tell him that, though, because Ms. Langford's Honors Speech and Debate class came in. Matthew Weir came to sit by Brij, and then they were discussing what it was like to be a five-hundred-level mage in a two-hundred-level wench world. Or something. I wasn't really paying attention.

Love,

Twinkle

Thursday, June 4
My room

Dear Sofia Coppola,

Maddie and I are going to a paint-and-sip event tonight. Usually it's just old married people or working women in their thirties who go there to basically get drunk and paint pictures (why are adults so strange?), but Maddie goes to these things to unwind. She says she didn't inherit the Tanaka creativity gene (which she also says does not exist but is just a figure of speech and I shouldn't get sucked into that misconception like so many laypeople do), but that's not true. Even though we're both following a template and we get a lot of help from the instructor, Maddie's bridge at sunset (for instance) always ends up looking like a bridge at sunset and mine somehow ends up looking like a puppet with dentures or something.

She was by my locker after school this time, but she didn't apologize for ignoring my call last night. It was like déjà vu.

"Hey," she said, texting furiously while she talked.

"Hey. Oh, it's working?"

She raised her eyebrows without looking up. "Huh?"

My heart raced for a second while I debated changing the subject. Then I went for it, feeling reckless. "Your cell. I called yesterday."

She stopped texting. "Oh. Right. I'm sorry. I was at Hannah's and she was upset about this final in chemistry. . . ."

I waved her off. "Yeah. Sure. Okay."

Slipping her phone into her pocket, Maddie came up to me and put her arm around mine. "I'm sorry. But you can tell me about the movie tonight, can't you?"

I looked at her sweetly smiling face and knew I should say something more. I shouldn't just accept this weak apology. But did I mention before that I'm desperate to hold on to my old BFF/sister from another mister? I didn't know how to *not* be Maddie's friend anymore. "Sure," I said, feeling all crumpled.

Artsy Fartsy has 50 percent off their admission for Teen Thursdays and Dadi gives me the ten bucks if it's to spend some quality time with Maddie. Dadi acts like Maddie is her lost grandchild. That's why I haven't told her that Maddie and I hardly ever hang out anymore. It would devastate her. And then she'd probably want to burn a couple dozen candles and make me dance around them, and we all know that would end up with the cute firefighters storming our house again.

Anyway, I'm wearing my old Nora Ephron T-shirt (the unintentionally creepy one where her eyes have chipped off; I really should throw it out) with leggings tonight, my DIY glitter Keds, and my movie-reel earrings. I went downstairs to get a drink of water—dressing up makes me thirsty—and Mummy and Papa, both of whom were miraculously off work, were sitting at the kitchen table, reading and drinking chai, while Dadi fed Oso bits of Parle-G biscuits under the table. (Papa frowns on feeding dogs people food, so Dadi does it when he isn't looking and he pretends he doesn't know.)

So then Mummy looks up at my shirt and smiles and goes, "Oh. Princess Diana. Very nice."

I've worn this T-shirt *so* many times. How could she think it was Princess Di? When have I ever expressed an interested in British royalty, a concept with which I don't even agree on principle? I stared at her, realizing that it was because she'd never asked me, not once, who it was on my T-shirt. We don't talk about my movies or filmmaking or anything of substance. So I literally didn't even know where to start. It was this gigantic sign of how Mummy and I are like two ice floes, passing each other, cold and silent. Even when we try to make a connection, we can't get any traction. That's our relationship. It sucks, but what am I supposed to do?

Oh, and get this. Papa looked up from his book and his face broke into a grin. "You have leg pain?" he said, between guffaws.

You know, because my leggings remind him of compression bandages. Har de har.

Then Dadi looks at me and says, "Oh! Princess Diana!

Chandrashekhar says she has a very regal and respected presence on the other side."

I smiled. "That's great, Dadi." So what if she got it wrong? At least Dadi shows up. At least Dadi *tries*.

The more I think about it, the more I wonder if my mother and I are related at all. I bet I was dropped on her doorstep, like Harry Potter, and she just hasn't figured out how to tell me yet.

I walked off to my room to look for my lightning bolt scar. Because that is the *only* way any of this makes sense.

And I didn't even get my cup of water.

Love,

Twinkle

Five

Thursday, June 4

Artsy Fartsy

Dear Kathryn Bigelow,

Maddie's in the bathroom. She always drinks way too much Sprite when we come here and then spends 10 percent of the time peeing. So I'm just hanging out, sorta painting (that's the best I can do) and petting Roux, the adorable red Lab that belongs to the lady who owns this place. He keeps putting his gigantic head in my lap every time I pick up my brush and looking at me, like, *You can't resist this, Twinkle. Let's be real.*

Anyway, I've been subtly probing Maddie's interest in Brij all night by asking sly questions, such as, "Hey, wasn't that binder Brij made so cool?"

Maddie's entire face lit up. "Oh my gosh, yeah, it was! Do you think he does that for every subject or just econ?" (Do I know Maddie or do I know Maddie? I asked Brij the EXACT SAME question in the library because I knew she'd want to know.)

I played it casual. "Oh, I'm pretty sure he's a well-rounded organizer. Rumor has it he even has those Post-it flag thingies and a personalized memo pad." Maddie was practically fanning herself. They should make a Hallmark movie out of their budding love story.

So now I'm trying to figure out what the best way would be to get Brij and Maddie together. I have to be sly, though. If I try to force it, Maddie'll buck and run. Kind of like those wild horses that can never be tamed. They always end up kicking some well-meaning horse whisperer in the head and getting put down.

Hmm.

Thursday, June 4
Still at Artsy Fartsy, 2.5 Sprites later

Dear Claire Denis,

Maddie's in the bathroom again. My field of sunflowers looks like a toxic waste dump, which might turn out to be a cool statement on society's unthinking gluttonous exploitation of our planet's natural resources. Maddie's looks like Monet helped her paint it. It's so unfair. Why did she have to luck out in virtually every department?

Hold on. Roux's chewing on my journal. He is such an attention hog.

Okay, I'm back. The owner lured Roux away with a shriveled pig's ear, which is apparently a canine delicacy? Dogs seriously have no standards.

So, anyway, Maddie and I were talking and being all open and honest, and she told me how she went to get fro-yo with

Hannah, Victoria, and Francesca the other night. What sucks is Hannah's having a birthday party at Victoria's parents' cabin in Aspen in two weeks but it's on the same night that Mr. Tanaka has a gallery showing in Denver, so Maddie said she couldn't go. Hannah didn't understand and thought it was because Maddie was mad at her about sitting on her turkey sandwich that one time (it was in a sandwich bag, but still). The way Maddie tells it, Hannah pitched a little fit.

I *knew* I shouldn't say what I was thinking. Hadn't I learned my lesson at Mr. Tanaka's birthday party? But the words were out before my brain could sound the alarm. "Why do you hang out with her?"

Maddie looked surprised. "What?" Her gold eyeshadow and purple silk dress made her look like royalty. I felt a little dowdy in my clothes, tbh, which was crap because it's what's inside that matters and I'd been proud of my T-shirt and glitter Keds at my house, parental comments aside.

"You can't go because it's important that you support your dad. So why can't she understand that? Hannah sounds like a total jackass." I stopped talking all of a sudden and my eyes went wide. Papa should have replaced *my* filter when he replaced our fridge's because mine is obviously completely worn out. Speaking up about her dodging my call must've unlocked something reckless in my brain.

Maddie's cheeks turned this light pinkish color. (Unlike mine, which turn a deep shade of purple instead. Dadi calls it my *baingan*, aka "eggplant," look. I think she means it in an endearing way, though.) "I can't just *stop* hanging out with her," she said, stabbing her brush on the canvas, her charm bracelets clinking angrily together.

"Why not?" I was thinking "in for a penny, in for a pound" at that point, which, in retrospect, was totally stupid. I *should* have changed the subject to syncope in older adults to take Maddie's mind off the fact that we are so far apart now on most issues that we practically live on different continents.

"Because!" Not meeting my eye, she kept stabbing at her canvas. "If I want to hang out with Victoria and Francesca and that whole crowd, I have to hang out with Hannah, too. It's sort of a package deal." She glanced sideways at me. "And Hannah is . . . She gets, I don't know, possessive. Maybe it's because she's an only child and she gets lonely."

I wanted to say, *You so don't have to put up with that.*

Or: *Is that why you won't hang out with me around your other friends? Because Hannah won't let you?*

Or even: *Hey, you may have noticed, but I've got a BFF spot vacant. No friendship with Hannah required.*

But my fearlessness evaporated and I didn't say anything. We painted in glum silence until Maddie sighed and put her brush down. She bumped my knee with hers under the table and smiled when I looked up. "So, you never told me how your meeting with Sahil Roy went."

I let my breath out in a whoosh. Okay, so she didn't pick up when I called to talk about it, but this was progress—at least she was asking now. "It was amazeballs." I filled her in on the gender-swapped Dracula idea. "And he gave me a DVD of the original movie to watch at home."

Maddie sat up straighter and clutched my shoulder. "Ooh! You guys should watch it in my home theater!"

Maddie's home theater setup is epic. You didn't need to shell out twenty bucks for a movie ticket at the real theater because you got all of that in much more lux surroundings at her place. "Are you serious?"

"Absolutely! How about tomorrow night?"

"Sure!"

She grabbed her cell off the table. "What's Sahil's number?"

I'd memorized it in case I needed to call it at any point, so I gave it to her. She typed in the message, her fingers flying over the keyboard. Her phone beeped almost immediately.

Sounds good! How about 7?

I nodded and she confirmed with him and then set it aside. "Done."

"Thanks, Maddie." I clapped my hands together (gently, so the brush didn't spray paint all over Maddie's expensive dress). "This is going to be awesome. Sahil's cool. I think I'm gonna enjoy working with him."

She raised an eyebrow at me, teasing, and I waved her off (still being mindful of paint and silk). "Nah," I said. "Sahil's just Sahil." Even if he is cute and totally gets my need to punch back at the patriarchy with excellently made movies.

"Riiiiight," she said, arching her eyebrow even higher until it nestled into her bangs. "I forgot you're holding out for the *other* Roy brother."

"Shut up!" I said, laughing.

She's right, though. I *am* holding out for Neil. I *am* holding out for that shiny, non-groundling future self I'd always pictured, the one people can't just ignore. That future Twinkle Mehra? Maddie would *never* leave her behind.

Love,

Twinkle

Thursday, June 4

My room

Dear Valerie Faris,

I hung my toxic waste dump painting on the wall. It goes well right next to the shelf with my vintage 1950s Kodak Medallion 8 camera. (Dadi bought it for me at a flea market four years ago to remind me of "the vast unknowingness of the human experience and how you must always strive to capture it, Twinkle.")

Oh, wait. My computer just *ding*ed with an incoming e-mail. I love e-mail. I know most people my age are all about the texts, but as someone without a cell phone, I have to take what I can get. Brb.

OH MY GOD. YOU ARE NEVER GOING TO BELIEVE THIS.

I, Twinkle Mehra, wallfloweriest of wallflowers, have a SECRET ADMIRER.

This is not a drill.

I repeat: *I have a secret admirer*.

I printed out the e-mail, and I'm pasting it below:

From: binadmiringyou@urmail.com

To: twinkiefilmfan@urmail.com

Subject: Hello!

Dear Twinkle,

Hi! How are you? You're probably wondering who I am,
and you will find out. Just not yet.

The first thing you should know about me: I think you're
pretty. And funny. And I like the way you wear your hair.
PPC is a vast and germy pit stop on the highway of life, but
you make it a little cooler. (I got your e-mail from the school
directory, in case you're wondering.)

Secondly, please don't try to guess who I am. I'll reveal my
identity at the perfect time, but if you try to guess, I'll have to fade
away and this will be game over. :(So I hope you'll play along!

I'll write again soon!
Your secret admirer,
N

Do you see how he signed off? N!! And he called me *pretty*,
just like you-know-who did at the lockers yesterday! Do you
know what this means?

It's Neil. It has to be Neil. IS IT NEIL??

I wrote back immediately. I'm stapling my response below.

From: twinkiefilmfan@urmail.com
To: binadmiringyou@urmail.com
Subject: ????

Hi, N!

I know you said you don't want to say who you are and I promise I get it (and I love surprises so it's totally cool), but can you give me a hint?? You're my first secret admirer and I don't know all the protocol, but I'm hoping you'll make an exception!

Love,

Twinkle

He hasn't written back yet. I went and looked up Neil's e-mail in the school directory, but there isn't one listed. I mean, I know he's using one he made up specifically for this purpose (if it's even Neil), but I just hoped! AAAHHHH. I'm not gonna be able to sleep tonight.

Love,

Twinkle

FriYAY, June 5
Homeroom

Dear Nora Ephron,

N never wrote back. Grrrrr. I've chewed my nails to little stubs. It has to be Neil. He's not at school, so I can't even just go up to him and ask. I mean, not that I would. Because (a) that would be embarrassing if it isn't him, (b) I am, after all, the Greatest Coward West of the Mississippi, and (c) I kinda like the mystery and he clearly does too, so who am I to ruin it?

You were always super good at showing the relationship between guys and women, Nora. I wish you were here to give me some advice. Because I feel like I'm in a movie and I'm the main character.

I'm used to being invisible, you know? Papa works a lot—he has since I was a baby—and Mummy's always been . . . Mummy-like and distant. People at school constantly looked through me, but I didn't care much because I had Maddie. But now she's semi-gone and . . . I'm not okay with being overlooked anymore. And all of this—Neil (potentially) e-mailing me, the movie, and my new friendships with Sahil and the rest of them? It feels like my life is *finally* getting on track.

Besides, what girl doesn't want to be the object of someone's affections, secretly or otherwise?

He-he-he.

Love,

Twinkle

Friday, June 5
Lunch

Dear Sofia Coppola,

I'm not sitting alone at lunch anymore. I'm sitting at Sahil Roy's table, with him and Skid and Aaron! They just casually waved me over and I just casually walked there.

Maddie was watching me, so I waved. And guess what? She glanced at Hannah and bit her lip, like she was afraid to say hi or something. And then *Hannah* saw me and did this obviously fake laugh and grabbed Maddie's arm so they could look at something on her phone together. And Maddie went along with it. *Totally* uncool, but that's how it's been—I've learned to accept that Maddie is completely different from the Maddie I know when her other friends are around. I'm hoping she'll realize that this blows as a long-term strategy, but in the meantime, I just go with the flow.

Brij and Matthew came over too, even though the invitation was not *exactly* meant for them. Maybe Brij is trying to get some more info on Maddie, which I am okay with. Maybe he can loosen Hannah's hold on her like I haven't been able to. We scooted over and made room.

"Man, I do *not* want to do that project for Cultural Studies," Skid grumbled, shoveling some pizza into his mouth.

"Show-and-tell for high school," Aaron said, shaking his head and scoffing.

"What are *you* complaining about?" Skid elbowed him. "You were all excited last night about getting to talk about your underground bands."

Aaron blinked and looked momentarily caught out. "Uh, yes, but . . ." He looked around. "Sahil's going to talk about Roger Ebert, an old dead guy who loved movies way more than a normal amount!" he blurted out suddenly. "He's bringing in the poster and everything."

Every head at our table swiveled to look at Sahil. "So what?" he said, thrusting his chin out. "The man's a legend. Our loss is tremendous."

Brij and Matthew snorted, but I smiled. "I agree with Sahil. I mean, there are some people who deserve legend status and that's nothing to be ashamed of. I'd bring in my poster of Ava DuVernay if it weren't falling apart."

He bumped me gently with his shoulder. "Thanks, T. I knew my director would have my back."

Brij was watching us intently. "Well, I'm going to be bringing in my E-3000 Digital Study Buddy," he said, looking directly at me. "It has a built-in bank of SAT vocab words."

Everyone just stared at him. "Er," I said finally, because he was still looking at me. "Great, Brij. That's awesome. You should remember to tell Maddie about it too."

"So, what are you bringing in?" Aaron asked me, folding his giant pool-noodle arms on the table.

"I'm not sure yet," I said, taking a swig of milk.

"Maybe you could bring in your camera," Sahil said. Our arms were resting on the table together, and the hairs on his brushed mine lightly. An interesting and not altogether unpleasant little ripple went up my spine, but I ignored it.

"My Canon?" I said. "I don't know. . . . I need it to make our film." I'd gotten it for a total steal on Craigslist because the lens cap was missing and the handle was broken, and even then it had wiped out my entire savings account.

"No, I mean the other one," Sahil said, his brown eyes sparkling as he looked at me. "That vintage Kodak you brought to school in eighth grade?"

I shook my head slowly. "You remember that?" I'd been so ridiculously excited that I'd slept with it for a week.

He cleared his throat and rubbed the back of his neck, looking down at his food. "I mean, yeah," he said softly. Brij and Matthew were arguing loudly about cryptocurrencies and Skid and Aaron were debating which was more important to society,

66

botany or music, but I could barely hear them. Sahil glanced at me from the corner of his eye. "It seemed important to you, so."

I didn't even know Sahil had seen it or realized it meant so much to me. Dadi buying it at the flea market was the first time someone in my family had acknowledged my dream of becoming a filmmaker. I'd leveled up that day. I wasn't even sure Maddie remembered anymore that I had the Kodak. "That's sweet," I said, looking down at my food too. It was hard to meet his eyes all of a sudden. "Maybe I will bring it in."

"Grab," Sahil said, and I heard the smile in his voice.

"Definitely grab," I said, smiling too.

Your movies were a lot about insider/outsider status, Sofia, and I wonder what you'd say about me sitting at this table (ostensibly a loser table, but populated by some of the funniest, kindest, most talented people I've ever met). I tossed my hair and laughed extra hard just so Maddie could see how happy I was, even though half my heart was over there, beside her. It's not the most mature thing I've ever done. I'm running out of ideas, though, to show my ex-BFF that I won't just wait around forever. But at the same time? I'm not ready to let her go.

Love,
Twinkle

Friday, June 5
AP Econ
Dear Dee Rees,
After lunch, Sahil and I talked about our movie project and how

we were going to watch *Dracula* together tonight at Maddie's. (But then Mr. Rivers poked his head out of class and told Sahil to *stop flirting and get to class*. Sahil and I both turned red and purple respectively. Come on, Mr. Rivers. Don't you recognize a *BUSINESS MEETING* when you see one?)

We decided that we're going to take notes on iconic scenes, costumes, and anything else that sticks out to us that we want to include in our movie. We were both *so* excited, we were talking over each other and laughing all giddily and stuff. I have never had anyone be as exhilarated about making a movie as I am. This must be how Dean and Sam Winchester feel every time they go on a hunt together. (I am the cooler, bad-boy Winchester and Sahil can be the tall and gawky-but-still-kinda-built Sam.)

Only six more hours till *Dracula*!

Love,

Twinkle

Six

Dear Nora Ephron,

Tonight was the *most* fun I have had since . . . I don't know when.
So Papa dropped me off at Maddie's place—

Oh, wait. I do know when. Tonight was the most fun I've had
since that time in fifth grade when Maddie and I were having a
sleepover at her place but then sneaked off in the middle of the
night (Mr. Tanaka was in his studio, and when he's painting,
nothing gets through to him) and walked around her super-fancy
neighborhood drawing "edgy" Dr. Seuss quotes on the sidewalks
using sidewalk chalk (my favorite: one fish, screw fish, red fish,
fool fish). Then the next morning we watched from the window
as Lyla came out and just stared and stared at our artwork, this
stupefied look on her face. It was hilarious and we laughed soooo
hard. Actually, I peed my pants a little, but then I took a shower
and changed into Maddie's clothes and she swore she wouldn't
tell anyone. (She didn't.)

Anyway. This was just as fun as that.

So, as I was saying, Papa dropped me off at Maddie's place, and there was a blue SUV in the driveway. I figured it must be Sahil's, and then my stomach did this weird fluttery thing, thinking of our conversation in the caf. I muscled through it and rang the doorbell, and Maddie answered wearing a gorgeous pink halter dress and wedge sandals.

"You're here!" she squealed, and leaned in to kiss me.

"Yeah." I followed her in. "Are you going somewhere?" Lyla, who had also been an artist and an intellectual in her home country in Eastern Europe somewhere and was now Mr. Tanaka's creative consultant/household manager, had put some fresh orange hibiscuses in the vase on that big table in the foyer. I knew for a fact she did this only when Maddie had guests over. It was kind of a big deal when she stopped doing that when I visited because she considered me family at that point. Seeing them now hurt my feelings, but I figured—and hoped—she'd done them for Sahil more than me.

"No. I thought I could hang out and watch with you guys?" Maddie darted me a look as we headed downstairs. "If . . . that's okay?"

Ugh. It was hideous that we were having this conversation, both because I wasn't sure if Maddie wanted to hang out with me and because *she* wasn't sure *I* wanted to hang out with her. "No, yeah. I want you to stay."

She smiled a small smile. "Good. Sahil's already downstairs."

Wow. I'd forgotten how fancy Maddie's house was. The walls were lined with super-expensive-looking paintings, both Mr. Tanaka's and from other artists, and there were little lights beaming down on them like we were at an art gallery. Maddie's basement is bigger and nicer than my entire house. We hung left and then passed through big double doors under a sign that said, THE THEATER in big gold letters.

Sahil was in the theater, making a fresh batch of popcorn with his back toward us. He was wearing a blue T-shirt that hugged his shoulders and shorts that skimmed his hips and fell to his knees. One of his gigantic sneakers was untied, which would never happen to Neil. I felt a squeeze of affection for Sahil.

He looked over his shoulder and his face blossomed into a crazy brilliant smile. "Hey, Twinkle!" He gestured to the popcorn popping behind the glass doors of the machine. "Hope you guys are okay with extra butter, 'cuz that's the only way I fly."

"Well, then, I hope *you're* okay with M&M's in your popcorn," Maddie said, looping an arm around my shoulders, "'cuz that's the only way *we* fly. Right, T?"

I was in total shock that Maddie's arm was around my shoulder *and* that she'd said "we" about her and me *and* that she still remembered our popcorn ritual from our sleepovers. We hadn't had one in more than a year.

I was starting to get emotional whiplash. Maybe a braver person would confront Maddie head-on. But I just wanted to hang on to the moment as long as I could.

"Right," I forced myself to say, just before the silence became a little too long and awkward. "Definitely."

"Hmm, all right. Well, I'm an open-minded dude. I can try that."

71

I laughed and walked up to him and the popcorn machine and grabbed a bottle from the lower shelf. "But you also have to add the caramel sauce or it's no deal."

Sighing, he said, "Well, they say sugar comas are manageable these days," as he reached in to grab the popcorn with a scoop. His hand hit the hot metal part, though, and yelping, he jerked back. "Holy mother of kilojoules, that's hot!"

"Oh my God, are you okay?" Without even thinking about it, I grabbed his hand and closely inspected the red part. "Oh, whew. It doesn't look too badly burned. You should still run some cold water over it, though, just to be sure."

Letting go, I looked up at him. His hand remained suspended between us, and he had a goofy expression on his face. "Um," I said, pushing my braid over my shoulder and feeling self-conscious at the way he was looking at me. I mean, he's a boy. Who knows why they do half the things they do. He could've been thinking any number of unflattering things about me. Though, to be honest, he just looked sort of . . . amazed. And I was beginning to realize I'd extended unasked-for physical contact. *Again.* Like I hadn't learned my lesson with that whole pencil on the thigh thing. I mean, not that Sahil didn't have nice, big, manly hands that I 100 percent did not regret touching. But still. "Are you okay?"

"N-no, yeah, no. Absolutely." He let his hand drop and reached for his popcorn, but his expression didn't change. Something about the way he kept darting sidelong glances at me made butterflies jam out in my stomach.

Maddie was watching us with a sly little look on her face, so I cleared my throat and immediately put three feet between me and Sahil. Still looking smug, she walked over to the bar and asked, "You guys want a drink?"

For a minute I didn't know if she meant a *drink* drink. So, I just said, "Um . . . I'll have a Coke?" and then wished I'd said it less like a question and more like someone who's completely comfortable with the fact that she doesn't drink alcohol. I'm usually okay with my choices. But sometimes around Maddie, I forget that.

"Me too," Sahil said, bringing three bowls of popcorn over to the theater seats. He handed one to me and set another one down. "Okay, these have been carameled and M&M'd, so I think we're just about ready to begin our sugar inhalation."

Maddie brought us three glasses with little umbrellas in them, all set on a nice glass tray. "Okay. Drinks are a go. You guys ready?"

I smiled at Sahil and then at my ex-BFF as I caught our reflections in the TV screen. Our faces were shiny, three pairs of brown eyes glowing. I took a deep breath. "Ready."

Okay, so I knew *Dracula* was a classic. And I knew that Bela Lugosi was an epic actor from the ancient world whom people like Sahil still look up to today. I knew the director of *Dracula*, Tod Browning, was talented, because people have been talking about his work for decades now.

But somehow, I never connected all those facts with the idea that *I'm gonna have to do him justice.* And not just that, but I've now undertaken the task of gender-swapping this brilliant movie, which means people are going to be doubly interested to see what I do with it.

If I do it right, it could be like this giant coup for the women of PPC and beyond. It'll say to the world, "Look, a movie by a teen girl of color! Yes, women direct movies too! And we don't have to rely on the same old tropes—Dracula can be Dracu-lass!" But if I do it poorly . . . maybe saying I might never want to direct anything else ever again is too extreme, but I might never want to direct anything else ever again.

During the best scenes, Sahil would meet my eye in the dark. I couldn't tell what he was thinking; I just knew my pulse quickened every time. And one time he looked at me, I smiled, and he almost upended his entire bowl of popcorn.

But during the bad scenes, I'd laugh and roll my eyes at him. That bat? So fake. Also, I had no idea how much people in the thirties liked melodrama. When I did *that*, Sahil would throw popcorn at me. On purpose this time.

Eventually the credits rolled and Maddie switched the lights back on. I sat there, staring straight ahead. "Um, Sahil?"

"Yeah?"

"You're going to hate me."

He swiveled in his seat. "Impossible." We looked at each other for a beat, my mouth going dry. "Ah, I mean, why do you say that?" he amended hastily. Maddie snickered, but I chose to ignore her.

"There is no way *I* can do Browning or Lugosi justice. Zero chance." I shook my head. "He's a superstar, you guys. And I'm just some . . . some kid from Colorado Springs. I've never even directed a real movie before!"

Sahil came to sit by me. "If anyone can do this, it's you," he said, leaning forward. "So maybe you haven't directed a movie before. But that's just mechanics. You have the *soul* of a storyteller, Twinkle. I've watched your YouTube videos, okay? You have the ability to make people bare their real selves when you're holding a camera, and not many people can do that. You and Browning aren't as far apart as you think."

I swallowed, touched that he'd checked out my videos. I'd mentioned them in passing at lunch. "You really think so?"

"I know so."

We gazed at each other, the moment stretching on. I forgot Maddie was present, watching everything. I forgot what a Maddie even was. What was happening? *Sahil* was not the Roy brother I needed. But somehow, when I looked into his eyes, I saw myself the way he saw me: as someone talented and capable, as someone who could *do* this.

We sat there in silence until Maddie burst into our moment like a rampaging elephant. "Um, excuse me? Did you two watch the same movie I watched?"

We looked at her. "What?" I said.

She laughed. "Oh my God. That was so over-the-top and ridiculous! T, you're a *wayyyy* better filmmaker than that guy Brownie ever was."

Sahil pinched the skin between his eyebrows. "Browning. His name is Browning." Then he looked at me. "Is she for real?"

I nodded. "Maddie thought *Psycho* was stupid too."

Sahil clutched at his chest. "You . . . you didn't like *Psycho*?"

"What?" Maddie said, sipping her Coke. "Anyone could tell there was something very, very wrong with that Norman Bates.

Like any woman would even stay at his creepy-ass hotel in the first place!"

Sahil stared at Maddie, and I laughed. "Okay, whatever our feelings about *Psycho,* can we just focus on *Dracula* right now? Now, Maddie has a point. Some of those scenes were pretty hilarious." When I saw Sahil open his mouth to verbally murder me, I hurried on. "But others were classic. Like that line, 'I am Dracula. I bid you welcome'? We *have* to shoot that."

Sahil's face lit up like Dadi's face at Diwali. (It's all about the sweets for her.) "Yes! That's exactly what I was thinking!"

I nodded, pointing to the notebook page on my lap, which was filled with scene-blocking diagrams, bits of dialogue, and costume ideas. "We need to keep it creepy, but charismatic creepy. Whoever our Dracu-lass ends up being, she needs to be just as captivating as Bela Lugosi."

"You mean like this?" Maddie asked, whipping a throw around her shoulders and tying it at the hollow of her throat. Her entire persona transformed. Suddenly her eyes had a flinty look, and her smile was predatory. She shook out her hair and stalked over to Sahil. He pretended to swoon, just like Mina in the movie, and Maddie bent close to his throat, pausing just short of putting her mouth on his skin.

I was enchanted.

Okay, so if I'm being *completely* honest (which I think is the point of a diary), I felt two things. Enchanted was 99 percent. I was also . . . well, if you wanted to put a label on this sort of thing, I guess you'd say jealous. Just 1 percent, though. I think it was something about seeing Maddie so close to Sahil after we'd just shared that moment, which was ridiculous, obviously. But I was definitely not more than 2 percent jealous. Three percent tops.

So, anyway, I sat up straight and stared at Maddie. Sahil was doing the same thing. She tucked a lock of straight, shiny black hair behind one ear and laughed. "What, you guys? Was it bad?"

"Um, Maddie?" I said, my voice sounding faint, even to myself. "Can you pretend to be Dracula and say, 'I am Dracula. I bid you welcome'?"

She took a deep breath and that steely-eyed, creepy seductress was back. "I am Dracula," Maddie said, her voice reverberating with power and dominance. "I bid you welcome."

She paused, and then she was just Maddie again.

"Sahil?" I said, and this time my voice was squeaky. "I think we've found our Dracu-lass, don't you think?"

"Um, *yeah* we have," he said, his voice full of awe. We were both staring at Maddie, our mouths hanging open.

She clapped her hand over her mouth. "Are you serious? *I'm* going to be the lead in your movie?"

I nodded. "Do you have any other hidden talents you aren't telling us about? Can you build a stage using your bare hands? Manufacture a full house out of thin air?"

She laughed. "I don't think so." Then, after a pause, she squealed, "I'm going to be an actress!"

That sort of broke Sahil's and my paralysis, and then we all began jumping up and down and shouting and yelling until Lyla came downstairs and shushed us, saying that Mr. Tanaka was on the verge of a breakthrough about how his latest piece might be about the Dadaists' unwitting altruistic donation to the modern zeitgeist. He absolutely could not be disturbed, she said. Then she bribed us with homemade strawberry lemonade slushies if we'd go out in the backyard for the next hour. So that's where I am now.

I can't believe it. Our lead actress, and she was hiding in plain sight. Also? I get to work closely with my ex-best friend again. Do you know what this means? Maddie's going to see how much fun we have together, she's going to remember all the good times, and things might just go back to normal. This is going to *rock*.

Friday, June 5
My room

Dear Mira Nair,

Holy crap. This night just keeps getting better.

So, out on the balcony, we were all so excited that we kept discussing what we were going to do next. So Maddie said, "Costumes! We need costumes!" And I said, "Well, okay, but Thoroughly Thespian is the only local place that sells theater costumes that don't look like Halloween rejects, but you have to be famous or have an agent to shop there because all their stuff is so professional." Sahil pulled up the Thoroughly Thespian website and we all drooled over the stuff they have to offer.

I said, "See? It's *perfect*. It would take our stuff to the next level." Then I sighed. "Oh, well. Guess we'll have to go to Goodwill or something." I know I sounded like a brat when I said that because there's nothing wrong with Goodwill and I shop there lots, but for such a life-changing project, I wanted something a little more special.

Then Sahil studies my face and he says, "Hey, it'll be okay. We'll come up with something good."

So I sort of shrug and force a half smile and say, "I know."

Then he nods, picks up his cell phone, and begins typing something.

"What are you doing?" I ask, frowning.

He smiles super mysteriously. "They're open till ten tonight." Then he pushes speaker and I hear, "Good evening. Thank you for calling Thoroughly Thespian. How can I help you?"

And I stare at him and then at Maddie, who's staring at *me*, and then I stare at him again and he puts one finger on his lips and says in a confident but snooty voice, "Yes, hello. This is the Zenith Talent Agency calling on behalf of Twinkle Mehra. Ms. Mehra is in the Springs for just a few days and would love to stop by to sample your wares for her newest movie."

I clapped a hand over my mouth to keep from laughing, and Maddie giggled and stepped away to get ahold of herself.

"Right," the female voice on the phone said, sounding suspicious. "*Who* did you say you represent again?"

"Twinkle Mehra, darling," Sahil said, sitting back and kicking his feet up on the table. "She's very avant-garde, very new, but *so* up-and-coming. You know, there's already Sundance buzz for this project and you *would* be credited. Of course, if you're too busy, Karen at Perfect Props in Denver already has her scheduled first thing tomorrow." It was like watching a magic trick. Sahil had completely transformed, his confidence like new clothes on him.

"No, no," the voice said quickly. "We would love to have, er,

Ms. Mehra come look at our, er, wares. What time is good for you?"

I almost peed my pants just like that one time at Maddie's. I couldn't believe Sahil was pulling this off. "Let me check her schedule . . . ," Sahil said, riffling the pages of my notebook, which was on the table, and looking at me questioningly. *Anytime is good,* I mouthed. He nodded and got back on the phone. "How does eleven a.m. tomorrow sound?"

"Perfect," the voice said, sounding relieved. "We'll see you then."

"Excellent. See you soon." Sahil pressed end, swung his legs back down, and we all burst out laughing at the same time.

"Oh my *God*," I said, kicking his shoe. "I can't believe you did that!"

"I think *you* need to be in the movie," Maddie said, almost choking with laughter. "You were so smooth! 'Twinkle Mehra, darling'!"

"No, no, I'm just the producer," Sahil said, chuckling. "And part of being the producer is taking care of my director." He winked at me.

"This is so cool of you," I said.

"I just want to make a great movie," he said, reaching for his lemonade slushie and shrugging. "And I want to support you so you can bring your vision to life as much as possible."

Something inside me blinked awake. Here was someone who was so passionate about his art, he refused to let small things like obscurity hold him back. He just leaped into it, somehow *knowing* he'd make it all work.

I want that, I realized. I want to be honest and brave and confident in my art.

Laughing a little, I said, "You know who you reminded me of a little right then, with your legs on the table and everything?"

He grinned. "Michael B. Jordan. I get that a lot, actually."

"No," I said, swatting at him. "Neil. You had that same confident, 'you *will* do as I ask' air that I could never pull off in a million years."

His smile got dimmer and dimmer as I spoke. "Oh," he said, itching his ear. "Right."

I glanced at Maddie and then back at him. "Are . . . are you okay?"

"Yeah." He forced another smile, but I could see his heart wasn't in it.

There was a beat of silence, but no one rushed to fill it. I looked at Maddie again, but she shrugged lightly. Sahil was looking off into the distance.

"You guys," I said finally, eager to break this weird little moment. "We could have costumes from Thoroughly freaking Thespian tomorrow! We're so legit!"

"We're so legit it hurts," Sahil said, holding up his glass of lemonade, thankfully having shaken himself out of that stupor. Maddie and I clinked it with ours. "To new partnerships," he said, but he was looking just at me.

"To new partnerships," I said, grinning. "And fabulous costumes."

"And lead actresses!" Maddie said, and then we all laughed again and happily slurped our slushies.

. . .

Things are finally falling into place and I'm over here like, *Is this life?* I can't wait for tomorrow! Saturday-morning costume shopping—huzzah!

Love,

Twinkle

Seven

Saturday, June 6

21 days until Midsummer Night!

My room

Dear Valerie Faris,

I should *not* be allowed to talk to boys. There should be a federal law. The Twinkle-Versus-Cute-Boy-Communication Act. You may think I'm being dramatic, but I assure you I'm not.

This is what happened: Sahil picked me up at ten thirty this morning. He came in and said hi to my parents and Dadi and called them "Uncle and Auntie," which made their day. Dadi offered him some of her Parle-G biscuits, which she only does to the most deserving visitors—and Oso. (That's because we have to go all the way to the Indian market in that shady plaza with the exotic fish store. It's owned by this guy with orange hair and gold teeth who freaks Dadi out.)

He looked nice today too. He was wearing a cool *Blair Witch Project* T-shirt, which I secretly coveted the entire day. And his hair was gelled. I'd never seen it like that before, but it suited him. I kept sneaking peeks at him as we drove from my house to his place.

It was hitting me, for the first time, how . . . um, *attractive* I find Sahil. I mean, I know he and Neil look alike. That's the whole thing with identical twins. But it wasn't *just* about his nice shoulders or his hair or his square jaw. It was like something happened last night. I saw what Sahil's made of on the inside, and . . . I don't know if this is gonna sound gross, but his insides match mine. I don't know how else to explain it. I see what he's made of, and it's the stuff I'm made of too, I think.

But that doesn't help me with the whole "leave the groundlings behind and get on Maddie's level" plan. Only Neil fits into that plan. It's not that I need him to get to Maddie. It's just that if I date someone like Neil, things will be so much easier between me and her.

We drove past the city to this tiny town north of the Springs. It's where Sahil and most of the other, richer people live, and I realized something.

"Wait. Is this where Thoroughly Thespian is?"

"Yep, just five minutes away. Why?"

"Don't you live up here, too?"

Sahil nodded, looking a little confused.

"You didn't have to drive all the way down to get me and then come back up here. I could've asked my dad to give me a ride."

"Nah, it's okay, Mehra," Sahil said, grinning at me. "I couldn't leave my director hanging like that."

My face felt hot and sweaty. "But . . . I mean, I *can* get my own rides. Just because I don't have my own car doesn't mean you need to bail me out or anything." I swallowed. I half couldn't believe I'd said all that out loud—actually *calling attention* to the fact that I don't have much money. But the other half of me was proud for speaking out.

"Twinkle." Sahil looked at me as long as he could without driving off the road. "I just wanted to hang out with you. I like spending time with you. All right?"

My cheeks were still hot now, but for other reasons. "All right," I said softly, feeling a little shy.

He smiled at me, and even though I knew it shouldn't, it felt like moonbeams straight through my heart.

We pulled into the parking lot and walked up to the store, which is this weird warehouse-looking thing with rusted metal steps leading up to it. "Huh." I tipped my head back and took it in. "Are you sure we're in the right place?"

Sahil checked the GPS on his phone. "Yeah. Unless the Google gods have steered us wrong."

Shrugging, I reached out and pulled the door open. It creaked like we were in a haunted movie. I stepped into the space—and gawked.

I was expecting something dinky and dark, to match the outside. But this space was enormous, all of it brilliant white. It was like being stuck on Iceland. Not that I've ever been to Iceland. But the name implies a land of white ice, and that's exactly what this looked like.

Along the wall, oversize mannequins with blank white faces stared at us with their eyeball-less eyes. They were all dressed in gorgeous costumes, with Victorian-era thick, brocade dresses and fancy, elaborate hats with fake fruits and birds on them.

"Yikes," I said at the same time that Sahil said, "Awesome!"

I shuddered as he ran up to one and poked it in the face. "Those things are so freaking creepy." I sidled over to a shelf along the wall and picked up what looked like a solid gold staff with rubies encrusted on the handle. "*This*, on the other hand, is cool."

Sahil bounded over to me. He was an oversize puppy in a pet shop, running from toy to toy. "It is!" He reached behind me, his arm sliding over my shoulders, to grab something else off the shelf. "And look at this!" He showed me a hypnotizing mask that looked like it had raindrops (made out of crystal and light-blue gems) pasted in an ombré pattern down the right side.

"Wow," I breathed, running my fingers along the bumps of the rhinestones. "That is *stunning*."

Suddenly it hit me. We were here, in this fabulous warehouse with all these incredible things surrounding us that we could pick and choose from, because of Sahil and what he'd done last night. I reached out and squeezed his arm on an impulse.

He looked at me, surprised.

"Thank you," I said, grinning up at him. "This is . . ." I shook my head. I needed a thesaurus. "What's a word for 'so awesome it makes you speechless'?"

"Hmm," Sahil said, a small smile at his lips. We were so close I could smell his soap. *Focus, Twinkle.* "Grab?"

I laughed. "This is extremely grab, then."

We were both looking at each other, and slowly, our smiles faded. My heart trip-hammered. Sahil took a step toward me.

And then I remembered.

I had a secret admirer—N. And he might just be Sahil's twin freaking brother. Also? I have a grand, master plan to leave my current self behind by joining the ranks of the silk feathered hats. *And* I'm beyond tired of being a groundling and blending into the walls all the time. What about N/Neil being a part of that dream? What about all of that?

I put my arm down quickly and stepped away, doing that tittery-nervous laugh I do when I'm super uncomfortable, like that one time I walked in on Mummy and Papa and I'm pretty sure they were doing *it*. (In my defense, none of the Mehras knock because Mummy, Papa, and Dadi say that is a silly Western rule that has no place in our house.) In that case, I'd wanted an extra pillow out of their closet, but I'd just done the silly tittery laugh thing and stumbled backward, closing the door behind me super quick. Here and now, I ran over to the other wall and began to stare at a peacock-themed tapestry as if it were the lost treasure of Tutankhamun.

Sahil cleared his throat, like he was going to say something, and I just thought, *Please, Sahil, there* cannot *be anything between us, so can we just ignore that ripple of electricity between us?* when someone behind us said, "Hello? Can I help you?"

I recognized the voice from the phone call yesterday. We both spun around. Sahil straightened his shoulders, and I could see him morphing into Agent Sahil again. "Hello," he said, all snooty. "I'd rung yesterday. This is the talented Twinkle Mehra, come all the way from Sweden just for a few days."

Sweden? Did he think I could *speak* Swedish? At least I was wearing these cool skinny-fit black trousers and a mustard-yellow polka-dot top that Maddie had gotten me once for a gallery showing we went to together for one of Mr. Tanaka's girlfriends, so I looked the part of worldly European filmmaker. Even if, inside, I was a trembling mound of teenage insecurity.

"Oh, yes," the woman said, eyeing both of us up and down like we were trolls who'd come tearing out of the forest—a little disgustedly, but also warily, in case we were a big deal. "I am Violet Hayes."

That could *not* be her real name. Violet Hayes? Like Purple Haze? Anyway, focus. It was time to play the part. I squared my shoulders, held out my hand, and said, *"Enchanté."* Crap. That was French, wasn't it? "Um, *bienvenue.*" Nope, still French. And also not making sense anymore. "Uh . . . thanks for having us."

Violet, who was tiny and thin and had a lavender-colored pixie cut, smiled haughtily. "It is my pleasure."

Why do you look like you ate a rotten lemon, then? I wanted to ask but didn't. I don't have a problem communicating with *women.* Just cute boys.

"Miss Mehra's working on her first movie, which will explore gender relationships in old cinema," Sahil said, stroking an imaginary beard.

I bit the inside of my cheek and tried not to laugh. Ms. Haughty Smile turned her icy blue eyes on him. "Indeed," she said. "Well, I could escort you around or . . ."

"No, we can find our way," I said, a little too quickly. Then I added more coolly, "Gender relationships are a very . . . private matter for me."

She nodded, bowed—bowed!—and then left us.

Sahil and I grinned at each other and then whispered, "Yaaaay!" and then we began to explore.

We quickly found that everything we wanted would be on the second floor. Instead of white floors, this level had a black stone floor with threads of red glinting in it. Very Dracula-y. All the props were dark and mystical too. Sahil was immediately drawn to a cyclorama—a curved backdrop—of a landscape that had a moon painted on it that looked like it was screaming.

"Oh my God, I need this," he said, his eyes lighting up. Then, when I looked at him, he said, "Um, I mean *we* need this?"

I laughed. "Are you joking? I think something like *that* is the one that fits our vision." I pointed at a flat scene, this one with just a regular moon. "It even has lights from a distant village against those hills."

"Oh, well, we can talk about it," Sahil said, because he obviously disagreed with my artistic vision, which is a huge mistake, but whatever.

I left him to drool while I went off to the far-right side, where tons of racks of costumes were hanging, all of the clothes in shades of deep purple or inky black or blood red. I'd riffled through about fifteen different dresses and was just about to give up when . . . You know how TV shows have brides shopping for these overpriced white dresses and they always say some variant of, *I knew the moment I saw it that it was* the *One*? And it sounds like they're talking about their fiancés, but they're talking about a frothy mixture of tulle and lace? And it feels sort of ridiculous? Well, I apologize to all the brides I ever judged before because I so felt that.

My heart beat faster. My palms got sweaty. And I knew. It was *the One*.

"Sahil?" I called, my voice quavery. He came over, and I held the dress against me. It was tight to the ankles and then flared out in a swath of purple-black silk, and it came with a little faux-fur capelet. It was *perfect*.

"That's it," he said, a slow smile spreading across his face. "That. Is. It. You found it."

"And look," I said, pulling the capelet off the hanger to show him. Unfortunately, because I'm a *total* klutz, I dropped it on the floor.

Sahil and I both went to get it, and as I reached over, his legs got tangled in the long dress I was holding. He began to fall, his eyes wide and panicked, and he reached out and grabbed my arm.

I yelled out some expletive or other, trying to find my center of gravity, but it felt like I was on an ice rink without skates on. Stupid, slippery dress.

And then we were lying on the floor, and somehow I was on top of him. My hair made a curtain around his face. In the hazy corners of my mind, I knew I should be completely and utterly humiliated. I mean, my *boobs* were pressed into his chest. I could feel his thigh muscles under mine.

His face was flushed, his eyes wide, like a cornered bunny. "I—I am so sorry," he said. "That was just, um . . . I'm so sorry."

"No, it's—it's fine," I said, my own face getting hotter and hotter as I tried to get off of him. Only the dress had somehow *trapped* both our legs inside it and all I was doing was gyrating uselessly on top of him. *Oh my God, Twinkle,* my brain yelled. *Could you make this any* more *awkward?* "Sorry," I said now. "I'm really . . . I'm trying . . ."

He kind of turned his head away and bit the inside of his lips like he was trying to maintain some semblance of control. Arrrgh. Did he think I was being a total perv? What was that look about? "It's—it's okay," he said, his voice strangled. "Um, take your time."

Thankfully, my legs broke free and I was able to scramble up to a sitting position *off* of Sahil. I couldn't look at him as I gathered up the dress and the capelet.

He was on his feet in half a millisecond, straightening his shirt without looking at me either. (I could see him from my peripheral vision.) "So!" he said, his voice high and squeaky. "I'm just gonna . . . pick out some props." And then he walked off to the other side of the room.

"O-okay." I stood looking after him, a giant tangle of feelings inside me.

Disappointment. Relief. Confusion. Exhilaration.

What was happening between us? Why did those annoyingly persistent butterflies hang out with me every time he was around? Why couldn't my brain just remember that he was Neil's brother and therefore 100 percent off-limits?

I put the capelet up to my face and made a long, tortured groaning sound.

"Are you . . . okay?"

Oh crap. Whipping the capelet away, I stared. Of course. Of *course* Sahil was back, and he'd seen me acting like the mayor of Freakville. "Oh, sure," I said, smiling brightly. "Just . . . you know, I wanted to check if we needed to dry-clean these, but nope. Downy fresh!"

"Oh, okay." He looked a little confused, but had the grace not to call me out on my dubious behavior. "Um, I was gonna go tell Violet some of the stuff we wanted. That cyclorama okay with you?"

He was talking about the curved backdrop with the evil moon. Arrrgh. I *super* didn't want that one, but things were awkward and uncertain right now and I was feeling even more "puddle of embarrassed goo" than usual. "Sure," I said, wishing I could rent a backbone from here too. "That works."

"Awesome."

While Sahil was downstairs, I finished picking out the rest of the costumes and a couple more props. We didn't talk about what happened; the ride home was almost completely silent. It's obvious Sahil thinks I'm a huge pervert and can't stand me anymore.

The good news is we're all set up to begin making our movie. The bad news is I'm turning my room into an airtight container from which escape will be impossible.

Love,

Twinkle

June 6
The Reel Deal Blog
Posted by: Rolls ROYce

The good news is Sparkle made full-on-body contact with me and didn't run off screaming disgustedly. The bad news is I was so shocked I morphed into a wax museum exhibit of myself.

I can't help but feel optimistic anyway. Because something happened today. Something shifted.

I'm not one to make up crap in my head. I can see reality pretty plainly. For instance, I know my brother is the epitome of the golden boy: He's athletic and smart and Harvard bound and does SAT practice tests "for fun, dude." Girls regularly swoon over him like he's . . . oh, what's that character who died because Kate Winslet wouldn't scoot the hell over on that door? Oh yeah. Jack. Which is hilarious because we are the *exact* same from a genetic perspective, but I digress. Basically, everything has always come easy to him, and okay. Am I bitter? Nope. Do I *like* it? No, but I accept it. We all have our roles to play and stuff.

So you'll believe me, then, when I say that something was *definitely* happening between me and Sparkle today. I'm not deluded. I know girls usually just dismiss me as "that geeky dude who has a thing for horror movies." But she didn't. The way she looked at me . . .

Okay, so I was having a hard time, no pun intended, when she was on top of me. I wanted to say *something* to her in the car, anything that would let her know that I was on board. Like:

Sparkle, I am a lovelorn fool, so could you just put me out of my brain-numbing misery already by telling me what you're thinking. Just a sliver of a thought would be nice.

But instead I sat there in silence. I'd glance at her occasionally, but that girl is a closed book.

That's okay, though. I'm gonna make a game plan and go with it. What I need to do is come up with a campaign to approach this in an organized fashion so I don't blow it. Oh! I just thought of a slogan: "I like you, too, Sparkle, but not in a needy way. Also, I'm the cool, geek-chic guy you never knew you always wanted." Or something with less suckage, but that's essentially the heart of the message. Never again will she say I remind her of my brother because *he* will remind her of *me*, instead. A subtle but very important difference, my friends.

I can do this. I am so there. I'm feelin' it, as my friend Slide would say. Sparkle, here I come.

Sunday, June 7
My room
Dear Nora Ephron,
Eep! Another e-mail from "N."

From: binadmiringyou@urmail.com
To: twinkiefilmfan@urmail.com
Subject: An ode to you

Twinkle, Twinkle, little star

Right now you might be oh so far

But soon in your beauty my eyes will bask

And then at last you'll see me unmasked

—Your Secret Admirer, N

There's no doubt in my mind: It *has* to be Neil. Let's dissect this poem, shall we?

First, my secret admirer says that we are "oh so far." Ahem. Neil is *away at a pre-Olympic summer swim camp*. I never get to see him.

Second, N says "soon our eyes will meet again," because Neil is *coming back* to school at the end of the month.

And third, "unmasked"? Neil couldn't be more obvious if he tried. He's trying to tell me he remembers that one time we danced at the masquerade ball back in sixth grade, just like I do! (Or maybe it was fifth? And did I dance with Neil? Minor details.)

This *has* to be Neil. It just has to. And if it is, then . . . I don't know. I think I might expire from happiness or something, because if it *is* him, my shiny, future self might be materializing before my eyes. The movie stuff is going well so far, which means my message will get out to way more people than ever before. With Maddie as the lead, maybe most of the rest of the cast could be silk feathered hats too. Maybe they'll finally begin *seeing* me. Maddie's and my friendship will hopefully be back on the right track. And now Neil? It feels like the last piece of the puzzle has just landed in my lap.

Okay, so there's a *tiny* part of me that's like, okay, cool. Maybe Neil is e-mailing me. But . . . do I really want that anymore? I mean, my life is already pretty sweet right now for the first time in forever. I have new friends I click with. And . . . I like hanging out with Sahil. A lot.

But that's crazy, isn't it? This, *Neil*, is what I've wanted for so long. The part of me that isn't ecstatic about the e-mail just needs to be squashed. Maybe the problem is that I've become too unfocused. Maybe I'm spending too much time thinking about Sahil when I need to be thinking about his brother instead. Sahil needs to remain just a friend. I can't let it progress any further. No more looking deeply into his eyes. No more falling on top of him. Focus and maintain my balance. That's what I need to do.

Love,

Twinkle

Eight

Sunday, June 7
Backyard

Dear Mira Nair,

I walked out to get a snack and saw Dadi on the couch, reading *Lentil Soup for the Reincarnated Soul*, with Oso curled up like a little prawn by her feet. I asked her where Mummy and Papa were, and she said, "Papa is at the youth home." Papa works as an aide at a center for runaway teens. He takes his work very, very seriously and goes in a lot even when he isn't technically on shift. Which is good, because those kids don't have any reliable adults in their lives. But sometimes I wish I had more reliable adults in mine.

"What about Mummy?" I asked, noticing that she'd purposely left that part out.

Dadi's eyes got that shifty, darting look they do when she's trying to cover something up. "She's . . . sleeping."

"Sleeping?" I glanced at the clock on the wall. "It's eight thirty."

Dadi shrugged, looking pained. She held out one arm to me and I went to sit by her, curled into her side. "Your mummy has a lot of pain in her heart, Twinkle. I wish it did not affect you so, but I am afraid we must all carry our burdens in each lifetime. Sometimes we must carry a bit of our parents' burdens as well."

My throat got all choked up like it does a lot when we talk about Mummy. "Right. Burdens."

As usual, Dadi read my mind. "Oh, *munni,* of course I don't mean *you.*" Dadi rested her head against mine as if she could beam love through her skull into mine. Knowing Dadi, she probably believed she could. "You are the greatest source of joy in her life. But she cannot help it. She has left behind a part of herself in India."

"Ever since Nani died," I said, swallowing away my tears, "she's been so different."

Dadi smoothed a strand of hair back from my forehead. "*Haan.* When your mother dies, it is as if a part of you has died too. And because she could not go to India to be there . . . she blames herself. It is not her fault, but she cannot see past her pain." Dadi put a hand under my chin. "But, Twinkle, none of that has to do with you. None of it is because of you. You are faultless."

I snorted and rolled my eyes, mainly to keep them from filling with tears. You once said, Mira, that nostalgia is a useless thing. It doesn't move you forward. I so get that. I just wish Mummy did, too. Pulling away from Dadi, I put my feet up on the couch and reached for the remote. "I know. Anyway, I'm done talking about all that. Let's see if we can find a Mira Nair movie on the Hindi channel."

I felt Dadi watch me for a good long time, like she was trying to decide whether to say anything else on the subject or not. Thankfully, she just put her arm around me and said, "Okay, *munni*. Let's see."

So what if Mummy's asleep and Papa's at work? I have Dadi. I have Oso (and Dada by extension). I have my new friends Sahil, Skid, and Aaron. I have my movie. And I have N, my secret admirer. What else could a girl want?

Love,
Twinkle

Monday, June 8
Honors Calculus

Dear Sofia Coppola,

Today at lunch Aaron was trying to, as usual, convert me to listening to his alternative heavy metal bands. He is six four and he maybe weighs only, like, 140 pounds tops, but he's got this giant, booming voice I hope (for his sake) that the rest of him will grow into. "Empty Plastic Bottles!" he bellowed around a mouthful of mozzarella sticks. (He was stuffing four at a time in there.) "Just give them a chance!"

Sahil laughed beside me as I made a face. "Aaron. Empty Plastic Bottles?"

"Don't judge!" Aaron yelled.

"No, forget about all that for a minute," Skid said, leaning forward. "You've *never* tried truffle balls?" As a chocolate fiend and our resident sweet tooth, Skid lived in a constant state of bewilderment that I was firmly committed to my Reese's and/or other peanut butter and chocolate sweets.

"Nope," I said, popping a chicken tender in my mouth. "Aren't truffles mushrooms or something?"

Skid clutched at his heart all melodramatically.

"Dudes, leave her alone," Sahil said. "She's my director. I'm gonna have to start making appointments for you plebs to talk to her."

"*Plebs?*" Skid said, glaring at us. "Don't forget who's editing the freaking thing."

"Sahil didn't mean it," I said, smiling sweetly. We could *not* afford to annoy Skid. He's a genius of video and photo editing. The yearbook group pays him a retainer because he says his time is too valuable to work on puerile and fleeting pursuits like the high school yearbook for free. "There's definitely a trip to Rocky Mountain Chocolate Factory at the end of all this. . . ."

Skid looked placated. "All right, then," he said, and then he and Aaron got into a conversation about some football team.

I'd been stealth studying Sahil the entire time in the caf, but thankfully, he did not seem to hold any lingering awkwardness over our incident from Saturday. If anything, he was even friendlier today than he'd been before. Which I didn't get, but I wasn't going to question either.

"I hope we get at least ten people at the auditions Wednesday," I said to him, glancing over my shoulder at Maddie. She was sitting at her usual table, but she'd laid out the capelet from her costume (which she *loved*) for everyone to admire. She was doing a great job as our PR person. The other girls kept touching the capelet, and I could tell a bunch of them would probably show up to audition now that Maddie was the lead and it didn't look like we'd dress her in anything hideous. "Anything less than that and we won't have our pick of who we want, I think."

"Ten is a good number." Sahil nodded. "I think we'll get ten."

He's one of those eternal optimists, which is another one of those cute Sahil things I'm trying not to notice too much. "So . . ." I cleared my throat. "About that cyclorama you ordered? The one with the evil moon?"

Sahil grinned. "Yeah. They'll deliver that Friday to Ms. Rogers's room. She gave me the okay."

"Yeah . . ." I stabbed my chicken tender with a fork. "Um, do you think we could swap it out for the other one?"

"You mean the one with the plain moon?" Sahil asked, frowning.

I nodded. "And the village lights in the distance."

Maybe I should just let Sahil have the cyclorama. I know this isn't just *my* movie. In fact, if it hadn't been for Sahil, I wouldn't even be doing this in the first place. Besides, I ended up choosing most of the props and costumes because Sahil kept going for these totally creepy, Victorian-era-esque masks and things. They would've just freaked the administration out and then we'd probably be banned from Midsummer Night. Sahil agreed with me in the end, but still. He obviously cared about the cyclorama a lot. And it was the one thing he *did* pick out without my help. *But*.

This movie's my big shot. I'm ready to show the world what I have inside me, to reach out and make that connection. And

Sahil had just taken over that piece of it. He didn't even have a conversation with me like I did with him about the rest of the costumes and pieces.

"Hmm," he said, his eyes flickering with annoyance. "I already placed the order. I don't know if they'll let me swap now. You know how they are over there."

"Well, maybe I'll call them anyway," I pressed, even though my underarms were beginning to prickle with sweat. This was toeing the line of confrontation land, and I was completely out of my element. "Just to—"

"T, would you let it go?" Sahil's voice was brittle, on the edge of snapping. I stopped short, surprise and hurt churning inside me. I glanced at Aaron and Skid, but they were still deep in a conversation about touchdowns. "I don't know why you can't see this," Sahil continued, just barely meeting my eye before looking down at his food. He stabbed a piece of broccoli with his fork. "The fanged moon is the only way to go. It's got that shine, that pizzazz we want. The other one is so plain it's just going to fade into the background, and that is *not* the message we want to send. Okay?"

I gripped my own fork, unable to speak for a second. I had a thousand things queued up behind my lips. But in the end, the only thing that came out was a thready, "Okay."

Ugh. I should've said something. I know that. Sahil was so out of line, it was ridiculous. I don't even know what that was about; I've never seen him talk to me—or anyone—like that before.

Besides, do I really want to see that moon grinning at me with all its ten thousand and sixteen fangs? No, I do not. But if

I want things to change, I have to speak up. And I really don't know how to do that.

Love,

Twinkle

Monday, June 8
Honors Spanish II

Dear Mira Nair,

Well, now I know why Brij and Matthew weren't at lunch today. I was walking from calculus to Spanish when I saw them in the hall-way, sitting behind a long table. That's when Brij took off his head.

Lest you think this journal has taken an unexpectedly dark turn, I should hasten to explain that he's fine. They were both in *costume*.

Brij looked like a screaming blue toad, but he was actually "Poliwhirl, a water-type Pokémon that is also bipedal and whose abilities include the swift swim, which is, in fact, a hidden abil-ity." I nodded extra and showed a lot of interest because I think he was a little embarrassed when I said that thing about the screaming toad and I felt bad. Matthew, on the other hand, was Pikachu, and I guessed that one on the first try.

I thought maybe it was just another Monday for a couple of computer science geniuses, but Brij told me that they were fund-raising to build the school a better firewall because apparently our security posture is sorely lacking and is an utter disgrace to the school district.

"Okay, Nath, I'm sure the girl understands all the big words you just said," Matthew said, rolling his eyes at me.

"Hey," I said, leaning forward so Pikachu and I were eye to

nose, "I may not be a computer prodigy, but I *do* know what a firewall is. Furthermore, I do not appreciate you saying what you said on the basis of my gender. Let's not further those out-dated patriarchal stereotypes here in the sanctified institute of learning that is PPC, Matthew."

Okay, so I didn't say that. The most nonconfrontational girl in the world, remember? Mostly I just glared at Matthew, which was hard to do because I did not know whether to look into Pikachu's eyeballs or his nostrils, which is where *Matthew's* eyeballs were.

Matthew appeared not at all intimidated (as far as I could tell, given the stupid costume), but then Brij said, "Dude, Twinkle's a genius in her own way. I bet you don't know the first thing about filmmaking," which I thought was super nice. Standing up to your friends is not the easiest thing to do.

I passed Maddie, Hannah, and Victoria in the stairway as they were heading off to art. "Hey," I said to Maddie. She was now *wearing* the capelet, the faux fur swishing around her elbows as she strutted around. "So, is that, like, method acting?" I joked. "We don't have a replacement, so just remember that Dracu-lass probably wouldn't get paint on her clothes."

Hannah rolled her eyes and looked at Victoria, who didn't respond, but just wrapped her already luscious red curls around each finger to curl them more. *Excuse me, Hannah? What was there to roll your eyes about that joke?*

I *know* Maddie saw her, but she didn't say anything. Well, she did, but it was to me. "I won't!" she chirped, and then they all headed off downstairs together. She didn't stop to talk to me about the movie or anything.

And when they were at the bottom of the stairs, Hannah laughed. I thought I heard Maddie say, "Come on, Hannah," in a slightly irritated way, and then Hannah started to argue. Embarrassingly hopeful, I held myself still so I could hear more, but they were too far away by then.

Come on, Hannah. It doesn't sound like much. But I feel like maybe Maddie at least stood up for me a bit. Kind of? I don't know. Sometimes I feel like I'm trying to clutch at drips and drabs of my old best friend, hoping she's still in there somewhere.

Love,

Twinkle

Monday, June 8
My room

Dear Haifaa al-Mansour,

I have an e-mail from Maddie. Stapling it below:

> From: futuredoc20@urmail.com
>
> To: twinkiefilmfan@urmail.com
>
> Subject: Today
>
> Hannah was only joking today in the stairway. I just wanted you to know.
>
> <3 M

Okay, so first: Great. Take Hannah's side, Maddie. Right when I thought you'd been a friend to me today. Fabulous.

Also? An *e-mail*? Maddie almost *never* sends me e-mails. She's avoiding me because *clearly* her conscience is eating away at her and soon she will be nothing but an oily husk of regret.

And third, this isn't an apology?? What does she expect me to say, *Oh, no problem. It's all good. I thought it was pretty funny how she was rolling her eyes and laughing at me anyways because you know how I love to pulverize my already sketchy self-esteem?*

I don't even know how to respond to this. Seriously, I don't. There's nothing I can say. If Maddie can't even put herself in my shoes for more than half a second—ugggghh. I'm just not gonna respond.

A bit later

Obviously I responded. See below.

> From: twinkiefilmfan@urmail.com
> To: futuredoc20@urmail.com
> Subject: Re: Today
> Right. Okay. But just so you know, it's never okay to roll your eyes or laugh at someone. I mean, that's just rude.
> —Twinkle

I bet she won't respond to that. I mean, what could she even say?

Still later

OMG she responded.

> From: futuredoc20@urmail.com
> To: twinkiefilmfan@urmail.com

Subject: Re: Today
Hannah was doing that at something else, not you. She
told me.

—M

So Hannah just *happened* to roll her eyes at the *exact* same
time I made that joke? Mm-hmm. Super believable. And she just
happened to make a joke and laugh right after, but that also had
nothing to do with me.

What does Maddie not understand about how *awful* it feels
to be made fun of for just *existing*? Why is this something I have
to spell out for her?

Also? *Still no apology.* I'm not responding.

My computer just *ding*ed. I thought it was an e-mail from
Maddie again, maybe detailing exactly what joke Hannah *was*
laughing at, or, if the universe liked me, another e-mail from N
(I still haven't responded to his poem; I'm trying to think of a
cute thing to say), but it was Sahil!

From: reeldealsahil@urmail.com
To: twinkiefilmfan@urmail.com
Subject: Font
Hi T,
Which font do you like better? See samples attached.
—Sahil

From: twinkiefilmfan@urmail.com
To: reeldealsahil@urmail.com

Subject: Re: Font
Font? Why do you want me to pick a font?
—Twinkle

From: reeldealsahil@urmail.com
To: twinkiefilmfan@urmail.com
Subject: Re: Font
All will be revealed soon! Pick, *por favor.*

From: twinkiefilmfan@urmail.com
To: reeldealsahil@urmail.com
Subject: Re: Font
Hmm, #1.

From: reeldealsahil@urmail.com
To: twinkiefilmfan@urmail.com
Subject: Re: Font
Excellent.
Wanna hang out after school tomorrow? Skid, Aaron, and I
are going hiking at Red Fox Trail.

From: twinkiefilmfan@urmail.com
To: reeldealsahil@urmail.com
Subject: Re: Font
Sure! But *hiking* after school?

From: reeldealsahil@urmail.com
To: twinkiefilmfan@urmail.com

Subject: Re: Font

I know, I know. Skid's into botany and there's an elusive variety of musk thistle that he's desperate to track down. Aaron and I mostly just laugh at him and his nerdy plant guidebook the entire time, but it's pretty fun.

From: twinkiefilmfan@urmail.com
To: reeldealsahil@urmail.com
Subject: Re: Font
You had me at musk thistle. I'll be there.

From: reeldealsahil@urmail.com
To: twinkiefilmfan@urmail.com
Subject: Re: Font
Awesome! I'll give you a ride after school if you want.

I can hang out with Sahil without all that electricity crackling between us. I'm sure I can do that. Also, I know I was being facetious about that whole musk thistle thing, but hiking with them does sound fun. (Even though most days I'd rather die than go outside to wheel the trash can to the curb.)

Love,
Twinkle

<Text message 10:13 p.m.>
From: Sahil
To: Skid, Aaron
Dudes. She's coming on the hike with us tomorrow

\<Text message 10:13 p.m.\>
From: Skid
To: Sahil, Aaron
yeah but is she coming as a friend or as a PGF?

\<Text message 10:13 p.m.\>
From: Aaron
To: Sahil, Skid
PGF?

\<Text message 10:14 p.m.\>
From: Skid
To: Sahil, Aaron
potential girlfriend

\<Text message 10:14 p.m.\>
From: Sahil
To: Skid, Aaron
Idk but I'm gonna make it clear that I like her as
a PGF

\<Text message 10:14 p.m.\>
From: Aaron
To: Sahil, Skid
Oh yeah? How are you gonna do that?

\<Text message 10:15 p.m.\>
From: Sahil

To: Skid, Aaron
Idk but I've got moves you guys haven't even seen yet

<Text message 10:15 p.m.>
From: Skid
To: Sahil, Aaron
lol right like how you knocked over the napkin dispenser at
Perk? Come to think of it I HADN'T ever seen that move before

<Text message 10:16 p.m.>
From: Sahil
To: Skid, Aaron
HILARIOUS

<Text message 10:16 p.m.>
From: Aaron
To: Sahil, Skid
Aw come on we're jk. Gl bro. We'll keep our distance so we
don't impinge on your moves

<Text message 10:16 p.m.>
From: Skid
To: Sahil, Aaron
yeah or accidentally steal her away. Girls just can't resist
me. it's like this musk I put out or something

<Text message 10:17 p.m.>
From: Sahil

To: Skid, Aaron
You probably got it from your musk thistle gtfo skidmark

<Text message 10:17 p.m.>
From: Skid
To: Sahil, Aaron
did I tell you to never call me that on pain of DEATH

<Text message 10:18 p.m.>
From: Sahil
To: Skid, Aaron
Jeez. I'll leaf you alone now but maybe you should just dill with it

<Text message 10:19 p.m.>
From: Aaron
To: Sahil, Skid
Yeah Skid don't forget the tree of us are best fronds

<Text message 10:20 p.m.>
From: Skid
To: Sahil, Aaron
haha the botany puns never get old y'all are idiots

Nine

Dear Jane Campion,

Brij just asked me if he could audition for *Dracula*! Apparently he saw one of the many, many flyers Skid and Aaron helped us plaster all over the school. Sahil and I were a little worried we'd get a ticket from Principal Harris for littering or something because so many of them fell off (cheap dollar-store tape), but they must be working. Of course I told Brij yes. I even said Maddie would be there and winked at him, and he just stared at me, all openmouthed like he tends to do. He must be so smitten. I mean, I'm still mad at Maddie, but (a) she brought me my favorite Peanut Butter Chocolate Mountain Majesty cupcake from the Cupcake Doctor, and I know she had to wake up an hour early to do that and (b) I can't let an opportunity for true love pass her by. Look, it's a choice I've made. Maddie with her friends is not the Maddie *I* know.

Anyway, that's one-tenth of the people we need to show up so we can have our pick for the remaining four roles. We're ten percent of the way there! Huzzah! If I wasn't so nervous about tomorrow I might pay attention in econ. Poor Mr. Newton just can't compete with auditions for my first-ever paid gig though. Not even if there's a quiz next week, which I am sure to only squeak by with a C on.

Brij just passed me a note. Wow. I didn't think he was a note-passing kind of guy.

> *Do you want to study together for the quiz?*
> *Sure. But I bet Maddie might want to come too.*
> *Is that okay?*
> *Yep, no worries. I can bring Matthew.*
> *Okay, cool. How about Sunday afternoon, maybe around two? We can meet at the library.*
> *Sounds good.*

Muahaha. Now I'll stick them together and neither Maddie nor Brij will know what hit them. I should consider opening a matchmaking thingy on the side. Ooh, and maybe I could invite Sahil, Skid, and Aaron too. They've all been complaining about econ being overwhelming. Misery loves studying econ together.

Love,

Twinkle

June 9, 11:07 a.m.
From: twinkiefilmfan@urmail.com
To: binadmiringyou@urmail.com
Subject: Re: An ode to you

Dear N,

I love that poem. You are clearly extremely talented. Here's
one for you:

I wish I knew who you were

Your masked identity is like a burr

In my soul, dear N,

Please come forward and let this end!

Not that I don't enjoy our e-mails. I just *really* want to know
who you are. When can we meet up?

Love,

Twinkle

Tuesday, June 9
Honors Calculus

Dear Nora Ephron,

You are never going to believe what just happened.

So, I was at my locker getting my books when Sahil stopped by.
It's funny. I never noticed that his locker was so close to mine, but
now that there's less than a month and a half until school gets out,
we're friends who eat together and hang out and stuff. Go figure.

"Hey," he said, smiling at me. "Meet me here after school and
I'll give you a ride to Red Fox."

"Sure," I replied, thinking inside how Sahil wouldn't forget
and ditch me like Maddie had. I mean, it's *Sahil*.

And then, almost like my thoughts had conjured her, Maddie
walked by with (as usual) Hannah and Victoria.

"Hey, Maddie!" I called, raising my hand to get her attention.
There was a pause after she looked my way, and my heart

clenched. She wouldn't ignore me when we were two feet away, would she? *Of course she would*, this cynical part of my brain said. *She's Maddie 2.0 around Hannah.*

After another millisecond of hesitation, she smiled. "Hey, Twinkle." I let out a breath as she walked over, trailed (reluctantly) by Hannah. Victoria came, too, but she looked neither pleased nor displeased to see me. Victoria's teenaged Switzerland, I think.

I kept my eyes on Maddie, ignoring Hannah as completely as she was ignoring Sahil and me. My philosophy was that it was best not to give people an opportunity to act their worst. "Thanks for the cupcake. It was delish."

"You're welcome." Even as she smiled, she darted an uneasy glance at Hannah, who'd sighed loudly and stepped away to talk to Victoria. Sahil shifted beside me, probably not used to being so close to Hannah's irk. I, on the other hand, was a professional irk-bearer.

"So, I'm studying with Brij and Matthew on Sunday," I said, closing my locker. Glancing at Hannah, I lowered my voice and waggled my eyebrows. "Do you want to come? I know how much you liked his *binder*." I stretched the word "binder" out to about twenty-two syllables.

Maddie gave me a look, like she was plotting something deep and dark. "Yeah . . . and how's the planning for the movie coming along? Because, as I recall, there are some *perks* to doing it for a *pretty* girl like you. . . ."

Oh my God. She was teasing me about Neil right in front of Sahil, and she was using those puns to torture me. Tit for tat—you got me, Maddie.

My cheeks fiery hot, I said quickly to Sahil, who was watching us in confusion, "Um. Do you, Skid, and Aaron want to come, too?"

"Sure," Sahil said. "Thanks. But what perks is Maddie talking about?"

I widened my eyes, and Sahil and I looked at her together. My heart thundered. I wasn't completely sure I wanted Sahil to know about my centuries-long unrequited crush on his brother.

I mean, yes, there was definitely something between Sahil and me. But I'd already decided that we were just going to be friends. So telling him would be better. So he'd know there was no chance for us. But a small part of me just kept thinking about how, if I told him, there would be *no chance for us.* That felt too . . . final. I wasn't ready.

"Oh, that. I just, um, it's not—" Maddie started to say, and then Hannah grabbed her by the arm. Maddie shot me a guilty look, but then Hannah said, "*Maddie,*" and she, Hannah, and Victoria all began to talk, their backs toward me. It was pretty obvious I was being purposely excluded from that conversation.

Don't get me wrong. I was glad for the interruption. But also? It was super rude. And it made me feel like total crap. Did that guilt cupcake offering mean so little, Maddie? I suppose you're right back to being Hannah's doormat at my expense again.

I glanced at Sahil, a hot, liquidy feeling of utter humiliation rolling over me in a nauseating wave. His face was neutral, but his eyes were moving from Maddie to me. Slowly, as they kept talking, his face got steelier and steelier. "They're just going to . . . ignore you? It's been, like, a full minute."

I shrugged and glanced down at my tattered shoes. My face

was purple. I could *feel* it. "Ah, that's . . . that's okay. It happens."

Sahil looked at me disbelievingly. "Yes, but it shouldn't."

And seeing him looking at me like that, hearing his words—*yes, but it shouldn't*—I realized two things: (1) He was absolutely right and (2) So what if Maddie was too scared or intimidated or felt bad to stand up to Hannah? That didn't mean *I* couldn't.

My hands were shaking, but I forced myself to go up and tap Hannah on the shoulder. My heart was pounding so hard, I was sure my shirt was shaking.

She turned, her thin blond eyebrows sky high when she saw it was me.

"It's not okay to interrupt someone's conversation like that." I heard the quiver in my voice, but I kept going. "Also? It's not okay to roll your eyes or laugh at people. We learned all of that in kindergarten, Hannah. Or at least, we were supposed to."

Maddie's face was pale. Victoria's eyes widened, and she whipped out her cell phone and hid behind it, even though her tall red hair gave her away. I could see Sahil smiling encouragingly in my peripheral vision, and I straightened my shoulders. I had *no* idea what had come over me. But I was starting to get reeeeally tired. There's only so much being invisible you can take before you just want to go supernova so no one can ignore you anymore.

(Not that this sweaty, shaking confrontation in front of my locker was *exactly* going supernova, but still. You had to start somewhere.)

Hannah looked so at ease, it was like she was born confronting people. (She probably was, now that I think about it. I could see her as a wrinkly newborn, demanding that the nurse wash her *immediately*.) She crossed her arms over her chest, and her fifty-two charm bracelets clinked together. "Why are you so angry, Twinkle?" she asked, smirking.

Because you've turned my smart, funny, confident best friend into a total bowl of Jell-O, I wanted to yell. *Because you just take and take and take and never stop to think who you're hurting. Because you're a spoiled little brat.* "Why are *you* so mean to me?" I asked. "What have I ever done to you?"

She just shook her head and yawned. She actually *yawned*. "Let's go," she said, and began to walk away. Victoria quirked her mouth at me, shrugged, and left.

Maddie stayed for a moment. "You . . . Don't, Twinkle."

I waited, but she didn't say anything else. "Don't what?"

"You're just . . . You're not helping."

We looked at each other. Disappointment burned inside me. I don't know what I'd expected, but it wasn't for Maddie to just stay quiet the entire time and then imply I was making things worse.

"Fine," I said, but my voice was so quiet, I wasn't sure she heard me. Hitching her backpack up on her shoulders, she walked away.

I looked back at Sahil, my throat sore and tight. I wouldn't cry in front of him. I would *not*.

"Wow," he said, looking a little shell-shocked. "Are you okay?"

I shrugged. "I think so. That's the first time I've ever done anything like that. Figures that I suck at it."

"Hey. You don't suck at it. You were *awesome*," Sahil said, grinning.

I looked up at him. "Even though Hannah wasn't swayed at all?"

"*Pssh*. Maybe she gets off on making people feel small. I don't know. But you're not small, Twinkle." His eyes got serious, and my breath caught in my throat as I studied his face.

"Thanks," I whispered. I knew there had to be people milling all around us, but I didn't see any of them.

After a pause, Sahil nodded, still smiling. "I'll meet you by your locker after school."

I opened my mouth, but nothing came out—apparently my voice had pulled an Amelia Earhart. So instead, I just watched him walk away, my head all muddled and swimming.

Love,

Twinkle

Tuesday, June 9, post-hike at Red Fox Trail
My room

Dear Ava DuVernay,

Um. Whoa.

More soon. A *lot* more. But for now—whoa.

Love,

Twinkle

June 9
The Reel Deal Blog
Posted by: Rolls ROYce

I knew it. I just knew it. It wasn't my imagination.

Sparkle likes me. SHE LIKES ME.

Still Tuesday, June 9
Later, still my room

Dear Ava DuVernay,

Okay. I think I can talk about it now. I'm still not even *close* to being done processing it, but . . . maybe writing to you will help.

So Sahil and I went off to Red Fox Trail like we'd talked about. He met me at my locker (he was there even before I was—yay!), and we didn't speak while we drove. The silence was easy; he mainly just played some new music he'd downloaded.

When we got there, Sahil texted Skid and Aaron, but they didn't respond. So we just began walking, figuring they must be out on the trail, which didn't have the best reception from all the giant pine trees and stuff. I asked Sahil if he knew what musk thistle looked like so we could keep an eye out for Skid, but he just laughed and said no, he did not.

It was nice. The air was cool and I was perfectly comfortable in my T-shirt and shorts. Then something rumbled.

"Is that thunder?" I asked, frowning up at the sky. Sure enough, these giant black clouds were rolling in, and lightning was glittering in the distance. "We're pretty far into the trail. I don't think we can make it back to your car in time."

"It's all good," Sahil said. "We can take cover under the trees."

I was beginning to panic. Colorado thunderstorms are freakishly fast. There are many things that don't scare me, but being outside in a lightning storm is *not* one of them. I have seen way too many charred and splintered husks of trees to be blasé about something like that, let me tell you. "I don't think so, Sahil."

"Hey, it's going to be okay." Sahil smiled his gentle, calm smile.

"No, you don't understand," I said, finding it not a bit calming. "I think standing under a tree is the exact *opposite* of what you're supposed to do in a lightning storm." The first drops splattered on my skin.

"Serious?" Sahil's smile faded. "Crap." The drops turned into streaks of rain. The *ssshhhh* sound of them hitting the trees intensified.

Another bright flash of lightning split the sky, and right on cue, we both grabbed the other's hand and began to run just as a huge clap of thunder rumbled the ground under us.

"Um, where are we going, exactly? The car's too far away, right?" I huffed after a while. I wasn't even well-endowed, but my boobs hurt from running without a sports bra.

"It is! Let's just find some other shelter!" Sahil said, shouting over the thunder and deafening rain. "I know that's at least the right thing to do!"

"Stupid Colorado summer storms!" I yelled back.

"You're joking." Sahil glanced at me as we ran. He was barely breathing fast at all, but I felt like I was dying. Well, if you looked at our legs, mine were about half the size of his stilt-like numbers. It was no wonder. "That's one of my favorite things about this place!"

"Let's take it down a notch, please," I panted, holding my side, and Sahil immediately slowed to what for him was a leisurely pace and for me was still a brisk walk. "I like storms when I'm inside and drinking chai and reading a book or watching a movie. Not when I'm apt to be the latest lightning victim. Although I did read once that this guy got zapped by lightning and when he woke up, he could suddenly paint and speak five different languages he couldn't speak before. That's the only way this will be okay."

Sahil laughed and pointed with his free hand. "Hey, a cabin! Perfect!"

I looked at it through the needles of rain and then at Sahil. "Um. Doesn't that remind you of the cabin in any number of horror movies?"

"Beggars can't be choosers," Sahil countered. "Especially *wet* beggars."

He had a point there.

The cabin was old and the floor was full of pine needles and the walls were full of spiders' webs and it smelled like green, sludgy stuff, but at least if we stayed in the center, away from the holes in the roof, we would be dry. And I was fairly sure we were safer in it than out.

Sahil closed the crooked door behind us and blinked in the dim light. I could barely see him. I looked down at myself—and almost died. No. *No.* I was wearing a white T-shirt . . . which was now soaked through. My tattered old bra, the one I'd had since eighth grade, was on display. Immediately, I crossed my arms over my chest and tried to act casual.

Sahil was poking around. "Just looking for a lantern or something," he explained. "It would be nice if we could *see*."

"What? Nah," I said with a flick of my wrist while still keeping my arms locked firmly around my torso. "This is fine. It's a nice rest for my eyeballs anyway. I mean, they're always *on*, you know?"

I thought Sahil was giving me a weird look, but I couldn't be sure. "Um, okay," he said, coming to stand with me in the center.

A sudden wind gusted through the single open window (the glass was completely missing), and I shivered.

It didn't even seem like Sahil thought about it; he just put his arms around me. I froze again, but this time it was a *totally* different kind of freeze. "Are you cold?" he asked, rubbing his big, warm hands up and down my arms. Goose bumps sprouted immediately.

I tried to think about Neil in that moment. I did. The slight problem was, all I knew about Neil was that he had nice abs and calves. And all I knew about N was that he had questionable poetry skills (though of course I'd never tell him that) and favored an air of mystery. But Sahil? He made me laugh. I looked at things differently because of him. He supported me as an artist. How was Neil supposed to compete with that?

Oops, Sahil had asked me a question. "Um, yep," I said, my voice all high and squeaky as I tried to remember to breathe. I don't think he noticed, though, because he didn't say anything. "I just hope this cabin doesn't flood. That would be bad."

"Very bad," he said softly. "I can't swim."

I laughed a little. "You can't? But Neil's a swimming superstar."

Sahil's hands stilled and then dropped; his body tensed. "Yeah," he said, his voice hard. "*He* is, not me."

I looked up at Sahil. His eyes were glowing in the dim light, a drop of water on his thick eyelashes. The same thick eyelashes I'd always admired on Neil. "What's that about?"

His face was closed off now. "What?"

I studied him carefully. "You don't . . . you don't like talking about your brother?"

A muscle in his jaw jumped as he looked somewhere over my head. He looked down at me a moment later. "No, I don't. I'm sorry, though. I didn't mean to bring that here."

I shook my head and wrapped my arms around myself, shivering a little. "Don't be sorry."

"It's just . . ." He sighed. "I've always been compared to him. It probably happens with all siblings, but it's worse when you're a twin, I think. And it *really* sucks when your twin is a rock star and you're just an average nothing."

"You're *not* an average nothing," I said vehemently.

He shrugged.

"No, look. Neil's the kind of person who maybe ends up on the Fortune 500 list by the time he's thirty. But you're the kind of person I'd want holding my hand in the hospital if my grandmother was sick. And you tell me, which one's more meaningful?" As I said the words, I understood how true they were. I'd trust Sahil with anything.

He met my eye and gazed at me for a long moment, his eyes softening bit by bit. "Thanks, T," he whispered.

Outside, the thunder rumbled and lightning cracked into something. A tree, I think. I reveled in our cleverness at having come in here. Well, I sorta reveled. My brain was pretty tied up with other matters, to be honest. Like how I'd just gotten Sahil's eyes to soften. How I seemed to be able to get to him just like he got to me. How he was still standing extremely close, and I didn't know whether that was for warmth or . . . other reasons.

Smiling, I said in a slightly trembling voice, "I think I just heard a tree get smoked. Aren't you glad we're not out there?"

He didn't return my smile. His eyes were intense, and he was studying my face. "I'm glad I'm here with you," he said, coming closer.

His body heat was making it hard to think. I was beginning to lose sight of why, exactly, this was a bad idea. I should've thought of all the reasons kissing Sahil would be a bad thing, not the least of which is one of Dadi's maxims: *Desire has brought great women to their doom as surely as the Germanic leader Odoacer brought Rome to its knees.* (It's not very pithy—I mean, you couldn't embroider it on a pillow or anything—but she swears it's true.)

All I thought about, though, was Sahil's eyes. How kind and funny and talented he is. How he lets me sit with him at lunch now. And so I leaned *in* when I should've leaned *away*. And I kissed him.

My first-ever kiss, and it takes place in the middle of a freaking thunderstorm, in a deserted cabin. And not an ax murderer in sight. How romantic is that? Nora Ephron couldn't have planned it better. And all those things they say in romance novels about how your heart beats faster and your knees get wobbly and the boy's stubble against your chin is the most delicious sensation ever? All of that is 100 percent true.

I sank into that kiss. It was perfect.

And it can never happen again.

Because in case you missed it, shiny, future Twinkle dates Neil. *Neil*, not Sahil. Maybe my heart didn't care about that, but my brain did. My brain remembered just how long I'd been ignored and belittled. It remembered how badly I wanted to break free. And it knew my time to shine, to do what I was meant to do in this world, was just around the corner.

For some reason, though, when it came to Sahil, it was getting really hard for me to hold on to what my brain was saying. Something was happening between us, something very real, and it was getting more difficult to ignore. But maybe until I figured it out—whatever "it" might be—I should be more careful.

So as soon as we pulled apart for breath, I put a hand up to my mouth and stepped back, my eyes wide. "Whoa."

"Are you okay?" Sahil asked, frowning slightly. I looked at his reddened mouth and felt my cheeks grow warm. I did that. *Me*, Miss Wallflower. "Was that . . . okay?"

Oh God. Now he thought I was reacting like that because he was a bad kisser. Which was so not the case it was almost funny. "N-no! I mean, yes!" I corrected when I saw his face fall. "Sahil, you're . . . you're a good kisser."

"You mean that?" His face lit up so much, the cabin almost brightened. He took a step closer to me. "Then . . . why . . . ?"

I opened my mouth to say, *But . . . there's something you should know. I have a secret admirer, and it's probably your brother. By the way, I want to date him*. Only how could I say that to Sahil now that my heart and my brain were warring? And after he'd told me about Neil and their sibling rivalry?

So I chose another, smaller truth. "We work together. And if we . . . do this . . . it might complicate things."

"I can keep things professional."

I took a deep breath as I looked into his clear brown eyes. It would be so easy to say yes. It would be so easy to be with Sahil. "I'm sorry," I said instead, the words physically hurting me like they had sharp edges.

He studied my face for a long second and then nodded. "So . . . are you saying we can go out *after* Midsummer Night?" He grinned mischievously.

I laughed and pushed his chest, avoiding an answer.

Sahil's phone beeped in his pocket. "Huh. I must have reception again." He fished it out and looked at the screen. "It's Skid and Aaron. 'Did you see the news? Apparently big storm on the way.' They want to postpone so no one gets drenched."

We looked at each other, our cold, wet clothes clinging to us, our hair dripping, and then burst out laughing.

Sahil typed back a response and slipped the phone back in his pocket. "It would've helped if they'd sent that text about an hour ago."

"Ah, well. Next time we'll know to check the weather before we come."

Sahil smiled a half smile that made my heart stutter. "I enjoyed being stuck here with you, though. I'd do it again."

I bit my lip. "So would I."

That's when I realized the truth: I'd get stuck with Sahil in a cabin any day of the week, anytime. I'd even get stuck with Sahil in an econ class because I like being with him so much. I'd choose spending time with him over peanut butter chocolate ice cream. And over the Peanut Butter Chocolate Mountain Majesty cupcake.

So where the heck does that leave me with Neil?

At least I've managed to put Sahil off for now. I think what I need to do is meet up with N. See how I feel. Maybe?

Love,

Twinkle

Ten

From: twinkiefilmfan@urmail.com
To: binadmiringyou@urmail.com
Subject: Sorry to bug you
I know I just wrote to you, N, but I think we need to meet up.
Certain life situations have made things all jumbled up in my
head (and my heart). I just need to see who you are.
—Twinkle

Wednesday, June 10
17 days until Midsummer Night!
Homeroom

Dear Mira Nair,

I know my life is a mess right now with Maddie, Sahil, N, etc.,
etc. But I cannot even worry about that because . . .

TODAY IS THE DAY I HOLD MY FIRST AUDITIONS!

I hadn't expected this day to come for many, many years. But
today I get to sit in a room and watch people perform. And based
on my decisions, a film will evolve—one that has the power to

start conversations and get people talking about things like feminism and art.

Have I mentioned I'm a sixteen-year-old girl from Colorado Springs? A junior at PPC?

I keep wondering if I'm qualified to do something like this. This is a huge, huge responsibility. It just keeps hitting me that this isn't a two-minute video I'm going to upload to my YouTube channel. This is big. Hundreds of people are going to see this at the end of the month. This is going to influence how people *think*. What if I ruin it? What if I have nothing to say?

What if, what if, what if?

Arrrgh. It's too late to back out now, even if I wanted to, which I don't—not 100 percent. And like Dadi says, I have a feeling that if I don't take this opportunity, I'll look back and kick myself.

So here I go, onward and (hopefully) upward! Wish me luck.

Love,

Twinkle

Wednesday, June 10
AP US History

Dear Ava DuVernay,

I need to reread the story about how you got your start making films. In the meantime, let me tell you a little story about mine. You know how I was hoping at least ten people would show up to auditions?

Well.

So Sahil and I were sitting in Ms. Rogers's classroom at lunch, waiting until 12:20, which is the time we put on the flyers that people should show up and wait outside the door. We kept looking at each other, smiling, and then looking away, both too nervous to talk about the cabin and all that stuff (even though every time I looked at Sahil my gaze automatically fell to his lips—traitorous boy-oglers.)

Sahil sat there, too tall for the desks (his legs and arms jutted out and he kept jittering because he was so nervous), and I just closed my eyes and tried to visualize success because I read that all the big athletes do it and it's not hokey like I used to believe. I visualized the door bursting open and this horde of people swarming in and begging to audition. I could hear some noise, but I knew what it was: people going about their business in the hallway. Would *anyone* come to our audition?

Then Sahil said, "It's time!" He leaped up, bumped the desk with his thighs, and sent it sliding off toward the corner. His face flushed, he dragged it back into place.

I stood and took a deep breath. *Forget ten*, I said to the universe as we walked to the door. *Just give me* six *people. Just so I don't look like a total failure.*

We opened the door. And stared.

It was like a tsunami of noise. I'm not even lying. And it wasn't because people were loitering in the hallway at lunch either. They were all there for us. For my film, mine and Sahil's. I just stared at them. Sahil's paralysis broke first. He turned to me, grinning widely.

"A *little* more than ten," he said, giggling. He giggles!

I shook my head slowly. "How are we even going to manage

this?" I said faintly, and Sahil leaned forward because he legit could not hear me because it was so *loud*.

But then Skid and Aaron, who I had not seen come up, began shepherding people into a semblance of a line and Sahil hopped into the fray going, "Okay, people, let's have some order. No, don't break the producer, please!"

"Wow, check out the crowd," Maddie said, pushing her way up to me.

"I know, right?" I decided to put aside our differences for the sake of our professional relationship. Maddie had clearly turned it off, and I could too. Besides, I was fairly sure this was all part of being a director. I couldn't let my personal feelings get in the way of my art. "Oh, and thanks for showing off the capelet." Most of the people in line were from Maddie's social circle.

She waved me off. "Ah, it's no big deal. People are super excited to include this in their college apps, too. It's so different." She tucked her hair behind an ear and half smiled at me. "So, are you psyched? This is what you've always wanted, coming to life."

"I'm so psyched," I said. And then it hit me that we sounded like acquaintances who'd run into each other at a restaurant. Ugh.

"Cool," Maddie said, wrapping her arms around herself. "So . . . I'll go wait in line. See you inside?"

I thought about saying yes. But I could feel it—my best friend slipping further away from me. So, on impulse, I said, "Um, do you want to come inside? Maybe help us pick the roles?"

"Me?" Maddie said, holding a hand up to her chest. "But I'm

just an actress." I could tell by her exultant smile that she liked calling herself that.

"So what? Perks of being the lead."

She looked at me for a beat and then said, "Squee! Okay."

I felt a tug of affection for her, despite everything. Maddie is the only person I know who *says* "squee" instead of just typing it. Smiling, I put an arm around her and led her in.

Maddie turned out to be very helpful in casting. For instance, when Sahil and I had difficulties deciding between two people, she'd say stuff like, "Oh, Olivia just got grounded for going to a frat party without telling her parents, so she probably won't be able to make practice for a week or two." So we chose Francesca instead. Or "Mike told everyone he thinks this whole gender-swapped idea is crap but he needs to beef up his college apps," so we chose Brij for the role of "Morris" (Mina in the original).

Oh, and speaking of Brij—he completely captivated us with his acting! Even Maddie, who's not into films like Sahil and I are, was leaning forward and watching him. The only reason we'd been considering Mike a little more is because Brij has a tendency to mumble. But better a mumbler than a hater, I say.

Oh, and guess what? Victoria Lyons came up and *apologized* to me after she auditioned. Maddie was in the bathroom and missed it. Victoria basically said, "That was pretty crappy how we interrupted your conversation yesterday. I'm sorry. Hey, by the way, you should come to Hannah's birthday party next Saturday at my parents' cabin. Okay?"

First I just stared at her in utter shock. Not only was Victoria

Lyons apologizing to *me,* but she was also inviting me to a *party?* Then her words sank in. "Oh, it's Hannah's party?" I asked, thinking about our moment in the hall yesterday.

"Yes, but it's *my* parents' cabin," Victoria said. She put a hand on my arm. "Please, Twinkle. Let me make it up to you."

I said okay because I'd be *crazy* to refuse an invitation to a party at Victoria's parents' cabin in Aspen. Plus, *she* wanted to make something up to *me?* It was finally happening, wasn't it? The movie was helping elevate me past groundling status, just like I'd hoped. Maybe I could hang out with some of her friends, show her that I could fit seamlessly in with the silk feathered hats. I could probably just avoid Hannah most of the time anyway.

Plus, on a professional note, it'll be a good time to get some behind-the-scenes interviews with the cast members, like that extra footage at the end of DVDs, to make our film stand out at the festival.

I ended up casting Victoria as Renfield, but the invitation had nothing to do with it, promise. I mean, honestly, I would like to cast *Hannah* as the character who eats live animals with the hopes of obtaining their life force, but she didn't show up. Big surprise there. Why would she want to go to Twinkle Mehra's auditions? Maybe I should be thankful she even let Maddie come. Anyway, Victoria is great at styling her hair and she promised she could style it to look like a rat's nest to suit the character's chaotic mind.

We begin filming tomorrow—my first real movie and chance to be a director! This is so surreal, I keep looking around for

Salvador Dalí to make an appearance. I just hope I can live up to expectations—everyone else's and my own.

Love,

Twinkle

Thursday, June 11
Homeroom

Dear Valerie Farris,

I ran into Sahil today before first bell. "Hey, T," he said, his mouth quirked in a mischievous half smile. "Where're you rushing off to in such a hurry?"

Do not be taken in by his charm, I told myself. *You have something important to do. Stay focused.* "Um, I was hoping to catch you on your way to class."

His smile got brighter and he took a half step toward me. "Oh, yeah?"

"Yeah." I kept my face serious and looked straight into his eyes. His gorgeous, soft brown eyes. Those eyes I'd fallen into right before we kissed. *Focus,* Twinkle. "Look, I know the other day at lunch I might've seemed like I didn't care too much, but . . ." I took a breath and said the rest in a rush. If I waited, I'd lose my nerve and change the subject to the cafeteria's chocolate milk or something. "Sahil, it was a big deal to me that you chose the cyclorama over the backdrop I wanted. I mean, I'm not saying that you bullied me into it or anything—I should've spoken up at Thoroughly Thespian. That's something I struggle with, so that's what I'm doing now. I'm speaking up. I wanted the backdrop, not the cyclorama. And I didn't like the way you spoke to me at lunch the other day when I brought it up."

He stepped back and shifted his weight. "Look, what's the big deal, Twinkle? It's just one prop in the movie. I thought we talked about this in the caf."

"I know we did. It's just—Sahil, the big deal is that it's not what I wanted. And I feel like you're just rolling over me with what you want. You're not even hearing what I'm saying."

He shook his head. "Well, you picked out the majority of the props."

"Right, but you agreed the creepy stuff probably wouldn't fly with the administration, remember? You wanted to change those out after we talked about it. I didn't want to change this. Why are you so attached to this cyclorama, anyway?" My voice shook a little, but I held steady. This was important; I had to speak up and hold my own here. Sahil was being weirdly pushy, but that didn't mean I was going to let myself be intimidated into silence. I'm sure you've dealt with the same thing, Valerie, as a woman trying hard to make her voice heard in what has been a boys' club for way too long.

He shrugged. "It's . . . bold. It screams, *Look at me!* And I feel like that's what we need for this movie. We need to be noticed. We need people to see us for who we are."

I got the strange feeling that there was a lot more under the surface than what Sahil was saying. But his eyes kept darting around, his jaw was clenched, and his arms were folded across his chest. It felt like he didn't want me to get too close.

I sighed, sensing that we weren't going to get anywhere right then. Maybe I could regroup and try again later, when we had more time. "Sahil, I don't know what's going on here, but I feel like you're keeping something from me. You're not even really listening. So fine. Let's just pick this up later. I gotta get to class."

"Okay," he said, his expression shifting, becoming more thoughtful. "Talk soon."

I don't know how this whole thing is going to play out in the end, whether Sahil will finally see my point of view or if we'll have to have some ugly argument, but at least I spoke up. Not too shabby for a groundling, eh, Valerie? I'm just trying not to be too disappointed at Sahil's response.

Love,

Twinkle

Thursday, June 11
AP Bio

Dear Sofia Coppola,

The polar ice caps must've shifted because Maddie just passed me a note. In *bio*. When Mrs. Mears is talking about the *genome* project.

I'll paste it in here when we're done talking.

Love,

Twinkle

The auditions were fun yesterday.
I'm psyched we cast all the roles. TY again for getting people excited.
Sure. Hey, did Victoria speak to you when I was in the bathroom?

About Hannah's party next weekend. Why?

I don't think it's a good idea for you to come to the party.

Oh. Why not? I was going to get some behind-the-scenes footage.

You won't have any fun, Twinkle. Why don't I throw you another, smaller party and you can get your footage extras there?

Why don't you think I'll have fun, though??

Don't get upset!

I'm not upset!

The "??" are clearly an indication of an upset emotional state. I know you.

Oh, right, just like you KNOW how I shouldn't go to this party. Because I'm too much of a groundling.

Of a what??

Who's upset now?? And let me just say, Maddie, that I'm going. And I'm bringing Sahil, who happens to be my producer. And if you or Hannah have a problem with that, you can just take it up with Victoria, who invited me in the first place and whose parents own the freaking cabin. Okay??

Thursday, June 11
AP English

Dear Sofia Coppola,

You may think I am upset, but I am, in fact, not. So I had a fight with Maddie. So she doesn't think I belong with her FANCY,

STUPID friends in their FANCY, STUPID cabin. So she thinks I'm the stuff you find under your shoe after walking around in a big city all day. Big freaking deal. We were growing apart anyway. Maybe that's just what happens to friendships sometimes.

If you think I'm going to break down and cry, you're mistaken. I was a total idiot to think this movie could mean good things for Maddie's and my friendship. I was an even bigger idiot to think she'd be impressed by me hanging out with her crowd at the cabin, obviously, because she doesn't even want me there. Apparently I'm that big of an embarrassment. When people show you who they are, you should believe them. I'm so sick and tired of being treated like this. Everyone has a breaking point, and guess what? I think Maddie found mine.

I mean, will it make it awkward when we have to spend an hour and a half after school today filming? Sure. But I am a *professional*, as we've already established. I can deal with this. I can make it a non-issue.

I can. Yep. I've got this.

Love,

Twinkle

Thursday, June 11
Honors Calculus

Dear Nora Ephron,

So I was walking to my locker when someone grabbed my arm. I thought it was Maddie, but when I turned, it was Sahil's goofy smile I was looking at. My heart was more leapy than I would've liked, but I managed to keep my answering smile normal and not oversize like it was trying to be.

"Come with me, quick," Sahil said, dragging me down the opposite way of my locker.

"Um, I have to get to class. School's almost out; what's the rush?" I followed him, but I frowned, just so he'd think I had reservations about going with him. (Spoiler alert: I didn't. Foolish heart. Desire=DOOM, how hard is it to learn that? It's even an alliteration.)

"I know, and I do too, but I want to show you this one thing in Ms. Rogers's room quickly." His voice was fizzing with excitement, so I figured he was over whatever was going on with him the last time we spoke.

I couldn't afford to miss anything in calculus so close to the final, but my curiosity got the better of me. "Okay. You've piqued my interest, Sahil Roy."

He chuckled. "Excellent."

We rounded the corner and he opened the door to Ms. Rogers's room, which was empty. "She's grading in the teacher's lounge," he explained. Then he began to walk toward a large plank of wood that had been covered with a tarp.

"Oh, is that the cyclorama? When did you get this?" I asked, excited to see it even if it *did* have an evil moon with fangs. It was still part of our set. Our *set*. We had a SET.

He ran a hand through his hair, looking away for a second. "I went and picked it up."

"You skipped school?" I was confused. "I thought they were supposed to deliver it tomorrow."

He shrugged. "Most of the teachers are just doing review anyway." Then he smiled at me and put one hand on the tarp. "Close your eyes."

I *rolled* my eyes instead. "I know what it looks like, Sahil. Just take the tarp off."

"Nope." He thrust out his chin in this stubborn gesture that I loved. Er, I mean liked. A normal amount.

Sighing theatrically, I closed my eyes and put a hand over them for good measure. I heard the tarp rustling. And then Sahil, his voice bubbling with glee, said, "Okay. Open."

I took my hand off and opened my eyes. And there in front of me was the backdrop. Not the cyclorama Sahil had fallen in love with, but the one *I* had chosen. The one with the village lights on the hill. I stared at it in complete shock. My voice went AWOL.

"Are—is this okay?" Sahil asked, frowning. "I mean, it's all paid for and everything. You don't have to do any—"

I shook my head. "No, it's not that. It's . . ." I swallowed. "How did you—why did you do this?"

He stuck his hands in his pockets and quirked his lips. "The how was easy. It wasn't anything Agent Sahil couldn't handle." He put on his snotty agent accent. "'This cyclorama simply doesn't work for Miss Mehra's vision, darling. We need something else. Something with more *je ne sais quoi*.'"

I snorted.

"As for the why . . . I was being a jerk before about it. You were right—I wasn't listening, and I realized I was being an idiot. The cyclorama wasn't about the cyclorama. It . . . Anyway . . ." Shaking his head, he took a step closer to me. "I heard what you said to me this morning, T. About needing to speak up? I heard you one hundred percent. And I want to give my director what she wants. I trust your vision all the way, and this is me showing you that I do."

I still had a million questions.

#1: Why did you do such a nice thing for me, Sahil?

#2: Don't you know how hard it is for me to not hop into your arms and kiss you right now?

Okay, so maybe only two questions.

Sahil had *heard* me. That was a way bigger gift than this backdrop even was. I just stared at him, rooted to the spot.

His face was anxious as the silence stretched on. "So, do you like it? I wanted it to be a surprise, which is why I didn't consult you. . . ."

That broke my paralysis. I stepped even closer to him. Putting my arms around his waist, I laid my head on his chest. I heard his heart beating in there, solid and steady and strong. "This is perfect," I said, and I wasn't just talking about the backdrop. "Thank you."

After a pause, Sahil's arms wrapped around me, too. My heart thundered at his touch, but I kept my breathing calm. This was a *friendly* hug. At least, that's what I wanted him to think. I stepped back. "So. You were saying how the cyclorama wasn't actually about the cyclorama? I thought that whole conversation we had earlier didn't seem like you. So what's going on? What's the cyclorama about?"

He looked at me, steady. "It's about . . . being noticed. Not being the kind of person who's going to fade into the background, overlooked for someone else." His phone *ding*ed in his pocket and he pulled it out. I saw NEIL on the screen, and a text message below that. Sahil put the phone back.

I smiled. "Talk about someone who doesn't ever fade into the background."

"What?"

"Neil. I saw the text was from him." I laughed a little. "Ironic. We're talking about being overlooked, and Neil texts you. I don't think he'd know the meaning of the word 'ignored,' unlike some other people." I was talking about myself, but Sahil didn't return my smile.

"Right."

"Anyway," I said, studying his expression. He'd said at the cabin he didn't like to talk about Neil, but I didn't know something this small counted too. "You were saying?"

He waved me off. "Nah, nothing." Raising his chin toward the backdrop, he said, "So, you want to check that out?"

Again, I got the feeling there was so much happening I couldn't see. Sahil was an iceberg. Ninety-seven percent of him was under the surface.

He clearly didn't want to talk about it, and I didn't want to be the *Titanic*, so I nodded and walked up to the backdrop. Running a finger along the (non-fanged) moon and (non-fingered) trees, I whistled. "Love it. Love. It. This is exactly what we need for our first scene today." Sahil came to stand beside me, and I smiled at him. "Thank you."

"Anytime, T," he murmured. "Anytime." And then he was back to being *my* Sahil, the soft, sweet friend I could share anything with.

Don't judge me, Nora. I know I've had that secret fantasy about Neil and me being this power couple for as long as I can remember. But what about the connection I'm making with his twin brother now? Aaaahhhh. Why is high school so *complicated*?

Love,
Twinkle

Thursday, June 11
My room

Dear Mira Nair,

My first day of filming is over. It. Was. Amazing.

I mean, sure, things were still pretty prickly between my lead actress and me. (She and Brij were talking up a storm, but of course I couldn't comment on that because we're not talking to each other.) Victoria wasn't on the same page as Maddie because she came up to me and said, "Twinkle, do you think my right side is my good side?" (She has one of the most symmetrical faces I've ever seen, Mira, so I'm not sure what she's talking about. All her sides are "good.") And then she said, "I love this white dress you got me" and "This scene is so *incisive!*" She even gave me her cell number in case I wanted to text her scene ideas for her character. (I didn't have the heart to tell her I don't have a cell phone; that probably wouldn't compute for someone like Victoria.) I think she was trying to be my friend. *Victoria Lyons.*

It's like becoming a director is making me someone even silk feathered hats like Victoria respect.

And what's weird is . . . *I* felt myself changing too. As the minutes wore on and I was directing people (as one does when one is the director), I felt like I was getting taller. My shoulders straightened out. I stopped caring about whether I'd say anything dumb because all of them were hanging on my every word. I *felt* like a director for the first time ever today. I wasn't a silk feathered hat person, but just for that period of time, I wasn't a groundling either. I'm never, ever going to forget this feeling.

Oh, and I found out why Sahil had e-mailed to ask me what font I liked. He, Skid, and Aaron had pitched in and gotten me a *director's chair with my name on it.* They made me cover my eyes and sit on it and they kept asking me questions like "Do you feel different?" before they'd let me uncover my eyes. When it sank in what they'd done, I almost cried. I just looked at them, all of their faces smiling and sweet and friendly. They'd planned this for *me*, and they barely knew me.

It's getting a treasured place in my room when we're done with the film, a reminder that there are people who believe in me and the message I want to send the world. And then if I ever win an Academy Award, I'm thanking them onstage.

So, after we finished filming the first scene and Sahil dropped me off at home, I had a surprise waiting—an e-mail from N! Pasting it below.

This has easily been one of the BEST days of my life.

Love,

Twinkle

From: binadmiringyou@urmail.com

To: twinkiefilmfan@urmail.com

Subject: You're not bugging me

Twinkle,

Okay, I'm convinced. Let's meet up. How about the carnival downtown Saturday night, 8 pm? I'll meet you by the carousel.

—N

Eleven

Saturday, June 13
Dressing room at Target

Dear Haifaa al-Mansour,

I convinced Dadi to loan me some money to buy a dress. She thinks I'm going to the carnival to hang out with Maddie. I don't like lying to her, but if I told her I was meeting some boy who's been e-mailing me on the Internet, she would probably keel over of a heart attack. So I'll tell her once it's all worked out, promise.

I'm not letting it dampen my mood because . . . it's Saturday, the day I meet N at the carnival!

It's not till later tonight, but I opened my closet, looked in there, and realized I have nothing to wear. Nothing that doesn't make me look like a twelve-year-old, anyway. So here I am, trying on clothes.

N *has* to be Neil, right? I mean, fixing the meeting for Saturday at eight p.m.? He's probably done with his swim training then.

I kept rereading his e-mails like some obsessed character from *Macbeth* (instead of "out, out, damn spot!" I wanted to yell, "hint, hint, one hint! That's all I want!"), until I made myself step away from the screen. I had to force myself to remember all the other cool stuff I have going on in my life.

So, okay, my ex-bestie (extie?) and I are still fighting. She wouldn't even fully look at me during filming yesterday. *But* we got one whole scene completed. And all the other actors were paying attention, especially Brij, who kept staring at me like he was trying to see into my brain or something, which was a little intense, but if that's what he needs to do to get into character, who am I to judge? I've slept in my famous female filmmakers T-shirt every night this week to get into the mind-set of a butt-kicking female director. Victoria casually let it slip that she'd told Hannah I was coming to the party and then later I heard Maddie tell her that it was a bad idea to let me come. Then she saw me and her eyes got all wide and she walked off. Whatever. I'm still going. I'm the director and I was invited.

See, I have a lot going on. I don't need to be nervous about N. But that doesn't mean I don't want to look as beautiful and sexy and "shiny, future self" as possible. Fake it till you make it and all that. This could be the beginning of the future, non-groundling me. Tonight might be the night I look back on fondly once things have turned around for me. Shouldn't I look my best for it? (No heels, though. That's where I draw the line.)

Love,

Twinkle

Saturday, June 13
Car ride with Papa

Dear Sofia Coppola,

Papa's driving me to the carnival. I would be more focused on meeting N in just half an hour, but I'm too busy being stunned by my unbelievably weird day so far.

I had no idea looking beautiful and sexyish was as complicated as solving a freaking differential equation.

It all started out pretty well. I got a cute dress at Target. It's sleeveless and purple lace with these tiny buttons at the back and falls to midthigh. I even picked up some lip gloss and eyeliner on impulse (the dress was on sale, so I was able to get all of that for less than forty dollars, which is what Dadi had given me). But when I got home and began to get dressed (at five p.m., just to give me plenty of time), I realized I'd forgotten a big part of my outfit: my hair.

I mean, it's long and thick and falls to just above my waist. I usually wear it in a braid so I don't have to deal with it. But I couldn't wear a *braid* to the carnival, for my first meeting with N. I looked up these YouTube videos that promised "5 EASY ways to style hair ANYONE can master!" I must not be "anyone" because I felt like I was wrestling an octopus. Or maybe I needed to *be* an octopus, because there is no way anyone without eight arms can do all the stuff the girl in the video was doing.

At one point I was in tears. This was *not* how the first night of the rest of my shiny, new, non-invisible life was supposed to start. Things were supposed to be easy and fun, but everything felt stressy and sweaty and annoying. Honestly? I kept wanting to call Sahil to vent. I longingly imagined him, Skid, Aaron, and me in Perk, just laughing and hanging out. But then I'd tell myself I was being silly. Neil and non-groundling status was what I've been dreaming of for so long. Maybe I'm just suffering from impostor syndrome.

Once I dried my tears I tried to recruit Dadi, who said she'd be happy to help and then braided my hair into two braids that were horrifyingly stuck to the side of my head. I looked like I belonged on the hills of Switzerland with milk pails. It was already well past six o'clock at this point and I was beginning to hyperventilate when it hit me: I had the number to an expert hair-doer-upper. Sure, this wasn't strictly why she'd given me her number, but I was desperate and ready to try just about anything. So I called Victoria Lyons.

At first she thought I was telling her that I had a wig I needed help with for the movie, but when she got that it was *my* hair that was in dire need, she immediately said, "Oh! Okay, gimme your address." She showed up twenty-five minutes later with—I am not even kidding—a little suitcase on wheels.

I stared at it because I thought she'd misunderstood and thought I'd asked her over for a sleepover or something. "Um . . . is that a suitcase?"

"It's a travel case of all my hair supplies," Victoria explained. Then, pointing to her luscious red hair, which was in a high, bouncy ponytail, the kind I could never pull off, she said, "Do you think all this magic happens without some serious tools?"

She walked in and looked around at my tiny living room and the attached kitchen. "Oh. This reminds me of this cute little cabin I stayed at in Amsterdam over last winter break. They misrepresented the picture online when I booked! My dad almost sued the pants off them." She beamed at me, and I realized she didn't mean any of that to be insulting.

"Um, my room is this way," I said, walking down the tiny hallway. Once we were inside and she'd had me sit on my desk chair, facing the floor-length mirror on my wall, I said, "Thanks for coming over, by the way. I know you must have stuff to do."

Victoria smiled slyly. "I figured this had something to do with a boy. And that adorable dress on your bed and this makeup here tells me I'm not wrong."

I felt my cheeks get warm. Thank goodness for dark skin; Victoria probably couldn't see it. "No, you're not wrong."

Her grin widened as she loosened my hair from the knot I'd tied after Dadi's disastrous braid attempt. "So, is it Sahil?"

I hitched in a sharp breath. Victoria watched me curiously in the mirror. "Ah, no," I said. "Not Sahil."

She nodded. "Okay. Well, you don't have to tell me if you don't want to. We'll just make sure you sweep him off his studly feet. Deal?"

I grinned. "Deal."

She paused with her hands in my hair. "Although . . . can I tell you something?"

I looked at her in the mirror. "Sure."

"You don't *need* all this stuff"—she gestured to her suitcase— "to sweep him off his feet. You're kind of cool in a weirdly quirky way. It draws people in."

I almost choked on my spit. "No, I'm not." Had Victoria not

noticed that people were so *not* drawn to me that I, in fact, seemed to repel them? Especially the silk feathered hats?

She smiled a little. "Yes, you are. You just can't see it. Sit up straighter."

I did as she asked, feeling warm and happy. Victoria, one of the silkiest, featheriest hatted, people thought I was cool and quirky? And she'd come all this way to help me. I felt the little bud of our friendship beginning to bloom, and I smiled to myself.

Victoria got into it. She began to pull sections of my hair this way and that and then she told me to close my eyes because she wanted me to wait to see the final product at the end. And *then*, when she was done with my hair, forty-five minutes later, she told me she'd brought makeup in her traveling suitcase and wanted to slather that on my face too. I asked her what was wrong with the Revlon stuff I bought at Target, but she just said, "No offense, Twinkle, but everyone knows NARS is where it's at."

"What's that?" I asked, grimacing while she dusted something on my face that smelled like roses. I kept my eyes closed though. "A club?"

Victoria snorted. "Never mind. Just keep your eyes closed."

She kept muttering things like, "No, no, plum is definitely her color, but I wonder if I have something with a little gold in it" and "Firecracker Copper is *so* you," and finally, just when I thought I couldn't take the suspense (and Victoria's not-very-gentle ministrations) anymore, she told me to open my eyes.

"That is not me" is the first thing I said. Victoria laughed.

I looked . . . like some magical fairy version of myself. My hair was in these long, loose curls that looked effortless (but obviously weren't), and one side was clipped back. My eyes were huge and expressive, dark brown popping against the copper-colored eyeshadow. I had dangerously sharp cheekbones that looked like Maddie's, and my acne scars—even the deep one on my nose—had been covered up.

"Concealer," Victoria said when I ran a finger over it. "I have a kind that works for most skin tones."

Something dawned on me. The reflection in the mirror? It was *her*. The future Twinkle I'd always dreamed about, the one who had ideas that other people listened to, the one who was *cool* because she made movies, not nerdy because she was always hiding behind a camera.

"This is . . . I don't know what to say, Victoria," I said, standing and facing her. "I feel . . . like a glossy version of myself, if that makes sense. Like I could go places the old me would never have been allowed." *Like your social circle*, I wanted to say, but didn't. Actually, I didn't even know if that was strictly true anymore. Things were shifting somehow. Victoria was here, in my house, being a friend to me. She'd invited me to her parents' cabin. Maybe the movie was magic, somehow doing what I'd never been able to do for myself.

"Makeup can do that," Victoria said, nodding knowingly. "But, Twinkle, you don't need it. It's not a golden ticket. You could've gone to the carnival in sweats and I'm sure you'd still be able to charm this guy, whoever he is."

I smiled. "Thanks. That's sweet."

"Ugh, don't call me that," Victoria said, making a face. "Speaking of makeup, I'm leaving the eyeshadow, blush, and lip gloss I used on you here if you ever want to try this stuff on your own. They don't work on me anyway, and don't worry, I always use disposable applicators, so it's all hygienic."

"Thank you," I said, feeling shy all of a sudden. I know I've always been all about the groundlings and the silk feathered hats, but right then Victoria didn't seem like a snob and I didn't feel like a groundling. We were just two girls hanging out and bonding. "You're like my teenaged fairy godmother. Only with makeup and hair spray."

Victoria laughed. "Hey, I like that! I always knew I was special." She winked and began packing up her stuff. "Now, get that dress on and go wow that boy, whoever he is."

"I will. And, um . . ." I wasn't going to say anything, but if there was ever a time, now was it. "I know you invited me to Hannah's party, but Maddie—"

Victoria turned to me. "Don't worry about Maddie. She's just paranoid."

"Paranoid?"

"Yeah. She thinks because Hannah doesn't want you there, it'll be weird or something. But it won't. You're *my* guest."

"I don't think she's afraid it's gonna be weird," I said, trying not to let my hurt show. "I think she just doesn't want me mixing with her friends."

Victoria put her hands on her hips. "Well, she doesn't get to make that decision alone." After a pause, she said, "Besides, Hannah just needs a chance to get to know you. In fact, I always thought you were this mousy, weak girl with nothing to say—"

"Thanks," I said, raising a combed and powdered eyebrow.

Victoria held up her hands. "—but you're this cool, creative, film genius person! Hannah just needs to see that too. Don't worry."

"Okay. Thanks for real then." I grinned at her. "I mean it. You're pretty cool too."

She smiled. "I know, right? Anyway, I'll get out of here now so you can go meet Prince Charming." Blowing me a kiss, she rolled her suitcase out into the hallway and was gone.

Holy crap, we're here.

Love,

Twinkle

Saturday, June 13
One fantabulous Ferris wheel ride later
My room

Dear Sofia Coppola,

I know, I know. You're probably dying to know who N is. But first, I must set the stage to tell the story.

So Papa dropped me off at the carnival. Right before I got out of the car, he looked at me and his eyebrows got all furrowed and he said, "Just you and Maddie? No boys?" I almost confessed everything right then and there because Papa was paying attention and he'd thought to *ask*, unlike another parent I have.

But if I told Papa the truth, he'd follow me around all night with that giant flashlight he keeps under his seat, and somehow I felt that might kill the atmosphere. I promised silently to tell him everything once N and I made it official instead.

After he was gone, I bought enough tickets for one ride and walked in. It was the usual hazy pink sky as dusk fell, the smell of fried stuff smothered in powdered sugar, people laughing and hooting and pushing past me. But it still felt magical. I felt different, like tonight all things were possible. Like every facet of my life would finally shape up and become clear.

For instance, the thing with Victoria showed me that not all non-groundlings are the arrogant, judgmental beasts I'd always thought them to be. (I never thought that about Neil, of course.) And maybe finally seeing N would put the Sahil problem to rest. Maybe I'd finally know what to do with my foolish heart.

It was weird, too, because as I walked, random boys kept looking at me. First I didn't understand what that was about, but after the fourth one I realized: THEY WERE CHECKING ME OUT. This has never, ever happened to me on such a large scale before. Am I "hot" in this outfit, makeup, and hair?? Weird, especially considering not a single thing about me has changed. I just have some paint slapped on me.

I wound through the crowd and found the carousel. (It was hard to miss because of the music and also because the entire top hooded part of it had been covered in these twinkly lights.) I checked the watch I'd borrowed (read: stolen) from Mummy's drawer: 7:50 p.m. I still had ten minutes. Was it uncool to get there ten minutes before my secret admirer? Probably. I thought about ducking into a nearby stall and waiting behind the stuffed animals, but decided that would be too weird, even for me. So, instead, I watched the little kids on the carousel.

It was pretty cool. Most of them had their eyes closed in total delight, like they were imagining themselves flying or something. Some of the more anxious ones kept their heads turned so they could see their parents at all times. I wondered which one I used to be when I was a kid. I had a feeling I was in the nervy group, constantly reaching for Mummy even if she didn't want me to. That's okay, though. Dadi always took her place.

Anyway, do you know they don't just have horses and pumpkin carriages on carousels now? This one had some *Pokémon* and *Adventure Time* characters.

I glanced at my watch again. Only three minutes had passed. This was *torture*. My palms had literally begun to sweat.

"Get ready, folks!" a voice said on the loudspeaker, startling me. "In just a few minutes, we're going to blow the horn and open the gates to the rides in this park for a full sixty seconds! That means you can ride for free, noooo tickets needed, as long as you get on the ride before the horn stops blowing! Once again, this is for *every* ride in the park!"

Huh. That might be fun. Maybe once N got here, we could do that. We could ride the spinning teacup ride thing and maybe he'd kiss me in it, setting my non-groundling future into full force.

Two more minutes left. He might be walking toward me at *this very moment*. I started to watch the kids again—and felt a big, warm hand on my elbow.

Twelve

Totally cheesy, but I swear time stopped in that moment. My breath caught in my throat. A loose curl blew across my face. I tucked it behind my ear, blinked, and slowly swiveled, the carousel music creating a perfectly surreal, magical backdrop.

Sahil grinned down at me, debonair in a yellow button-down shirt with the sleeves rolled up and plaid shorts. I didn't even think for a second that it might be Neil. I was getting to know all of Sahil's little quirks, like that silly dimple-like divot on the bridge of his nose when he smiled. "Hey!"

I blinked again. Huh? "Are you . . . ?" *Oh my God*. Was he N?? I felt a weird combination of confusion and hope warring in my chest. I tried the question again. "What are you doing here?"

"Oh, I'm supposed to meet Aaron and Skid to go ride the roller coasters. We do it every year. But Skid had a flat on the way here, so they're waiting for a tow truck. I offered to give them a ride, but they said I should just meet them here." He shrugged. "So here I am, ready to grab some fried goodness, get a head start on the food-coma train." He grinned. "What about you?"

My heart did this slow plummet as he talked and I realized that *duh* he wasn't N and *duh* that didn't even make any sense because his name is *Sahil Roy*. He doesn't have a single *N* anywhere in his name. Then I remembered he'd asked me what I was doing and I still hadn't answered. "Oh, right. I'm, ah, just meeting someone."

"Oh, cool." He looked me up and down for the first time and his eyes got wide. "Wow. I mean, you look—" Then he stopped and his face got this stiff, guarded look. "Is this a, um, date-type situation?"

I opened my mouth to respond. I didn't know *exactly* what I was going to say, but I'd figure it out. The thing was, I still didn't want to tell Sahil about N. I knew hiding this wasn't the most honest thing to do; it wasn't fair to Sahil. But there was so much tension between the brothers. Sahil had told me, in no uncertain terms, that their sibling rivalry was pretty bad. He didn't even like me bringing up Neil's name. So what would you do in my situation? Besides, I wasn't even 100 percent sure N was Neil. Was there any point getting Sahil hot and bothered about nothing?

But before I could answer, the voice blared over the loudspeaker again. "Okay! Time to go, folks! Three, two, and one!" A deafening horn blew, and the entire crowd of people who'd so far done a remarkable imitation of completely normal humans morphed into these rampaging beasts looking for free carnival rides. We were immediately—and I do mean *immediately*—swallowed up by the tsunami of the crowd. Thankfully, Sahil grabbed my hand at the last second or we'd have been utterly and irrevocably separated from each other. I couldn't see him; I just felt the steady pressure of his fingers against my skin.

"This way!" I heard him shout, and then something was yanking on my arm and I just blindly followed.

We broke free a minute later, making a left toward the Ferris wheel while the majority of the crowd turned right toward the more fun rides in the park. Sahil pulled me forward, and I saw the line to the Ferris wheel was tiny. I guess most people were going to get their money's worth from the ten-token rides. Once we were able to stop, he looked at me with wide eyes. "What the heck was that?"

"Something about free rides?" I said, brushing down my dress and adjusting the clip in my hair, which was coming loose.

He shook his head. "Wow. I don't remember that from last year."

I looked back toward the carousel, which was now quite a distance away. The crowds were still seething and surging. There was no way N would be able to find me anymore. The horn had stopped blasting, but people were still running every which way, trying to make it to a ride before they filled up. I thought about what Sahil had said when he'd first walked up to me. He'd asked if I was all dressed up for a date. If I were being completely honest, I was more than a little relieved that the horn had interrupted him. Because I didn't want to tell Sahil what I was doing here.

N would have to wait another day. Even if I did go back by the carousel when the crowd died down (*if* this murderous crowd calmed down), what were the chances that N would still be waiting? And I didn't have a phone to e-mail him and tell him to meet me somewhere else.

"Hey," Sahil said, interrupting my tumbling thoughts.

I looked at him.

"Want to go on the Ferris wheel with me?" He gestured at the giant wheel glittering with lights.

I smiled without hesitation. "Okay."

We got on—into a bright pink cab—almost immediately. I scooted in so Sahil could slide in beside me.

"Oh my God," I said, grabbing the bar with my free hand as soon as the wheel began moving. "I forgot how high up these things go."

Sahil laughed. "Are you serious? You couldn't tell from just, um, looking at it?"

"Shut *up*." I hit him on the arm, and he laughed harder. "It's different when you're in here, suspended in the air—" I cut myself off with a yelp as the sadistic operator jerked us to a halt, with Sahil's and my cab *as high as it would go*. Everything was eerily quiet except for the faint music from the carousel. Our cab swung lazily back and forth. "Oh my God," I said, gasping. "I think I have a slight fear of heights."

Sahil laughed. "So I shouldn't do this?" He shifted in his seat and the entire cab rocked dangerously.

"Stop!" I yelled, way too loud, and someone laughed from below. Far, far below us. "Not funny!" I said, glaring down.

Sahil grinned. "Oh, come on." He scooted gently over to me, so the cab didn't move. "It was a little funny."

A male voice from below floated up to us, saying, "There's always one." More laughing.

I glowered into the darkness. "Thank you kindly for your unsolicited opinion, sir! You can shove it right—" Even more laughing.

Sahil looked at me, his eyes serious. "Twinkle. I promise I will not let you fall."

He smelled like something warm and lemony and spicy. *"Swoony" is the word you're looking for, Twinkle,* my brain said.

"Um." I cleared my throat in an attempt to clear my head. "Okay. Thanks." Something about his presence felt anchoring. I felt safe, ensconced, and protected, even though I knew in my head that was idiotic. If the Ferris wheel failed, there was absolutely nothing Sahil could do to fight off *gravity*, unless he was hiding some major superpowers.

"Sure." I could hear the smile in his voice.

I let go of the bar and sat back reeeeally carefully as the wheel began to move again.

"Oh, hey, I wanted to tell you: I thought you did a great job on the analysis you gave everyone about the movie on Thursday," Sahil said. "I could tell you were drawing them in, especially when you said that thing about Dracula representing the untrustworthy foreigner who came to England to plunder and pillage."

"Ah, you think so?" I smiled, pleased. "I know how hard it can be to relate to older movies. I was hoping it would give them something to latch on to as they acted out their parts."

"That was excellent thinking." Sahil paused. "Something I've learned from studying the film industry is that directing's about helping your actors insinuate themselves into the parts they're playing as much as it is about getting them on film. I feel like you have this innate grasp of that process. You're going to touch so many people with your movies, T. I hope you know that."

I studied his face, my heart thumping. Sahil saw what I was doing—what I was *trying* to do as a director—and more than that, he believed I could do it. I'd been afraid of doing something as intimate as making art with him watching, but Sahil was one of the few people who not only saw Twinkle the artist, but *respected* Twinkle the artist. If Mummy's ignoring my art made me feel invisible, Sahil's recognition was like being surrounded by a million neon lights.

"Thank you," I said, looking away and out over the carnival, at the tiny people milling around on the ground below us. I was afraid he'd see in my eyes what I was beginning to suspect—that his heart knew my heart. That my soul was a piece of his.

"So," Sahil said after a moment of crystalline silence. "Do you ever think about what you want to do after high school?"

I shrugged and faced him again, now that the moment was broken. "I don't know. My dream is to go to USC, like George Lucas or somebody. But it's expensive. I'd pretty much need a full ride, and I don't think my grades are good enough for that." I tried to pretend saying all of this out loud didn't coat my mouth in the bitter taste of disappointment.

"My parents would call that a travesty," Sahil said, and I frowned at him questioningly. "Oh, they're big believers in higher education. Both of them teach anthropology at UCCS.

They sort of finance the education of one student every year. It's their mission in life to make higher ed accessible to everyone."

"That's so cool," I said. And crazy that they could do that. My parents couldn't even afford to put *one* kid through college.

"Cool, but also a little bit annoying. They want both Neil and me to go into academia. Neil's one hundred percent on board, but I want to be a film critic, which my dad thinks is just an excuse for me to sit around and watch movies and get paid for it. I mean, he's not wrong." We laughed. "But I don't get why that makes it a less valid profession than his. Anyway, what do your parents do?"

"Um, my dad's an aide at a center for runaway youth. And my mom's a substitute teacher. Dadi doesn't work."

Sahil didn't ask why I mentioned my *dadi* when he asked about parents, which was cool. He got the whole Indian extended-family thing. It was another example of how Sahil saw me in ways other people didn't.

We began our ascent again, and my stomach dipped uncom-fortably. I must've made a face because Sahil moved infinitesimally closer to me, the movement seeming completely subconscious. I, on the other hand, was hyperaware that our thighs were just a breath away from each other. My fists balled in my lap.

"And do they support your filmmaking?" he asked, in a way that told me he was trying to take my mind off the fact that we were, once again, *floating in the sky* in a creaky little metal cage.

But I played along. It helped. "Dadi does. My parents don't exactly support it, but they don't *not* support it either, if that makes sense."

"Yeah." He nodded. "It does. It sucks when parents aren't fully engaged in your stuff, even if it's so much better than hovering parents."

I looked up at him again. He was so right. I had cousins in California and Oregon whose parents were basically a subspecies of helicopter, they hovered so much. And that would be super irritating. But having parents who couldn't care less about what you were up to had its own levels of associated suckage. "Yeah. I know what you mean."

"You should come to breakfast at my place sometime," he said suddenly.

I glanced at his flushed face and saw this was a big deal to him. Sahil wasn't the type of guy to extend frivolous invitations. "Your parents wouldn't mind?"

"Nah. They're always telling me to broaden my friendship horizons beyond the same two I've had since second grade. Besides, my mom is impressed that you want to be a film director in the . . . how did she put it? Oh, right, the systematic racial and patriarchal system that has been curated to exclude women and especially women of color."

"Wow."

"Yeah." He smiled fondly. "Mom gets a little bent out of shape about the patriarchy. But I promise they're fun. And my dad makes *the* best peanut butter chocolate chip pancakes. Hands down."

"No kidding?" To be honest, I was curious about Sahil and Neil's parents. What must they be like to have raised two crushworthy boys? And okay. I was also into the idea of accidentally-on-purpose running into Neil. Maybe we could just talk about all the secret admirer stuff right there and things would *finally* be clearer. "All right. You've convinced me. Just let me know when."

He grinned, looking relieved. "Awesome."

The Ferris wheel stopped spinning and I realized we were at the bottom. We'd be getting off in a few short seconds. I felt a lurch of disappointment that my time with Sahil was almost over.

"Wanna go on another ride?" he asked.

I desperately wanted to. But another ride would turn into another one and then this would turn into a flat-out date. And I couldn't do that to Sahil or N. I just couldn't. I had to use the unspent money Dadi had given me for rides and stuff on a cab ride home. There were a bunch at the gate. "I . . . shouldn't."

His disappointed face matched mine. Only for a heartbeat.

Because then I blurted out, "Do you want to get some cotton candy?" *Twinkle, why? Why couldn't you just let Sahil go?*

His face brightened, like someone had turned up the wattage. "Sure."

We walked to the cotton candy stall slowly, people swarming around us like busy flies. Our arms kept brushing together, and I scooted in half a millimeter closer. It was chilly and he was warm, okay?

Sahil ordered two from the cotton candy vendor.

"Hey," I said as I paid for the cotton candies with the money Dadi had given me. Sahil made a motion for his wallet, but I threatened him with bodily harm and he laughed and surrendered. "I forgot to tell you, but Victoria Lyons invited me to Hannah's birthday party next weekend."

We began to walk again. "For real?" he said.

"I know. I was surprised too. But I think I've earned street cred with her because of this whole director shtick." I shrugged. "Anyway, I wanted to know if you'd come with me." When he seemed to get really happy, I hastily added, "Because I want to get that behind-the-scenes footage we were talking about."

"Oh, right," Sahil said, his mood dampening noticeably as we made our way through the crowd and the noise.

I took a big bite of cotton candy. "It's in Aspen at Victoria's parents' cabin, so it's a bit of a drive."

Sahil whistled. "And this is *Hannah's* birthday party? But *Victoria* invited you?"

He was starting to remind me of Maddie. Was it just so obvious to everyone else that I didn't belong with them? I felt a little silly in my shiny new dress and my perfectly done hair all of a sudden. Trying to ignore the sting of hurt, I said, "I know. It's so weird that they'd want me to go."

"No, that's not what I meant," he said, grabbing my hand to get my attention. "I just mean . . . Hannah's never been very nice to you. Are you sure she's gonna be okay with it?"

I shrugged. "Victoria told me not to worry about it, so I'm not worried about it. I'll just bring her a fabulous present or something."

"Hmm. Sure, I'll go. And I'll drive you if you want."

"That'd be great. Thanks." I took my hand away. "Sahil . . ."

"Yeah?"

"I don't think we should hold hands. I don't want to confuse things. . . ."

"Is this still about keeping things professional?" he asked quietly. "Because I get the feeling that there might be something else. Or someone else."

"There is the movie, but you're right. There's some other stuff I have to figure out too," I admitted, swallowing and keeping my eyes forward. My palms were sweating.

"But . . . you like me?"

I took a deep breath. "I do. I like you."

Sahil smiled. "That's good enough for me for now. And this stuff you need to figure out?"

"Yeah?"

"Will kissing help or . . . ?"

I laughed and pushed him on the arm. "Stop it."

He walked me to the gate. "So, I'll see you tomorrow?" he asked, stepping closer. I tried not to notice the way his eyes positively glowed as he looked at me. I was sure mine had a matching glow.

"Yes."

He tucked a curl behind my ear. It was like we couldn't stop finding excuses to touch each other. I should stop him, but I didn't want to. N and I didn't meet up. And Sahil was here. Sahil was *always* showing up for me. I stepped closer and wrapped my arms around his neck, pulling him in for a hug. "Bye."

"Bye, Twinkle."

I smiled and turned around to walk outside to a waiting cab. And all the way there, I felt Sahil watching me go.

Love,

Twinkle

Thirteen

Saturday, June 13
My room

Dear Nora Ephron,

I took a shower, changed into comfy pj's, and was sitting here doodling when my computer dinged. E-mails below.

> From: binadmiringyou@urmail.com
> To: twinkiefilmfan@urmail.com
> Subject: The carnival
> Hi Twinkle,
> I don't know what happened tonight, but when I got to the carnival, the crowds were impossible to get through. By the time I made it to the carousel and looked around, you weren't there. Do you want to try to meet up again?
> —N

From: twinkiefilmfan@urmail.com

To: binadmiringyou@urmail.com

Subject: Re: The carnival

They had some free ride thingy going on that apparently turned everyone into greedy, stampeding zombies. Anyway, on the one hand, I do want to try to meet up again. On the other, what if this is a sign from the *universe* or something?

—Twinkle

From: binadmiringyou@urmail.com

To: twinkiefilmfan@urmail.com

Subject: Re: The carnival

Since the universe is not a single entity, but rather a collection of nonsentient gases, rocks, galaxies, planets, moons, stars, and also encompasses all of space and time, I do not see how the universe could be sending us, mere specks of carbon, who, in the sheer scope of things, do not matter at all, a sign.

From: twinkiefilmfan@urmail.com

To: binadmiringyou@urmail.com

Subject: Re: The carnival

So . . . is that your way of saying you still want to meet up?

From: binadmiringyou@urmail.com

To: twinkiefilmfan@urmail.com

Subject: Re: The carnival

Yeah, I was thinking next weekend?

From: twinkiefilmfan@urmail.com

To: binadmiringyou@urmail.com

Subject: Re: The carnival

Sure. I'm going to Hannah's birthday party in Aspen on Saturday. Um, if you're not going to be there, we could meet Friday evening at the Perk? Maybe around 6?

From: binadmiringyou@urmail.com

To: twinkiefilmfan@urmail.com

Subject: Re: The carnival

The Perk sounds great.

See ya then, Twinkle.

From: twinkiefilmfan@urmail.com

To: binadmiringyou@urmail.com

Subject: Re: The carnival

See ya, N.

Is it just me or does he sound . . . less than enthused? And, okay, if we're being perfectly honest, *I* sound < enthused, too. Sahil's and my notes about scene blocking have more chemistry than that set of e-mails, honestly.

But . . . I mean, I'm not completely surprised. Sahil and

I shared something on the Ferris wheel. There's something between us that I've never felt with anyone else.

Still. I know I need to give N a chance. How can I give up on that picture of shiny, future Twinkle because of a boy I just met?

N and I need to meet soon and figure this out.

Love,

Twinkle

Sunday, June 14
My room

Dear Mira Nair,

I barely slept last night. I stared at my ceiling for hours, and then at the strand of twinkle lights on the wall from which I've hung pictures of Maddie and me, and Dadi, Mummy, Papa, and Oso. I have a few pictures of Sahil, Skid, and Aaron, and the rest of us on set from last week that I need to put up too. Then I stared at the wall beside my bed thinking the blank boringness of it would lull me to sleep, but *no*. My brain refused to shut off.

For a minute I had felt like my life was going according to plan. The movie was coming together, Maddie was going to be the lead, and N had begun to e-mail me. It felt like I was getting backdated karma for being a good person. But now? Everything feels muddled and confusing.

The movie is still going well, but Maddie being the lead has only led to even *more* distance between us somehow. And sure, N e-mailing me is still exciting because it might be Neil . . . but at the same time, I can't stop thinking about Sahil and me. How right that feels. How easy it would be. But then what about that image I've always had—of leaving the groundlings behind? Of being with someone like Neil? Of being seen for the first time ever in my life? No matter how hard I try, I feel like I can't make the different parts of my life work together.

So I just lay there and lay there and lay there and I had barely closed my eyes when the doorbell rang this morning.

I put one pillow over my ear because our house is tiny and anyone standing in the living room and talking at a normal volume basically sounds like they're standing beside me and talking into my ear. My door opened with a soft *click*, and I squirmed deeper under my covers. Hopefully it was just Mummy coming in to put my clothes away and not to wake me to see some horrible auntie who stopped by because she clearly has no sense of time or propriety. *Everyone* knows Sunday mornings are for sleeping in. Everyone except aunties from the Indian association.

But then I felt a small hand on my shoulder and smelled rose oil. "Dadi?" I said, my voice crumbly. I turned over to see her smiling exuberantly down at me, her eyes bright and shining. Dadi is 121 percent a morning person.

"*Desi ladka aaya hai*," she said, putting one hand under her chin like some coy Bollywood actress from the sixties. "*Bahut* . . . Oh, how do you kids say . . . *haan, bahut* cute *hai*! *Kehta hai tumhara* producer *hai*."

I sat up suddenly. A cute boy who happened to be Indian *and* my producer? There weren't too many of those. Oh my God, I must look—

"Beautiful," Dadi said, running a hand over my cheek.

I groaned. Dadi was never an objective judge of whether I

looked beautiful or perfectly hideous. And first thing in the morning surely fell in the latter category. "Dadi, why is Sahil here?" I asked, hopping out of bed and running to my closet.

"I don't know, *beta*," she said, looking surprised. "I came here to tell you."

I went to the bed and pulled her up gently by the hands. "Then can you please go out there and find out? And run interference for Mummy and Papa?"

She chuckled. "Okay, okay. I shall return soon." The voices swelled as she opened the door and then shut it again. What was Sahil *doing* here?

I wriggled into my jean shorts, pulled on my *Wadjda* T-shirt (one of the best films ever, and one of the only ones I've ~~forced~~ convinced Maddie to watch that we *both* loved), and threw on some of Mummy's magenta glass bangles that I stole a long time ago. Then I crept into the bathroom and brushed my teeth and washed my face in, like, twenty seconds. When I was done, I took a deep breath and walked back down the hallway. I could hear my heartbeat thudding in my ears, half in anticipation and half in dread. Because I knew I was going to be overjoyed to see Sahil, as I always was. And I probably would forget all my resolve to keep things strictly platonic until I could figure out where this whole N thing was going.

Sahil grinned at me from the couch and I instantly grinned back as if I'd learned nothing at all. "Hey! What are you doing here?"

"I thought I'd hold you to your promise to come to my place and eat my dad's pancakes. That is, if you still want to? I know this is out of the blue. . . ."

"Oh, yeah! No, I definitely want to." I went to sit by him on the couch, my mind thrilling as the memory from the carnival slipped back in. How he'd held me close on the Ferris wheel. How we'd finally just confessed our feelings to each other, one groundling to another, seeing and being seen. Even if I had told him things couldn't go further than that, it had felt *so good* to say the words out loud. And to hear what he'd said back to me, to see that softness in his eyes when he looked at me, the gentleness of his hand when he gripped mine. I smiled shyly at him. "You look pretty grab for so early in the morning."

He did too. He was wearing a button-down shirt again (green this time) with the sleeves rolled up, and khaki shorts. His hair looked like it had been gelled, and he smelled amazing. It was like he'd made an effort to come meet my parents. He's perfect boyfriend material, my heart said. Swoony, respectful, smart, kind, passionate . . . It was still extolling Sahil's many, many virtues when he said, "Thanks."

Mummy laughed from the armchair across from us. "Twinkle never wakes up at eight a.m. on the weekend!"

I glared at her, feeling this weird mixture of angry sadness I only felt around Mummy (and felt a *lot* around her, to be honest). Now that we had a visitor she wanted to talk like she knew everything about me? Now that Sahil was sitting here, she wanted to appear to be a mother, someone who gave a crap. But why couldn't she do that for me all the time?

"True," Papa added. "She wakes up at noon and has lunch directly!"

But before I could say anything salty about how would he

know because he was more concerned with the schedule of his kids at his job, Dadi came in with a silver tray completely buried in biscuits from the Indian store. "Sahil," she said. "Would you like some biscuits? We have *kaju pista*, chocolate bourbon, Butter Bite . . ."

"Dadi," I said, shaking my head. "He came over to invite me to breakfast that his dad's making. I don't think his parents would be too happy if he ruined his appetite here."

Dadi's face got all soggy like a piece of notebook paper left in the rain. "Oh . . ."

"No, no," Sahil said, hopping up from the couch and going over to her. "These look delicious!" He stuffed three in his mouth, gobbled, and swallowed them in record time. Then, looking around with a mischievous grin, he said, "Teenage boy's metabolism."

Everyone burst out laughing. Everyone in my family liked him right away, even Mummy and Papa, who were generally suspicious of boys. And how could they not? Sahil is like gentle sun on a winter's day. You automatically want to turn your face to it and soak it up.

Well, I left because I needed to get my shoes from my room and I've been in here a while, so I'm gonna go now. More later.

Love,

Twinkle

Sunday, June 14
Sahil's room (craziness!)

Dear Ava DuVernay,

We drove up farther north of the city, where some of the richer kids in school live. I kept glancing at Sahil as we drove; it was like my eyes were magnets and he was Iron Man. I'd never noticed before how the hair on his arms ranges from a deep black to a reddish brown, or how his fingers are just the right amount of big and gentle-looking. Occasionally he'd catch me looking and grin at me.

"I've been thinking," he said after a few minutes. "You can't deny it, T. You and me? We're like . . . like Dracula and his castle. Meant to be."

One thing that made my heart race was how Sahil could be so adorable around me sometimes, tripping over his shoes and stuff, and other times, he was so smoothly, dashingly confident. He wasn't afraid to take control, to tell me how he felt. It's like his personality was an aphrodisiac made specifically for one Twinkle Mehra.

I snorted to cover up how off-balance he made me feel. "You are such a dork."

"You know you'd miss it if it was gone."

I laughed. He was joking, but his words tugged at my heart as thoughts from last night filtered into my brain. After what we'd shared at the carnival, I knew losing Sahil would leave a gaping hole in my life.

I blinked back to the present moment as we pulled past the gates of Sahil's subdivision. It was pretty fancy, with big houses with outdoor fireplaces and big front yards and pillars and stuff. Things you never would see in my neighborhood, unless you counted Mrs. Wilson's rotting "deck" made of two by fours, which she began to put together herself but never bothered to finish. Mrs.

Wilson is a little flighty like that, which is why she sometimes pays me to go knock on her door and remind her to clean her hamster cage. She doesn't own a hamster. Yes. I have many questions too.

Sahil turned down a street and pulled up a driveway to this sprawling gray house with giant windows. "Oh my God," I said. "You have four garages?"

Sahil winced. "Yeah . . . but they're all really small?"

We both laughed together.

"Come on," he said, pulling into one of the garages and shutting off the engine. "Let's go inside so you can meet the parental unit."

Sahil's house was just as beautiful on the inside as it was on the outside. There were statues and pots and paintings all over the place, with spotlights shining down on them like in a museum. "Oh my God," I said again, walking over to a metal plate on the table with what looked like little vines etched all over it. Dadi had a similar one in her "room" (just a big laundry closet Mummy and Papa converted for her when she insisted I should take the second bedroom, which was too small for two beds). This one was much bigger, though, and looked like it was made of real silver. "Your house is so cool."

"That's from India," a female voice said.

A tall white woman in a gray tunic and white leggings was smiling at us. Her eyes were green and her brown hair was pulled back into an untidy bun. An oversize watch hung loosely from her wrist. She was beautiful in an earthy kind of way, like she enjoyed messy things that made you sweat—gardening and rock climbing and stuff. "I love it," I said.

"You must be Twinkle." She came forward, still smiling

warmly, and clasped one of my hands in both of hers. "Sahil's told us so much about you—"

Sahil cleared his throat theatrically.

". . . your directorial skills," his mom amended, laughing. "I'm Anna."

I laughed too, even though my cheeks were flushed. What would Anna Auntie say if she knew I was crushing on both her sons? I bet she wouldn't be so welcoming. "That's nice to hear. Sahil's been a great producer."

I followed her into the kitchen, where a man stood at the stove with a dish towel over one shoulder, flipping pancakes. He was almost as dark-skinned as me, with thick glasses and a balding head. "Twinkle!" he called jovially. His voice had just a bit of an Indian accent coating his American one. "How are you? My name's Ajit. I'm Sahil's father!"

"I'm fine, Uncle," I said. "Thank you for inviting me."

"Uncle!" He beamed at Anna Auntie and poured more batter onto the griddle. "What did I tell you? Indian kids, best manners in the world!"

Anna Auntie rolled her eyes good-naturedly, like she'd heard this a million times before. "Yes, dear, I know. Our kids aren't so badly behaved themselves."

"But being only half-Indian, my manners are only half as good," Sahil said. "But I did manage to call your parents Uncle and Auntie in the nick of time."

"That would explain why they were so obsessed with you." I turned to Anna Auntie. "My entire family loves Sahil. They usually don't even like boys."

Sahil took a mock bow and his mom flapped her hand at him. "No one likes a show-off," she warned.

"Except Twinkle's parents, apparently," he said, carrying a glass carafe of orange juice over to the table. Was a carton too trashy? We didn't even *have* carafes at my house. If I asked for one my parents would probably laugh until they cried and then say, *Why don't we just burn some money for fun?*

"I think it was more your charming producer demeanor," I said, just as Ajit Uncle brought over a platter of pancakes. I stared at him. Papa would *never* serve us, and especially not wearing a frilly apron around his waist. I hadn't noticed it before because he'd been behind the stove. It had *hummingbirds* and *hearts* on it. I averted my eyes so I wouldn't be rude in my staring. I mean, he'd just complimented me on my manners and everything. It was cool to see an adult man not caring about society's artificial rules for masculinity, though.

We all sat, with Ajit Uncle and Anna Auntie taking seats across the table from Sahil and me. Two chairs at the head and foot of the table sat empty.

"So . . . is Neil here?" I asked, trying not to be too obvious about why I was asking.

"He's at his friend Patrick's house," Ajit Uncle replied. "He's at practice so much that he tries to see them as much as he can!"

"Wish he felt the same way about spending time with us," Anna Auntie added, laughing. "Right, Sahil?"

Sahil, I noticed, had gone still. He wasn't looking at me as he poured himself some milk. Right. That whole sibling rivalry thing. "Yep," he said with forced heartiness.

I took a bite of the pancake and almost fainted. "Oh my God," I said, after I'd swallowed. "This is . . . You should open your own restaurant!"

Ajit Uncle laughed. "Oh, I don't know about *that*."

"Papa's being modest," Sahil said. "He basically cooks every meal around here."

"Hey, now," Anna Auntie said between bites. "I make mac and cheese."

Sahil snorted. "Out of the box."

"Yes, but I add hot dogs and red pepper flakes to it." Pointedly, she added, "My own recipe. That Sahil loved, FYI, until two years ago."

I laughed. "I think it's great that Ajit Uncle cooks. My mom and *dadi* are the cooks in my place. But they never make peanut butter chocolate chip pancakes."

"Twinkle's a bit of a peanut butter chocolate nut," Sahil said. "Skid's always trying to convince her to branch out, sweets-wise, but she's stubborn."

"I know what I like," I said. "I can't help it."

"A person who knows her own mind is a rarity," Ajit Uncle said, tucking into his third pancake. "Tell me, Twinkle, where do you plan to go to film school?"

"Papa," Sahil said, rolling his eyes. "Not everyone knows what their plans are down to the location of their future college at this point in their high school careers. And some people don't go to college right away." Speaking to me, he added, "Sorry. Hazards of having overachieving parents. Papa got his PhD at twenty-eight and Mom was the youngest person in her department to achieve tenure."

"No, it's okay—" I began, but Ajit Uncle cut me off by protesting mightily.

"Now, now, Sahil, I know college isn't the right path for everyone! But, Twinkle, I assume going to film school affords you some opportunities you wouldn't otherwise get, no?"

"It does, I'm sure," I said. "I mean, George Lucas is one of the most famous examples of someone who got his start at USC's film school, which also happens to be my dream school. But . . ." I shrugged, wondering if it was crass to say this in their circles. But then I decided I didn't care. This was my truth and I was owning it. "I'm not sure I can afford it, to be honest."

"That's a travesty!" Anna Auntie said, pouring herself a glass of orange juice. "The state of higher education in this country is enough to give anyone hives. The average college student—"

Sahil looked at me, biting his lip to keep from laughing, and I couldn't help the giggle that escaped my mouth.

Anna Auntie narrowed her eyes and gestured with her fork between the two of us. "What was that?"

"Busted," Sahil said. "Nothing. I just told—excuse me, *warned*—Twinkle that you guys can get a little intense about higher education."

"But," I hurried to put in, "he also told me that you guys sponsor one UCCS student a year. Which is amazing."

"In-state student," Anna Auntie said. "We also get a break from the university. It's the only way we can afford to do it. But we see it as a calling, being professors and all. It's all about making higher education affordable and accessible to more people."

I smiled and tucked into my second pancake. I liked Anna Auntie and Ajit Uncle. They felt like good people. And the way they looked at Sahil, it was obvious they loved him to bursting. It made me a little sad, too, as if my own family were two thousand miles, and not a twenty-minute drive, away.

Fourteen

After breakfast, Anna Auntie and Ajit Uncle melted away, making vague excuses about errands and the post office (which Ajit Uncle calls the "postmortem office," because apparently all the postal workers look like grumpy zombies. Also, the post office on a Sunday? The Roys were really bad at making believable excuses, evidently.). When they were gone, Sahil looked at me a little awkwardly. "So, um, you wanna see my room?"

There was a beat between us as the words "see my room" floated there. I couldn't shake the feeling that we were both thinking of all the different meanings behind that euphemistic phrase.

Sahil rubbed the back of his neck and dropped his gaze. "Ah, I mean, just, see my room."

I laughed way too loudly to cover my shyness. At least we were being awkward together. "Okay, then, show me your manor, kind sir," I said, putting on a fake-confident air.

He smiled, and I followed him down the hallway.

Once we were upstairs, I saw a bedroom with its door wide

open. Above the bed, which was covered with a green and black bedspread, was a painted wooden letter *N*.

N.

I stopped, transfixed, my pulse quickening.

Sahil paused. "Everything okay?"

I knew I should look away, but I found myself taking in all the little details of Neil's life I had never gotten to see before. His Michael Phelps poster. His entire wall of trophies. His lightly offensive Tomb Raider poster. "Um, yeah." I turned before it got weird, smiling at Sahil.

"You sure?" he said, smiling back hesitantly. His eyes ran over Neil's room, like he was trying to see what I was looking at. "You seemed spaced out there for a minute."

I took a deep breath and laughed, even though it felt kind of awful, not telling him the truth. "Nah, I'm good. So, where's your room?"

After a pause, he smiled and turned to show me the way.

Sahil's room was not at all what I was expecting. I'd thought, based on his affinity for all things horror, he'd have black walls and a red bedspread. Maybe some skulls? But instead his walls were this pale blue, and his bedspread was white-and-yellow striped. He had a killer film-reel table lamp that I would've *died* for too.

"I like your room," I said, going over to look at a colorized Frankenstein poster on the wall. "It's very . . . you."

"You think so?" he said, looking pleased. "Because Skid and Aaron always tell me it's too girly. I just like blue and yellow together."

I scoffed. "Too girly? What does that even mean? And why is that something to look down on, anyway?"

"No, you're right," Sahil said, frowning. "Why *is* that something to look down on?"

I clucked my tongue. "Sexism, dude."

"So, is that why you're doing this?" Sahil asked, coming to stand beside me. "Making movies, I mean? To fight the patriarchy?"

I smiled. He wasn't even being sarcastic or making fun of me. He genuinely wanted to know. Maybe having a mom who also wants to dismantle the patriarchy and a dad who wears frilly aprons will do that. "Kinda. I mean, women make up only seven percent of the directors who worked on the top two hundred and fifty movies. And that's a recent statistic. If you factor in race, that number goes way down. I remember reading about Ava DuVernay. She said one of the things she wanted to do was cater to people whom art houses and the film industry generally ignore. People who can't afford to go to fancy schools and expensive film festivals still deserve to see their stories on-screen. So that's what I'm hoping to do, too. Make stories about people who don't get to see themselves on-screen."

Sahil was staring at me, his eyes wide. "You know that video you made of your mom, where she's standing at a sink, washing tomatoes or something? It's on your YouTube channel."

I nodded; I remembered that one. It was from two years ago. I'd set the camera on the windowsill, so it was like an outsider was watching Mummy. She hadn't noticed the camera, so she was humming this *lori* to herself while she worked. When she finally noticed the camera, she laughed. "Oh, Twinkle," she said. "Is my lullaby that interesting?"

I loved that she'd posed a question to the viewer. I loved that I'd caught her in a rare moment, being carefree and unburdened.

"I love that movie," Sahil continued. "And the one with Dadi and Oso. And the one with Maddie trying on that big floofy white dress. And how you joined her, wearing a sari."

"Oh, yeah." I grinned at the memory. "That was from eighth grade. We found her mom's old wedding dress and so she made me go home and get a red sari so I could pretend to be a bride too."

"But then you caught her in the mirror, saying how her mom won't be able to see her on her wedding day. And it drew the viewer in."

"Maddie doesn't like to talk about it, but her mom died when she was two," I explained.

"I remember that from elementary school." He was still holding my hand, and he tugged on it, drawing me closer to him. "But you caught that on camera. You have the unique gift of catching the truths people keep hidden."

I looked up into his eyes. I was close enough to him that I could smell his lemon soap. "So, what's *your* truth?" I found myself asking, barely able to hear myself over the sound of my thundering heart. "What are you keeping hidden?"

Sahil looked down at our hands, clasped together, my dark fingers against his light-brown ones. "Sometimes . . . ," he said, his voice quiet and halting. "Sometimes I worry I don't know who I really am. Sometimes I'm afraid nothing I do will ever be enough to set me apart." I got the feeling he'd never said those words out loud before, that he'd probably never say them again.

I squeezed his hand gently, until his eyes found mine. "I understand," I said, "more than you know."

"I don't believe that," Sahil replied. "It's so obvious that the world needs your voice."

I shook my head. "I'm just as confident about you as you are about me. So if you don't know you who are, Sahil, ask me and I'll tell you.

"You'll go on a botany hike on a ninety-degree day or to a headache-inducing music festival even if it's not your thing because a friend asks you to. You'll go out of your way to pick someone up in your car because you know they need it. You're brilliant at giving your opinion on a scene we're filming, but you're equally good at stepping aside and letting me take over. You're one of those rare people who can see when they're being unreasonable and temper themselves. You see me as an artist in a way no one else has, and I think it's because you have an artist's soul too."

We were looking into each other's eyes as I talked, and when I fell silent, we were still gazing at each other. Sahil leaned in a bit, asking permission. After only the slightest pause, I leaned in too, giving it.

And then we were kissing, tentative at first, but soon hungrier, our arms snaking around each other, our breaths coming quicker and quicker. It was like a movie kiss. I don't even care if that sounds childish. You know how people are always swooning over that kiss in the movie *The Notebook*, the one in the rain? That one would rate a -2 on the romance meter compared to the one Sahil and I shared.

When Sahil and I came up for air, I leaned back, just like I'd done before. "Remember when I said I wanted to keep things professional? I'm pretty sure this is an HR violation," I said, but the fact that I was panting and flushed undermined my authority.

"Right," he said, his voice shaky. "Professional. Until you figure things out."

I nodded. "Mm-hmm."

"And . . . what are you figuring out again?"

I wanted to tell him. I really, *really* did. But how could I? After everything he'd just told me, I couldn't think of a single way to say I might want to date his twin brother without hurting him, and without hurting myself. Because I wasn't foolish enough to delude myself for this long—I was absolutely, totally, and completely falling for Sahil Roy.

"I just need some more time. And then I'll tell you everything."

I would, I decided. Even if I ended up with Sahil, I'd still tell him about my secret admirer and my struggle. Maybe it wouldn't be so bad because we'd have our happy ending. But not now. Not yet. I could *not* let go of the idea of Neil and me, the one I'd had for so many years now.

"Okay," he said. Then he smiled, this soft, sweet thing that made my heart squeeze. "Hey, T?"

"Yeah?"

"Thanks." Briefly, he rested his forehead against mine and closed his eyes. Then he pulled back. "I'm gonna go grab a soda. Can I get you anything?"

"Some cold water would be great," I said, and he nodded and left.

So that's where I am now. Sitting on Sahil's chair, disappointed at my own idiotic stubbornness and so confused, too. Because it would feel *so right* to let things progress with Sahil. It would feel so right to fall in love with him.

Love,

Twinkle

<text message 3:31 p.m.>
From: Sahil
To: Skid, Aaron
I spent the morning with Twinkle but . . . something's off

<text message 3:31 p.m.>
From: Skid
To: Sahil, Aaron
what do you mean? are you wearing deodorant like I said?

<text message 3:32 p.m.>
From: Sahil
To: Skid, Aaron
Dude enough with the deodorant. It feels like she's holding back but I don't think it's just the professional thing like she said before. Something else is up

<text message 3:32 p.m.>
From: Aaron
To: Sahil, Skid
Have you asked her?

\<text message 3:33 p.m.\>
From: Sahil
To: Skid, Aaron
Yeah all she says is she needs time

\<text message 3:34 p.m.\>
From: Skid
To: Sahil, Aaron
then you gotta give her time man

\<text message 3:34 p.m.\>
From: Sahil
To: Skid, Aaron
Idk what if she's not into me or she pities me or something man

\<text message 3:35 p.m.\>
From: Aaron
To: Sahil, Skid
Sahil. How long have you had a crush on this girl?

\<text message 3:35 p.m.\>
From: Skid
To: Sahil, Aaron
don't forget that time we found her yearbook photo in his room UNDER HIS PILLOW

\<text message 3:36 p.m.\>
From: Sahil

To: Skid, Aaron

That happened ONCE and I was 11! I hadn't figured out yet what was creepy when it came to girls

<text message 3:36 p.m.>
From: Aaron
To: Sahil, Skid

Ignore him. Look you said the other night that Twinkle sees you for you. Like she gets you. So don't throw that away man. She likes you. If she needs time just give her time

<text message 3:37 p.m.>
From: Skid
To: Sahil, Aaron

I'm with Aaron on this one bro

<text message 3:37 p.m.>
From: Sahil
To: Skid, Aaron

Okay you're right I can do that. She likes me and I can give her time

<text message 3:39 p.m.>
From: Aaron
To: Sahil, Skid

Good. Now that that's settled do you want to do something fun? Do you want to go to Taco Bell?

From: Sahil
To: Skid, Aaron
Taco Bell? Wait. Are you quoting Mean Girls again?

<text message 3:41 p.m.>
From: Aaron
To: Sahil, Skid
Well I mean it is the greatest movie of all time so

<text message 3:41 p.m.>
From: Sahil
To: Skid, Aaron
Yeah ok fine. Pick you up in ten, losers

Sunday, June 14
East library bathroom

Dear Sofia Coppola,

I didn't know if Maddie would show up to the study group. I mean, she didn't need it, let's be honest, *and* she's so mad at me. I'm mad at her too, for practically saying the one thing I've always been too afraid to confront head-on: that even if things changed for me with the movie, I wouldn't be good enough to hang out with her and her new friends. That at heart, I'm a groundling, and I'll always be one.

But I still love her. And I still want her to find her person. The one who'll make her life feel more . . . complete. The one who can see her like she wants to be seen. I mean, everyone deserves that.

She and Brij are so made for each other. I think they'd be happy together. Happier than her and *Lewis*, who brought her to study group today. And then they've spent the entire thirty minutes—that's how long we've been here—whispering to each other. She sat next to Brij, which was a good sign, I thought, until I saw her and Lewis having these hushed, private conversations. Poor Brij looked all wilted, too. But then she'd talk to him and laugh with him and put her hand on his arm to make a point. *Talk about confusing, Maddie.* Doesn't she care about *anyone's* feelings anymore??

Also, unintentional relationship potential—Aaron and Matthew! Apparently they already know each other from an LGBTQ youth group they're both a part of. Matthew's bi, but he doesn't talk about it at school (who can blame him? PPC thinks diversity means talking about Martin Luther King Jr. once a year in February). So they already knew each other and sat together, but then I kept seeing them touching each other and laughing at all these inside jokes. So maybe Maddie and Brij won't leave here in a relationship, but I'm counting Matthew and Aaron under my "win" column.

Side note: Matthew pulled me aside and, rubbing the back of his neck while his face turned bright red, he said, "Hey, T-Twinkle. I just, I want to apologize for what I said the other day."

"When? When you said my braid bun looked 'like a coiled-up cobra drawn by a kindergartner'?"

He turned even redder, like he was surprised I'd quoted him

word for word. He clearly didn't know about my grudge book. "Ah, I need to apologize for two things, then. That and how I said you wouldn't understand what Brij was talking about with the firewall the other day when we were doing our fundraiser. It was pretty uncool of me."

I smiled at him. "But it's pretty cool of you to try to fix things. So apology accepted."

(I love when people surprise me in a good way.)

Oh, and I helped Skid with a girl problem. Apparently there's this girl at the public high school, Portia? He basically said, "Twinkle, Portia's my future wife. I just know it."

To which I replied, "Skid, seriously? I didn't even know you wanted to get married."

And he said, "I do, but only to Portia." And then he whipped out his phone and showed me a picture and *wow*. She's this incredibly gorgeous black girl, with curly hair to her waist and the most fabulous taste in clothes. Way out of Skid's league, if I'm being totally honest.

He isn't bad-looking. He's just a little . . . skinny and sallow. And short. Not exactly your typical dreamboat. She looks like she'd be at home dating, I don't know, a Hollywood actor's son or something.

So he asked how he could get her to notice him (their families go to the same church), because he wanted a girl's opinion, and I told him what I value in my perfect guy: that his love for me would make him selfless; that he'd want to be better just for me, and that he'd challenge me to be a better person in return. Like, for Skid, that could mean getting her a juice if it gets hot in church or handing her a Bible if she forgets hers. And then to just use that interaction as a springboard for other interactions. He loved that idea.

And then I realized that's exactly what Sahil did for me the first time we talked. He bought me that coffee because he saw that I couldn't afford one myself. He saved me from having to leave the coffee shop empty-handed and humiliated in front of all those silk feathered hats. He could be my perfect guy. But his brother could help me feel like I'd finally left groundling-dom behind, the thing I've been dreaming of for as long as I can remember.

It sucks. I keep looking at Sahil and he keeps looking at me and our hands have brushed a thousand times as we both reach for the same pencil or highlighter. But that's it. We haven't talked about anything else, like what it means that we kissed *twice* or how I told him I like him and he told me he likes me or anything.

I keep telling myself this is a *good* thing. Because N and I are meeting in a week and then maybe my brain and my heart will stop fighting. When I see Neil's face—it *has* to be Neil; the universe isn't that cruel—things will fall into place once and for all.

I hope.

Okay, I better get back in there. Those free-market structures aren't going to . . . build themselves.

Love,

Twinkle

Fifteen

June 15
The Reel Deal Blog
Posted by: Rolls ROYce

There are two types of people: those who kiss and tell and those who kiss and run. I would like to be the former, but sadly, due to my kissing partner, I have been forced to become the latter.

I am *delirious* with joy that Sparkle and I kissed. Twice. Every time I see her, I want to pick her up. I want to swing her around. I want to scream to the world that we are together at last. But I can't. Because she doesn't want me to. And I am but a servant to her wishes and whimsies.

Slide says I'm being a wuss. A-man says straight people are weird. I suspect they're both at least partially right. But what neither of them sees is how my brain completely short circuits when I think about her. Or maybe they do. I don't know. I mean, Slide *did* call me out today because I kept spacing out in calculus and we have our final on Wednesday. All I can say is that Roger Ebert said it best: First love is sweet and valuable, a blessed, if hazardous, condition.

Speaking of Ebert, we are nearing completion on filming; in fact, we should be done by Friday, and then Slide and I will edit the thing to show at the festival. And you know something? I kick butt at being a producer. I thought I was all about being a film critic, but I'm great at putting out fires and getting my director anything she needs to do her job. I even weigh in on scene blocking and storyline issues. The other day someone— let's call her The Lion—even came to *me* for a costume issue. (The green wasn't the right kind or something and it was clashing with her hair, but still. It was important to the actress and she sought *my* counsel! We decided that she could wear a lighter shade of green. I mean, the film's going to be black-and-white, so no skin off my back, but she was insistent and said knowing she didn't look her best was interfering with her creative output. And then she proceeded to fuss over everyone else's costumes—buttoning sleeves and hitching up hemlines—and helped us look sharper as a group). It's like I'm slowly gaining a modicum of respect. Like people see me as an expert of sorts. It feels for the first time like I'm moving away from the shadow of my brother and coming to stand in my own light.

As for Sparkle . . . She sees me for me. When she looks into my eyes, I can tell she's just as captivated by me as I am by her. I don't know what I've done to deserve this, but when we're working together, I feel alive, like I'm *me* in a way I've never been before. Man, I can't believe I just typed that. But it's true. Sparkle sees me as I am, without seeing my brother first.

So all I can do is be patient and wait for her to realize what I've known for a long time: We're meant to be together. It's so obvious. I know she's going to come to the same conclusion, no matter what it is that's holding her back.

Monday, June 15
AP Bio
Dear Lynne Ramsay,

Mrs. Mears was having us watch a video about mitosis (or was it meiosis? Something with cells, anyway) and she let us all sit wherever we wanted. I was kinda hoping Maddie would want to sit with me even though we haven't talked since she told me I shouldn't go to Hannah's party. But she and Hannah ended up across from me, and I sat with Matthew (who began passing me notes; I was so surprised I didn't even realize the piece of paper he handed me *was* a note until he cleared his throat and nodded meaningfully at the paper). Matthew's note enclosed. *But* that's not even the most surprising part. As I was scribbling my response to Matthew, I overheard Maddie and Hannah's whispered conversation (I have batlike hearing). It went something like this:

Hannah: So what was up with you and Nath at the library?

Maddie: What do you mean?

H: Lewis told Desiree that you two were huddled together whispering or something?

M: *laughter* Um, no, I was just being nice to him. . . .

H: Okay, because you don't want to ruin things with Lewis. I'm pretty sure he's going to ask you to go out the night of my party.

M: I told you, it's not like that with Lewis and me.

H: But it could be. Unless you want *Nath* instead?

M: *laughter, more frantic and fake* No, obviously not. I felt sorry for him, that's all. He's Twinkle's friend.

H: Ugh, I don't know why you even hang out with her anymore. Anyway, so wear something hot to my party, and I'll make sure you and Lewis hook up.

M: Okay, but can we talk about this later? I need to watch this video.

H: *sigh* Whatever.

I was gripping my pencil so hard by the end that I was sure it would snap. I glared at Maddie and Hannah, but neither of them was looking at me.

It doesn't matter, I forced myself to think. *None of this matters.* I have my new friends. And soon I'll be able to leave groundling status, simply based on this movie I'm making, which'll force people to see me and the message I want to send to the world. That's all I need.

Love,

Twinkle

Note from Matthew to Twinkle

HEY. SO, NOT TO BE ALL MIDDLE SCHOOL, BUT DID AARON SAY ANYTHING ABOUT ME?

Besides asking if I knew where he could find a bare-chested photo of you, no.

HAHA. BUT SERIOUSLY, TWINKLE.

Seriously, he didn't. BUT he did have this goofy smile all day yesterday after you left and this morning when I saw him before homeroom.

ARE YOU SERIOUS?

Yep. If you like him, you should ask him out.

HE'S NOT SEEING ANYONE ELSE?

I don't think so.

YOU HAVE TO BE SURE!

Okay, okay. I'll ask him. Jeez. So . . . you like him a lot, huh?

I THINK SO. WE HAVE A LOT IN COMMON. THE FIRST TIME I SAW HIM WAS AT A CONCERT FOR THE DUSTY ARCHIVES. OR WAS IT THE PLATONIC PLANETS? OH, I REMEMBER. THE PLATONIC PLANETS OPENED FOR THE DUSTY ARCHIVES.

You two are definitely meant for each other.

YOU THINK SO TOO?? ALSO, NATH WANTS TO KNOW
IF YOU AND SAHIL ARE GOING OUT.

What?? No, we're not. And anyway, why does he care??

I DON'T KNOW. I THINK HE WAS CURIOUS.

Did he say anything about Maddie?

HE SAID SHE'S CUTE. AND OUT OF HIS LEAGUE. AND
PROBABLY GOING OUT WITH LEWIS.

*What? No, she's not (on both of those last two
counts)! Do you think he'll ask her out?*

ARE YOU TRYING TO SET EVERYONE AT PPC UP OR WHAT?

I should form a matchmaking LLC or something.

YOU'LL NEED SOMETHING WHEN YOU FAIL BIO
BECAUSE YOU'RE NOT PAYING ATTENTION.

You're the one who started passing me notes!

ALL RIGHT, ALL RIGHT. SORRY. BUT YOU'LL
FIND OUT? IF AARON'S SEEING ANYONE ELSE?
APPARENTLY THERE WAS A GUY FROM LAKE VALLEY
A FEW MONTHS AGO, BUT . . . AARON'S A TOTAL
ENIGMA, BUT I KNOW HE LIKES YOU. HE'LL TELL
YOU IF YOU ASK HIM.

*LOL at the idea of Aaron being an enigma but yeah.
I'll definitely find out for you.*

MERCI.

Tuesday, June 16
AP English

Dear Sally Potter,

Today we sat out on the green at lunch because it was such a beautiful day. I ended up sprawled on the grass, and Sahil came to sit beside me with his food, our legs touching casually.

"So, Aaron," I said, a little too loudly, trying to divert my brain's attention from the feeling of Sahil's muscled thigh against my own skinny one.

He looked over at me, his mouth full of burger.

"You have a not-so-secret admirer."

His eyes got wide and he swallowed his mouthful. "Oh yeah?"

"I think you have an inkling of who it is." I grinned and shielded my eyes from the sun with one hand. "What should I tell him? Are you interested?"

After a pause, during which Aaron looked everywhere possible but directly at me, he nodded. "I'll talk to him after school."

Sahil and I both *whoop*ed and Aaron threw a fork in our general direction. "Oh, shut up."

"That's just great," Skid said, popping a French fry into his mouth. "Why does it have to be so easy for some people? I can't even get Portia to *look* my way."

Aaron glared at him. "Easy? You think being a gay black guy is *easy*?"

Skid held up his hands. "Sorry, man. You're right. I wasn't thinking."

Aaron went back to his burger. "Forgiven. Continue."

"I took your advice," Skid said, looking at me. "But she didn't look too hot during service." He paused. "*Temperature*-wise, I mean," he said with a cocky sneer. I rolled my eyes and he continued. "*And* she brought her own Bible. It was nicer than mine. Should I steal hers so I can offer mine?"

I sighed. "No, Skid. Those were just examples. You should look out for your own opportunities."

"What's this?" Sahil asked, looking between us with interest.

"I was telling Skid a sure way to a girl's heart—if she's anything like me—is to do something selfless for her." I snapped my fingers. "I know. You can invite her to Midsummer Night. You said she's a catalog model. Tell her there'll be media people here to make it interesting for her. She can't turn something like that down."

Skid pointed a finger at me, grinning. "That's not a bad idea at all. I'm gonna do that. Thanks."

I was genuinely happy for Skid. I mean, why not? *Someone* around here deserves to be happy and in love if it's not going to be me.

Love,

Twinkle

Wednesday, June 17
10 days until Midsummer Night
My room

Dear Mira Nair,

I did not know it was possible to be as mad as I got today.

We were filming one of our final scenes after school at Victoria Lyons's house. Her parents are out of town at one of their French country homes, and she said she thought her living room would be the perfect setting for the scene we were doing. She was right; once we set up all the spider webs and stuff, it 100 percent looked like a room in a castle.

So, the scene had Lewis, who plays the role of Mina (aka

Morris in our film), Francesca, Brij, and Maddie. Sahil and I set up the scene and the camera and told them to take their places. I loved how the actors kept looking at me when they voiced an opinion, to see what I thought. There was no evidence of my social bottom-feeder status. Everyone knew that in here, I was the boss. Victoria was on the couch, texting. (Her thumbs were all blurry from the speed. How do people do that??) So I went and took my place behind the camera, and then Sahil did his clapboard thing and yelled, "Action!" before picking his way back to me silently, out of view of the camera.

"Morris must go to his room to rest," Francesca said, adjusting her fake spectacles.

"I don't think that's as important . . . ," Lewis began, and then stopped. "That's not as important . . ." He looked right at the camera and smiled, like he was all embarrassed.

I sighed. "He just broke the fourth wall."

Sahil called out, "Cut!"

Massaging my shoulders (we'd been working for more than ninety minutes straight at that point), I walked over to the actors. "What's going on, Lewis?" I asked, keeping my voice even.

"I'm having problems remembering my lines," he said, scratching his chest nonchalantly and grinning.

I considered him in silence for a second. "Okay, but . . . you have three lines in this scene."

He laughed. "My bad."

I put a hand to my forehead and took a deep breath. I wasn't laughing, and I was trying my best not to lose my temper. The other actors shifted uncomfortably. "You've had, like, five days to memorize them. That's when I sent out that e-mail saying we'd be shooting this scene today, remember?"

"I gotta be honest," Lewis said, still grinning. My blood pressure was starting to skyrocket. "I went to this frat party last night and it wiped my memory, man." He laughed again. "My bad, though."

Maddie, Brij, and Francesca all looked like they were hoping for a trapdoor to open and take them away from this hideous scene unfolding before us.

Something gave way inside me and my voice came out louder than I was intending it to. "That's *all* you have to say about it? 'My bad, though'?" This was everything I hated—that smug look on his face, saying his time was more important than mine. The entitlement that came with being one of the silk feathered hats—that all the groundlings were there simply to kowtow to your every need. The knowledge, once again, that I simply didn't register on their radars. That I was, effectively, invisible, no matter what I was doing or how much good a project like this might do. It was all secondary to Lewis's need to go out to a frat party and get his memory "wiped."

Victoria looked up from her phone. I only barely noticed her.

"Chill, dude," Lewis said. "What, is it your time of the month or something?"

Sahil walked up, his eyes glinting. I'd never seen him look so . . . fierce. He was usually so soft and gentle, like that puppy in the toilet paper commercials.

I put a hand on his arm. "I got this." When I looked back at Lewis, it was like this avalanche of rage just burst through me. It was like all the times I'd found Mummy sleeping when I needed her or Papa working when I wanted to talk to him, all the times Maddie had blown me off for her other friends, all the times Hannah had implied my hair was awful or my clothes belonged on Orphan Annie came rushing-gushing to the surface. I remembered years of being overlooked, of party invitations being "lost in the mail." All of those things were volcanic lava, finally erupting after ages of being suppressed. Because now I was *somebody*. I wasn't a wallflower anymore; I wasn't that girl they could just ignore and push aside and laugh at.

"How. Dare. You," I said to Lewis, and I heard the throbbing tremor of anger under my words. Pushing a finger into his chest, I continued. "You think just because your daddy is on the board of a gazillion hospitals and your mom was a model in the eighties that you own everyone around you? We're all on your schedule because this is the *Lewis Shore Show*. And you can treat girls however you want because they're just there to prop *you* up, to make you feel like a big man, right, Lewis? You never stop to think that you're nothing but a grunting *Neanderthal* just like your father. So maybe I *shouldn't* be surprised that you made that completely sexist, jerk comment."

Lewis's face was pale. To be honest, everyone looked like mannequins, staring at me in wide-eyed shock. It was like they couldn't believe those words had come out of my mouth. I was breathing hard into the silence. To be honest, I couldn't believe it either. All this stuff had just poured out, but it was all true. I mean, Lewis's family is a total clichéd joke. But . . . if it was all true, why did I feel this burning, cringing inside me like *I* was the one who'd done something wrong?

Sahil spoke first. "Twinkle . . . ," he began, his voice heavy with what sounded a lot like disappointment and shock.

"What?" It came out sharper than I'd intended because I was starting to feel weirdly defensive. Why was everybody staring at me? Hadn't they heard what Lewis had said to *me*? Hadn't they heard the misogynistic comment that came after I had told him to do what he was supposed to be doing in the first place?

Maddie spoke next. First, she huffed a laugh that made me ten times angrier. "You can't *speak* to people like that," she said, her face a mask of disbelief. "Who do you think you are?"

"Who do *I* think I am? That's hilarious coming from *you*, Maddie." I gestured around at all of them. "You're all so entitled. You think you can just behave however you want and say whatever you want. This movie means something to me. To you it's maybe just a bullet on your college applications. But this is the career I want, okay? This is serious."

Brij stepped closer to Maddie, almost unconsciously, I thought. His jaw was hard as he looked at me, shaking his head. But before I could call that out, Maddie was speaking again.

"Wow," she said, staring at me. "I get that. Okay? But you can't talk about people like that. It's not right!"

"Can we all just take a deep breath?" Sahil said, his voice deep and calm. "This is getting out of hand."

"What's getting out of hand is Twinkle's attitude," Maddie said, unbuttoning her cape. "And you know what? I don't need this crap." She let it drop and stalked off, out the door.

"You can't leave now!" I yelled at her retreating form. "This is the last week of shooting!"

The door banged shut.

Sixteen

After the door closed, I felt this wicked, dark sense of spite and anger building up inside me. "Fine!" I said, looking around at all of them. "If she won't come back in, I'll just scrap the whole thing. We've put all this time and effort into this, and no one will have anything to show for it!"

Sahil shifted beside me, but I couldn't look at him for some reason. Finally, Lewis spoke up. "We'll go talk to Maddie. She won't want to let us all down. She's cool." He, Brij, Francesca, and Victoria all walked out in silence.

I turned to Sahil and threw up my hands. "What?"

He raised an eyebrow. "I didn't say anything."

"I know, but I can tell you want to. So just let it out. Maybe you think I should take all of their crap but hold my own tongue. Or maybe you think strong women shouldn't be so strong?" I crossed my arms.

Sahil stared at me. "Don't put words in my mouth, Twinkle," he said finally, shaking his head. "Why are you looking for a fight anyway?"

I had my mouth open all ready to argue with him. But then I stopped short. He was right. I *was* looking for a fight. I was absolutely gunning for it. But why? Why was I so angry? And why was it all coming out now?

I didn't have time to say anything because I heard the front door open again. I waited, hardly breathing, to see who would round the corner. Lewis came first, followed by Francesca, and Victoria, and then Brij . . . and finally, Maddie. She didn't meet my eye as she walked up. "I wouldn't want everyone to have wasted their time," she said to Sahil. "So I'm in."

"Great," Sahil said, looking at me. "Why don't we pick this up tomorrow?"

"Yes," I said after a pause. "Let's take a break and do this scene over tomorrow."

Sahil and I loaded the gear into his SUV without speaking much once everyone was gone. The air felt all strange and prickly between us. "Two more days of filming," he said as he pressed the button to close the trunk.

"Yep. And then Skid's going to have to kick things into gear to get it all edited in a week."

Sahil nodded and brushed a strand of hair off his forehead. "He can do it, though. He's a genius at that stuff." He began to walk away. "Well, I'll see ya. Your dad's giving you a ride home, right?"

I put a hand on his arm. "Sahil."

He paused, his eyes wary. "Yeah?"

I had a million things I wanted to say: *I'm sorry I freaked out like that; I don't know what came over me.* Or, *I think Lewis is a total buttmunch, but I shouldn't have let him get under my skin and*

I definitely *shouldn't have been so mean to him, and I'm not sure why I was*. Or even, if I was being 110 percent honest, *I'm a little scared of how I'm changing*. Because I am starting to think I'm *better* than other people. Because of my talent. And I don't know how to stop because it feels *good*, for once, to be the one on top. It feels *good* to not be on the bottom being crapped on. When have I ever, ever been in this position in my life? When have people ever needed me for anything? When have they ever *had* to listen to me or else? So maybe I flew off the handle. But I wonder what anyone else in my position would've done.

But in the end, all I said to Sahil was, "I'll see you tomorrow."

His face sagged a little, like I'd let him down. "Yeah. See ya."

I feel like I'm in some *Alice in Wonderland* production where I can't tell what's right and what's wrong, what's up and what's down. Is it wrong for me to get mad at Lewis's obviously sexist comments? At the fact that he wasn't taking it seriously? I don't think so. But I think I took it too far. I shouldn't have said those things about his dad. I know that. It was wrong. The truth is, I have *power* for the first time in my life. And I can't seem to stop it from going to my head. It scares me, Mira. I don't want to turn into someone I hate. But I also don't know what to do about it.

Love,

Twinkle

Friday, June 19
Honors Calculus
Dear Nora Ephron,
Today we got a nice little reprieve from the horror that is calculus.

Mrs. Smith told us we could go to the library to "research one prominent figure in the field" (really she had a head cold and just wanted us out of her hair, I think). I was kids-cartoon-character-level happy. I mean, any day that I don't have to spend cooped up in a classroom under fluorescent lights learning about open versus closed intervals is a good day.

Then, on impulse, I decided to check my e-mail. I mean, today was *the day*. The day N and I were meeting at Perk. I'd been feeling this low level of excitement/nerves all day, but that was all it was: a low level. I figured rereading his old e-mails might make me feel something more. And when I logged in to my account, I had one new e-mail from late last night. Pasted below.

To: twinkiefilmfan@urmail.com
From: binadmiringyou@urmail.com
Subject: Perk
Hi Twinkle,
I'm sorry, but I don't think I can meet you at Perk today.
I will explain soon. I hope you can forgive me.
—N

That was it. That's *all* he said. Not even the courtesy of a plausible excuse! What the heck? Am I not even worth an "I've got swimmer's ear" or "My house is on fire"??

I sat there and stared at the e-mail for the longest time, feeling my cheeks burning. I could feel the rage bubbling up again. First Lewis, now N? Did Neil think I was another disposable girl from the long line snaking outside his door? Did he feel that, as a groundling, I should just be grateful for any attention he threw my way? I may have flown off the handle with Lewis, but I felt fully justified in my anger toward N now. Here's the thing: I was a freaking filmmaker. I was a director. I had talent, and I was out to change the world. I did *not* deserve to be treated this way and I wouldn't stand for it anymore.

I balled my fists on the table in frustration. And then I pounded out a reply.

To: binadmiringyou@urmail.com
From: twinkiefilmfan@urmail.com
Subject: Re: Perk
Fine, N. We don't have to meet. I want you to know, though—this is totally uncool. You do *not* just cancel on someone at the last minute. What if I hadn't seen your e-mail? And what sort of a non-explanation is "I'll explain soon"? But you know what? If this is how you treat people, good luck ever being happy in life.
—Twinkle

I wavered a second before hitting send, but then I did and sat back, breathing hard. Neil had to know I wouldn't stand for his crap. I wasn't that person anymore.

Friday, June 19
My room
Dear Haifaa al-Mansour,
I was in a bad mood when I got home. I mean, I had planned

to go downtown to the library and hang out reading romance novels to put me in the mood until it was time to meet N at Perk. But instead I'd ridden the bus home and had a whole afternoon of hanging out with Dadi to look forward to.

I walked in the door and Dadi looked up from her book (*Who Moved My Tofu?*) and immediately said, "Uh-oh, someone has a thundercloud face."

I glared at her and walked to the kitchen to get a snack. "I do *not*." Outside, Maggie the dog was barking her little head off, probably pining for Oso. "Does that dog ever *shut up*?" I slammed the drawer shut after I got a spoon for my yogurt.

Dadi waited till I was back in the living room to respond. She had set her book aside and was watching me with her head cocked. "Are you all right, Twinkle?"

"Fine. I'm just gonna be in my room."

"But there's a documentary film I thought we could watch together," Dadi said. "The TV guide said it's 'essential viewing for anyone interested in a career in films.'"

I sighed. "No offense, Dadi, but I think I know everything about what a career in films entails. I don't need to watch some documentary made for laypeople. Okay?"

Dadi shook her head. "*Ghamand achcha nahin hota*, Twinkle. Arrogance is not a worthwhile friend."

I threw my hands up. "God, I'm so tired of hearing that. I'm not arrogant! I just know that I'm *good*. Okay? For the first time in my life, my self-esteem doesn't resemble rotting roadkill. Why can't everyone just let me be?" I stalked off to my room and closed the door.

I felt immediately sorry Dadi had become collateral damage; I've never spoken to her that way. But I'd spent my entire life feeling less than those other people at school. And now I was finally in a position to call the shots. Why was everyone in such a hurry to take that away from me? It's so messed up! Do they think I'm just going to stand idly by and let them walk all over me?

Love,

Twinkle

Saturday, June 20
Sahil's car

Dear Jane Campion,

Sahil and I made a plan that he'd pick me up at six o'clock. There was no way Papa, Mummy, and Dadi were going to allow me to go to an unchaperoned party at someone's parents' cabin in *Aspen*, so I was a little nervous about what I should say. Would they believe I was going to a sleepover at Maddie's? She hadn't slept over at my house in a long time. And Papa would be sure to drop me off at Maddie's house, so should I have Sahil pick me up there? Would that be too weird since Maddie and I weren't even on speaking terms?

But in the end, I didn't have to worry about it. Papa took an extra shift at the youth home, Mummy wasn't home (she sometimes goes off on these day trips by herself and no one knows where she is), and Dadi went to some drum circle conference thingy with her friends from the Dharamshala Temple and told me she wouldn't be back till late.

I dressed in my glittery black skirt, my Sofia Coppola T-shirt (it has her picture and a quote that says, I'M ALWAYS A SUCKER FOR A LOVE STORY), and my DIY glitter Keds. My camera bag banged on my hip as I walked past Oso, who was curled up on the couch—sleeping on sentry duty. He picked up his head, but when he saw I didn't have any food, he huffed and lay back down. I took one look around the empty house before I opened the front door. It wasn't that I was lonely, exactly. It was more like I was missing someone without even knowing who I was missing.

I walked out the driveway just as Sahil's SUV rolled up. "Hey," I said, pulling the door open and hopping in. I glanced at him, wondering if things would still be prickly between us after what had happened with Lewis. "Thanks for the ride."

"Sure, no worries." He looked super cute, I noticed in spite of myself, dressed in a *Cabin in the Woods* T-shirt and dark-wash jeans. I smirked, trying for a joke to taste the air between us. "Are you trying to freak everyone out with that T-shirt or what?"

He laughed. "Just trying to be on theme, T."

I leaned back against the seat, relieved. Sahil, at least, seemed to be past the weirdness that had happened at Victoria's house. The others had still been subdued when we'd filmed the next day, but at least they'd all shown up, said their lines, and acted well. That was all I needed. I could deal with them thinking I was a pompous freak if they'd just play their roles like I told them to. I suspect every great director has had to deal with that at some point. And as long as I still had Sahil and my new friends, what did I care what Maddie or the others thought?

"So, you ready for the most epic road trip of all time?" Sahil asked, grinning at me as he pulled onto the interstate.

"Urgh. I'm more the type of person who just falls asleep waiting for the road trip to be over," I said. "Being stuck in a metal bullet hurtling alongside other metal bullets at eighty miles per hour is not my idea of fun."

Sahil snorted. "You know what I like about you? Your refreshing view on life."

I rolled my eyes. "I'm going to have to start charging you for my gems. Anyway, I don't think that's 'refreshing' so much as an accurate, objective observation."

"Okay, but you've never been on a road trip with me as your guide. That's what the problem is. I promise, by the time we get to Aspen, you're going to be *begging* me to go on another road trip with you."

I raised an eyebrow. "Challenge accepted."

Sahil grinned. "Okay, so the first thing we're going to do?"

"Yes?"

"Reach in that bag behind your seat."

I did as he asked, and found a plastic grocery bag. When I pulled it into the front seat with me, I found a bag of Cow Tales, some Doritos in assorted flavors, and a bag of Reese's Mini Peanut Butter Cups. Grinning, I pulled those out. "Oh, yeah. Thank you."

Sahil reached for the Cow Tales. I tried not to notice that his fingers accidentally brushed against my bare thigh. But obviously I noticed. What am I supposed to do? Get rid of all the nerve endings in my body? "The first rule of road tripping is—"

"There *is* no road trip?" I hazarded as I unwrapped my first PB Cup.

"Nooo . . . the first rule is, you *have* to have superior

road-tripping snacks. Otherwise you may as well turn around and go home."

I chewed the chocolate thoughtfully, letting the fabulous peanut buttery-chocolaty goodness wash over my tongue. "Hmm. I see your point."

Sahil bit into his Cow Tale and chewed. "So now we can get to the games."

"There are games," I said as I reached into the bag again. "Of course there are."

"Duh. So, you've probably heard of the license plate game, yeah?"

I tried not to groan. Mind-numbing games like that were invented to take your mind off the fact that nearly 3,300 people die in car wrecks *every single day* in the United States. But they didn't. If anything, playing the license plate game only made me feel both terrified *and* like I wanted to jump out of a moving vehicle to escape. "Um, yeah."

"Well, we're not playing that. I mean, what are we, seven?"

I laughed. "I have to say, little bit relieved."

Sahil beamed at me, and it made my traitorous heart stutter. "Instead we're going to play a game called 'Did You Hear.' So, basically, each of us will take turns saying 'Did you hear that _____?' and we'll fill in the blank with either a truth or a lie. The other person can then either accept the statement as a truth or reject the statement as a lie. If you guess correctly, you get a point. Otherwise the point goes to the other person."

I smiled. "So, like, a take on Two Truths and a Lie? I like it."

"Sweet. I'll go first?"

I nodded.

Sahil took another bite of his chewy candy and then said, "Hmm. Did you hear that I once ate twelve doughnuts in one sitting?"

"Twelve??"

Sahil smirked and nodded. "Accept or reject?"

"Hmm." I tapped a finger on my chin and unwrapped another Mini Cup. "On the one hand, twelve seems like it'd send you into a sugar coma. But on the other . . . I did see you inhale three cookies and then several loaded pancakes like it was nothing. So, I'm gonna say . . . accept."

Sahil laughed. "Yep. You're right."

"Yessss."

"Your turn."

I stared out the window at the open fields and munching cows zipping past us in the fading light. "Okay," I said, facing Sahil again and folding my legs up on the seat. "Did you hear that I'm a fantastic singer?"

Sahil looked at me for a couple seconds, his mouth quirked to one side as he considered. "Hmm . . . I mean, you do have a beautiful speaking voice, so it makes sense that you'd have a beautiful singing voice."

I felt myself flush and concentrated on unwrapping another Mini Cup to distract from it. "So, what's your answer?"

"Accept," Sahil said with finality.

I nodded solemnly. "I'm gonna demonstrate." And before I could chicken out, I began to sing "Over the Rainbow." Well, I *say* "sing," but I really mean "croak." It was weird, but before this,

I would never even have dreamed of singing in front of people, let alone a boy I had a crush on. It was like directing this movie had given me so much confidence in myself. It was okay that I wasn't the best at everything because at least I had one talent that I totally slayed at. You know? Plus, there was just something about Sahil. His eyes were kind and gentle, like he'd never judge me, no matter what I did.

He began to laugh. "Okay, okay, I get it! I was wrong! Mercy! Mercy! You don't have to rub it in!"

I laughed but kept on singing, even louder than before, my voice breaking horribly as I went into the chorus.

He grinned at me. "I love you." And his grin abruptly fell off his face.

Seventeen

I stopped singing mid-word. I couldn't do anything but stare at him.

Sahil glanced at me before looking back at the road. "Did you hear that," he said quietly, "I've only been in love once? It happened when I was eleven. And it's still happening."

I swallowed and shook my head. "Reject."

He smiled a little. "One point for me."

"Sahil . . ." I didn't even know what I was going to say exactly. My heart felt all melty, butterflies were wreaking havoc in my stomach, and I felt scared and exhilarated and like laughing and crying all at the same time.

"I know," he said, his voice barely audible, almost covered by the humming of the tires on the road. His big hands gripped the steering wheel loosely. "It's complicated for you. But, Twinkle, I just wanted you to know it's not complicated for me." He glanced at me again, his dark eyes sparkling. "It's never been complicated for me when it comes to you." After a pause, he said, "I just want to be honest. I'm not trying to freak you out."

He wasn't freaking me out at all. In fact, I'd been marveling at how brave Sahil was. How unapologetically honest and trusting. I felt a little shift inside me, a softening. Maybe I could let down a wall of my own. "Thank you," I said finally. "For telling me. For . . . loving me. I appreciate it more than you know."

Sahil nodded.

"Because . . . did you hear that my mom doesn't? Love me, I mean?" I said before I could stop myself. My eyes filled with tears, but I forced myself to not wipe them away.

Sahil looked at me, startled. "I'm sure that's not true. Your parents love you. And your *dadi*. I saw it when I came to visit you."

I smiled a little as a tear dripped down my cheek. "One point for me."

Sahil reached over and put a hand on mine, squeezing gently.

I laughed a weird, watery-sounding laugh. "My *dadi* does love me. And Papa . . . he loves me in his own way. But you shouldn't believe everything you see." I shook my head, not able to speak for a few seconds. My throat was painfully tight.

"Mummy used to be this talented artist. I still remember her painting banyan trees from her village and red double-decker buses with Indian people spilling out of them. I used to hang out with her behind her chair and just watch. Sometimes she'd dab my nose with her paint to make me laugh."

Sahil smiled.

"Everything changed when my *nani* got sick," I said, looking down at Sahil's hand over mine. A tear splattered onto his skin, but he didn't move. "My mom's mom died alone back in India when I was nine. My parents didn't have the money to visit for the funeral. And after that, Mummy just became completely withdrawn. It was like every time she looked at me, she remembered the reason my parents came here when my mom was pregnant with me was so I could have a good life. The reason she wasn't able to go back to India is because my parents spend all their money—and they don't have much of it—on me. And she's never forgiven me for it. Sometimes I tell myself that I'll earn enough to take her back one day soon. But who am I kidding? Most filmmakers don't make any money at all, let alone someone just starting out. So I'm doomed. We basically don't have any relationship at all." I sniffed, and Sahil reached into his center console to hand me a tissue. "Thanks." I dabbed at my nose. "Wow, sorry to unload on you like that."

He rubbed my back and then put his hand back on the wheel. "I'm glad you did. And I'm . . . I'm so sorry, T. I had no idea."

I shrugged. "That was one of the things I loved about Maddie. She doesn't have a mom, so I used to pretend in my head that I didn't either. It was just easier that way. She had her dad and I had Dadi and we had each other, so it seemed okay. But now Maddie's gone and my mom's still gone in almost every sense of the word and . . ." My voice wobbled. "It just feels sucky all around."

Sahil looked pained, like he might cry too. "Hey, T. For what it's worth, you'll always have me. Okay? I'm not going anywhere. I promise."

I smiled at him through my tears. And in that moment, I

completely believed him. Sahil was someone I could count on. He'd never let me down.

Oh, we're here. I better go.

Love,

Twinkle

Saturday, June 20, post-party
Sahil's car again (he's getting gas)

Dear Ava DuVernay,

In the history of horrible, obnoxious, hideous, loathsome nights, this one would get its own full-color page, complete with attention grabbing headlines smattered with !!!! and unflattering pictures of me stealing away into the darkness, my collar up and my head down.

It started out okay. Sahil and I got to the cabin (it was obvious which one was Victoria's parents' because of the thumping bass and ten shrieking teens trying to climb into the fountain in the front yard). It was one of those enormous mountain chalet getaway thingies, with huge windows and logs and stuff. As soon as we entered, Sahil left to talk to Victoria about setting up a quiet space for the behind-the-scenes interviews. I walked up to Hannah, who was surrounded by the usual gaggle of juniors and seniors, including Maddie. Apparently she'd decided her dad's show was worth missing for this party. Slowly, the chatter died down as they registered the presence of an intruder in their midst.

"Can I *help* you?" Hannah asked. She looked gorgeous, with this ombré lip gloss and a deep burgundy strapless dress that set off her blond hair. Her friends all stared at me, and Maddie shifted from foot to foot, looking like she was in pain. Which might have been because she was wearing six-inch wedge sandals or because she was uncomfortable with the situation.

"I just wanted to say happy birthday," I said, handing Hannah the small silver-wrapped box. Sahil and I had chipped in for a gift card to Nordstrom together.

She took it with a small smile/grimace on her face. "Thanks."

"That's cool of you," Maddie said after a pause. "To bring a present, I mean."

I stared at her in shock for a moment before recovering. Maddie was being nice to me in front of Hannah? Was it one of the signs of the apocalypse or something? "Um, yeah. No worries."

A glance passed between Maddie and Hannah, and then, sighing, Hannah said to me, "Help yourself to drinks or whatever."

"Thanks. I'm mostly here to do the behind-the-scenes interviews, but that's nice of you."

Apparently done with me, Hannah returned to her friends, and they closed ranks, their backs facing me like a wall. Maddie tossed me a small, apologetic shrug, but that was it. She didn't say anything else. I felt my new friend, anger, begin to bubble inside me. Why was Hannah so intent on excluding me when I'd never done anything to her?

I didn't break my stride as I tried to find Sahil, but the thought slammed into me, hard: That was the last chance. I'd been willing to just come here, do a few fun interviews, and leave, if Hannah could treat me nicely for once. But now? The gloves were off. *Now* I was in search of the truest stories, the ones that would best represent the silk feathered hats. And if Hannah and the rest of them weren't happy with the end results, I wouldn't feel guilty about it. I was here as a story-teller, a fly on the wall, not as a friend. Not anymore. And if they didn't like that, maybe it'd force them to think about how they treated people.

I grabbed an orange soda from a cooler in the hallway and walked into a small room off to the right. Sahil was in there, set-ting up the shot. He'd placed a chair in front of a bookshelf that was mostly full of expensive-looking vases and china figurines, and not many actual books.

"Hey," he said, beaming at me. "I thought maybe we could set up the camera in that corner." He pointed across to the chair. "Victoria has a tripod if you want to use it."

"Sounds good." I smiled and walked up to him, close enough that we were toe to toe. I put my hands on his chest, feeling his heart beating, strong and steady. Sahil would never treat me like the others. Sahil was always so good to me. I ran my hands from his chest down to his stomach and then around to his back. His smile faded as his eyes got heavy, his gaze traveling down to my lips.

"Did I tell you already that you look heart-stoppingly beauti-ful tonight?" Sahil said. "Mina Harker has nothing on you."

I laughed quietly. "I don't know. I don't have that whole inge-nue thing down like she does."

Sahil shook his head, his eyes never leaving mine. "You don't need it. You have something else . . . *Chamatkaar.*"

"*Chamatkaar?* What is that—magic? A miracle?"

He nodded. "When I was little, I thought the word meant 'golden fireworks.' I don't know why or how I connected the two. But when I see you . . . every *time*, Twinkle, I feel those golden fireworks inside me. And the only reason I can think of is that you have some kind of *chamatkaar.* You must be a special kind of miracle." He smiled a little abashedly, like he was afraid he'd said too much.

I didn't even think twice. I just laced my hands behind his head and pulled him to me. His eyes widened, surprised at first, but then he wrapped his arms around me and pulled me as close as I could go. Our bodies molded together, his fingers digging into my hips, his mouth just as hungry, just as fevered, as mine. The only thought going through my head was, *Finally.* What had taken me so long? Why had I been so slow to figure out that Sahil was the one, that he'd always been the one? No matter what connection I'd thought I had with Neil all those ages ago, it was *Sahil* who was here now. *Sahil* who'd *been* here, who was so my type it was like he'd been created in a matchmaking factory just for me. Just like Sofia Coppola, I was a sucker for a love story. I'd just been too blind to see the one unfolding right before my eyes.

I pulled back and smiled at him, my fingers still in his hair. "When I'm with you, I feel like I can breathe. And all of these people? They don't matter. They're . . . they're nothing."

Sahil's smile morphed into a half frown. "I wouldn't say they don't matter. I think Victoria's been pretty nice to you, yeah? Inviting you here, letting us do the footage, use her house . . ."

And she'd done my makeup and hair the night of the carnival, too, though Sahil didn't know that. "Sure, sure. But the rest of them? Hannah and Maddie and Francesca and the others?" I rolled my eyes. "Please."

Sahil put his hands on my shoulders, his eyebrows furrowed with what looked like concern. "You know, maybe you need a break from all this filmmaking stuff."

"Why?"

"I've just . . . I've never heard you talk about anyone like that. You sound so . . ." He looked at me.

"What?"

"Cold. You sound cold and unlike you."

I smiled, but I could tell it was hard, like a sliver of ice. Sahil had been right before; I'd been awful to Lewis. But now? He hadn't seen how Hannah had just treated me. He couldn't understand what it felt like to be me, how tiresome it got to play the leading role in *Invisible Girl* day after day, month after month. But somehow, I couldn't bring myself to tell him any of that. Putting my hands on my hips I said, "Oh, so now I'm cold? I thought I was *chamatkaar*."

Sahil stared at me. "Twinkle, I'm not trying to fight with you. I'm just saying—"

"I heard you, Sahil. But you don't know what those girls are like. You don't have to put up with it like I do. So do me a favor and spare me the sermon."

He laughed a little disbelievingly. "Wow. All right. I hear you loud and clear." He rubbed a hand along his jaw. "I'll get the actors for the interview."

I grabbed his arm, regret pinching in my chest. "Hey, look. I don't want to fight either. I'm sorry. I just want to get this done and wrapped up. And then we can enjoy the party, okay?"

He studied my face and then nodded. Planting a light, soft kiss on my forehead, he left.

While Sahil rounded up people for me to interview, I walked to the kitchen for a glass of ice; the soda I'd picked up was getting warm. On my way there, I happened to glance out into the dining room and saw Francesca standing by the sliding glass doors, her face a mask of complete anger. My pulse kicked up a notch; I could sense a story. I walked out there and stood next to her, looking at what she was looking at.

Her boyfriend, Tony, was in the backyard. Wrapped around him was Sherie Williams, a senior cheerleader. I blew out a breath. "I'm sorry, Francesca," I said.

She took a shaky sip of her drink. "I can't believe that little crap bag," she said in her New York accent, and I wasn't sure if she meant Tony or Sherie. "You know *I* convinced him to go out for the football team last year? He thinks he's such a gift to women, but he was nothing without me." She glanced at me. "And Sherie? Her mom is usually passed-out drunk on the couch whenever I go over there. She's obviously compensating."

Something heavy and oily squirmed in my stomach. I did not want to be here, listening to this. At least, a big part of me didn't. But there was a small part of me, a small, vicious, spiteful part of me that wanted more.

"You want a behind-the-scenes interview?" Francesca said.

"I'll give you one. I can tell you some stuff, Twinkle. But you gotta promise me you'll put it in the video."

Walk away now, a voice inside me said. It sounded like a weird mix of Dadi and me. *You do* not *want to do this, Twinkle Mehra.* But Francesca and Sherie were both a part of Hannah's friend group. When had they ever stood up for me? When had they *ever* told Hannah to not be so mean? Why should I feel any sense of loyalty to them? Besides, this was a truth waiting to be unveiled. This was what I'd wanted—to show the world how things looked behind the curtain. This was me, an artist, not pulling any punches.

I nodded at Francesca. "Sure. I'll give you the first interview. Want to get started now?"

She took a drink, smiled, and then followed me back.

"So not only is Sherie a boyfriend-stealing diva, but she also stole Taylor Packett's bracelet. Yeah." Francesca leaned forward. "It was this charm bracelet her dad got her from Tiffany's. The clasp was loose, so Taylor left it on her desk while she went to the bathroom. Sherie took it when she thought no one was looking and then helped Taylor look for it when she came back from the bathroom!" She laughed, the sound hard. "Who *does* that? And Taylor still doesn't know." Francesca looked right into the camera. "Well, guess what, Sherie? Someone *was* watching. And I'm done sitting back and being quiet for you, you thieving little witch."

I hit pause on the camera; I could hear people outside, probably waiting to come in and do their interview. Wiping my palms surreptitiously on my jeans, I smiled. "Great. This was great. Thanks, Francesca."

She threw me a peace sign and walked out.

"Okay, the next person can come in!" I said, turning toward the door. Sure, it wasn't exactly award-winning work I was doing here. But it was something that would get people talking. It would get people *really looking* at themselves and the choices they were making. I thought about Hannah and Maddie, how Hannah had said she didn't know why Maddie hung out with me and how Maddie had refused to speak up for me even though we were practically sisters until about a year ago. So why shouldn't I be the one to force them to look at themselves closely? To see their rotten reflections in the mirror? I mean, I was doing the world a service. So I wasn't one of the silk feathered hat people, but you know what? I wasn't a groundling anymore either. I was something completely different, an artist on an island, the only one brave enough to tell the truth.

Taylor Packett walked in, wearing a hot-pink one-shoulder dress and giant hoop earrings. She tucked one strand of long brown hair behind her ear and sat down across from me. Her phone *ding*ed, and she looked down at it, giggled, and began typing out a text. I waited one minute, then two, then three.

"Whenever you're ready to start," I said, feeling my face beginning to get warm.

"Sure, sure. Just . . ." She kept typing and giggling.

My heart pounded. "You know," I said, crossing my legs. "I heard something interesting about you tonight, Taylor."

That got her attention. She looked up from her phone, frowning. "Oh, yeah? Like what?"

"Have you ever lost anything valuable?" I smiled a thin-lipped, tight smile. "If you have, you might want to take a closer look at your friends. Maybe make sure they're not all in on it, all laughing at you behind your back."

Taylor set her phone in her lap, her eyes hard. The fingers of one hand clasped loosely around her other wrist. "Are you talking about my bracelet? Who took it? Was it Katie Walters? Because let me tell you something about Katie. You know how last winter she went on break early because she was supposedly visiting relatives in Utah? Well, she was actually visiting Planned Parenthood to *stop* the arrival of a relative, if you know what I mean. And Katie's dad is the grand poo-bah of the Mormon temple." Taylor leaned forward and spoke directly into the camera. "Don't screw with me, Katie. I will take you down."

There were three more interviews after Taylor's, each one just as bitter and scathing and gossip-filled. Each time that tiny voice in my brain would tell me to pay attention to the squirming, faintly nauseated feeling in my stomach. And each time I'd shut it up. Who ever said making authentic art was comfortable and cushy?

"Come on in," I yelled over my shoulder toward the door when Sherie Williams had left after dishing about Francesca's dad's gambling problem. Which apparently was a big deal because he was the treasurer of the country club.

But no one came in. Sighing, I got up, walked to the door, and found Maddie standing just outside, her arms crossed. She had on silver eyeshadow to match her silver dress, and her red-lipsticked mouth was set in a thin, hard line. People milled out in the hallway, talking and laughing, no one paying attention to us.

"Hey?" I said, raising an eyebrow. "Want to come in for your interview?"

"What are you doing?" Maddie asked, shaking her head.

"I'm . . . getting interviews—you know what I'm doing."

"No. You're getting my friends to gossip about each other. This isn't about the *film* at all, Twinkle. This is about some sick part of you wanting revenge for feeling like—like you do."

"And how is that, Maddie? Since you're the expert on me, how do I feel?"

Her eyes glittered. "You know."

"I don't. Why don't you enlighten me?"

"I'm not doing this right now." She began to walk away.

I barked a laugh. "Oh, big surprise. Maddie's running away! That's your MO anytime you come across something you don't know how to handle."

She whipped back around, her cheeks stained pink. "Fine! You want to know what I think? You're just lashing out at everyone because you feel like a loser inside. News flash, Twinkle. That's no one else's fault but your own. Maybe you should fix yourself before you attack other people!"

Anger exploded in my brain in a thousand colors. For a second I couldn't even *see* Maddie because of the thick fog of anger surrounding me. She'd called me a *loser.* "How dare you?" I spat, leaning forward. "You can*not* blame me for your friends being total douche bags. Am I forcing them to say these evil things about each other? Am I feeding them their lines? *I'm* not the loser here, Maddie. It's too bad you can't see that."

"Oh, *they're* evil for the things they're saying?" Maddie

scoffed. "What about you, Twinkle? What about the fact that you're sitting here, baiting everyone? What, that's for the good of the world?"

"It *is* for the good of the world!" I shouted. A few people looked our way and then went back to their conversations. "I'm doing your friends a *service* by showing them what they act like when things don't go their way. I'm forcing them to face the truth about themselves, and the truth isn't always pretty!"

"You're forgetting the nice things people have done for you, then," Maddie said. "Didn't Victoria come over one weekend to help you do your hair and makeup? Didn't Francesca help pay for the expensive lighting you wanted? And I helped you recruit most of the actors for your movie! But that doesn't fit in with this bullshit narrative you have going on, does it?" Her voice rose with every question until she was shouting too. "What the hell are you doing, Twinkle?"

"What are *you* doing, Maddie?" I yelled, gesturing at her short dress. "Who are you trying to impress by talking about your old friends behind their back to your new friends? By dressing like a teenage WHORE?"

We stared at each other in silence. I felt immediate shame, hot and choking, for the last thing I'd said. People should not be judged by what they wore. I knew that. I *hated* when girls, especially, were called out for wearing the "wrong" clothes. When *I* was called out for wearing cheap clothes. But I kept my face the same, refusing to give an inch. I couldn't back down over that now, or Maddie would think I was apologizing for everything.

She nodded slowly. "Right. You know what? I don't even know why I'm bothering. Just forget it."

"Yeah, just forget it!" I yelled at her retreating back as she threaded her way through the crowd. "Just forget *you*, Maddie!"

I put a shaky hand to my forehead and took a deep breath just as Lewis Shore walked up, grinning. "Yo. We still on for that interview?" He clearly hadn't heard anything Maddie and I had said. It was weird, how my entire world felt like it was collapsing and he was just standing there, smiling, happy to be at this party.

"Yep," I said finally, my voice muted. "Come on in."

Love,

Twinkle

Eighteen

\<text message 1:18 a.m.\>
From: Skid
To: Sahil, Aaron
yo the a-man wants to know if you made your move yet

\<text message 1:18 a.m.\>
From: Aaron
To: Sahil, Skid
I did NOT say that. I merely wondered if you're having a
fun time with Twinkle at the party

\<text message 1:20 a.m.\>
From: Sahil
To: Skid, Aaron
Idk man it's a bad vibe tonight. It started out great, we
kissed and stuff and I thought I was winning her over but
idk. We're on our way back. I'm getting gas rn

From: Aaron
To: Sahil, Skid
What do you mean bad vibe?

<text message 1:22 a.m.>
From: Sahil
To: Skid, Aaron
She's acting different like super pissed all the time? it's as if this movie thing is changing her or something

<text message 1:23 a.m.>
From: Skid
To: Sahil, Aaron
don't tell her that. take it from me girls do not like it when guys stick their noses in especially when they're doing something wrong

<text message 1:24 a.m.>
From: Sahil
To: Skid, Aaron
I can't just NOT say anything

<text message 1:24 a.m.>
From: Aaron
To: Sahil, Skid
So what are you gonna do

From: Aaron
To: Sahil, Skid
I get it. if you care about someone you can't just sit by
while they mess up

<text message 1:26 a.m.>
From: Skid
To: Sahil, Aaron
dude it's your funeral so I'll wear black the next time I
see you

<text message 1:27 a.m.>
From: Sahil
To: Skid, Aaron
thanks for the vote of confidence Skid

<text message 1:28 a.m.>
From: Aaron
To: Sahil, Skid
Don't you mean vote of conFIGence lol

<text message 1:28 a.m.>
From: Skid
To: Sahil, Aaron
was that another plant pun? smdh I'm out

Saturday, June 20
Sahil's car yet again

Dear Ava DuVernay,

Sahil's playing music and seems to be focused on the road, so I'm back.

I'm trying hard not to falter under his gaze. He occasionally glances at me and smiles hesitantly, so I haven't completely blown it with him. I hope not, anyway. I don't think I did much wrong besides what I said to Maddie, but . . . I don't know. Something just feels off. Here, between us, and inside me. Also, Sahil was texting while he was getting gas. Was he texting about me??

When I was finished with the last interview, I took my camera off the tripod and walked through the cabin, aimed for the back door. As I walked, I held the camera up and ended up getting quite a few other shots of conversations at the party. If nothing else, I can use some of it to pad out the footage at the end. Too much footage is always better than too little.

Lowering my camera, I opened the sliding glass door and stepped outside. There was a glass-walled room with a hot tub off to the right, but I avoided all the screeching, writhing bodies over there, picking my way through a long path that wound off to the left into a grove of aspen trees instead. There was a half wall there, and I sat on it, setting my camera down and wrapping my arms around myself. The stars were silver in the night, and I tipped my head back and studied them. There was a weird lump in my throat that wouldn't go away and I knew it had to do with Maddie's and my conversation (aka screaming match). Strange, because it was obvious even to the most unobservant person that our friendship had been on its last legs for a long time. No matter how much I'd rallied and fought and wanted to believe otherwise, I think I always knew that in my heart.

"Hey."

I started at the soft voice before taking in the *Cabin in the Woods* T-shirt and the shorts, the gentleness of his brown eyes. "Hey, Sahil."

"Mind some company?" he asked, gesturing to the wall.

"Nah. Come sit." I scooted over.

We sat in silence for a few moments, listening to the whisper of the wind in the aspen leaves. "This is nice," Sahil said. "It beats the shrieking hot tub chaos over there." He thrust his chin in the direction of the people. "Can't really hear it from over here, though."

I grinned. "That's why I picked this spot."

"Smart. I went that way first and saw Oliver in his leopard-print Speedo. More like Speed-No." He shuddered theatrically.

I laughed and bumped him with my shoulder.

"So, the interviews go okay?" His voice was suddenly more serious.

"Yep. All done."

He nodded; I could feel him watching me. "I ran into Maddie inside."

I glanced at him. "And?"

Sahil sighed and looked down at his hands, folded in his lap. "Twinkle . . . is this what you want?"

"I'm making the best movie I can make, and that includes the behind-the-scenes interviews. I thought that's what you wanted too, Sahil."

"I do. But what does getting people to backstab each other have to do with making a good movie?"

I rolled my eyes. "Okay, maybe that's not artistic enough for you, but this is the sort of thing that grabs people by the throat. This is a social commentary. It's a mirror I'm holding up for people to see how they behave when no one's around to watch."

Sahil studied me for a long moment, until I was almost squirming under his scrutiny. "So this is art?"

I couldn't believe he wasn't getting this. *"Yeah."*

"It's not revenge?"

I looked away and let my hands drop. "I already got the third degree from Maddie."

He put his arm around me and I snuggled up, feeling warm for the first time all night. "I just don't want you to do something that isn't you, Twinkle," he said softly. "It's not worth it."

"What's not worth it?"

"Changing who you are," he said, looking down into my eyes.

I swallowed and looked away again.

"Because I fell for *you*, you know." I started to protest, not wanting him to feel obliged to tell me what he liked about me just because we'd been arguing, but he continued, undeterred. "The funny, passionate, kind Twinkle Mehra. Not this new version of her that's all twisted up and angry."

I stared at Sahil, feeling goose bumps crawling on my skin. He was talking about shiny, future Twinkle just like I'd always talked about her to myself. Only, in his case, he thought shiny, future Twinkle sucked. Was he right? Was I losing myself completely in my desperate bid to become her? And was that what I wanted?

"Okay, look," he said when the silence stretched out, pulling out his phone. "I've got the classic *Frankenstein* on my phone. What do you say to a little midnight viewing?"

"Right now?"

He grinned. "You got somewhere else to be?"

Smiling, I scooted even closer to him. "Let's do this."

And for the next hour and a half, I forgot all about Maddie and Francesca and Taylor and Hannah and the film.

All I thought about was the monster coming to life before my eyes.

When we left later, I realized I forgot my camera bag in the cabin. "I'll be right back," I told Sahil, hurrying back inside.

Hannah and Maddie were standing in the kitchen and didn't see me walk in.

"Well, at least she showed you her true colors," Hannah was saying. "At least you know now for sure. And you don't have to feel guilty about leaving her behind and making new friends."

"It just sucks that she'd want to air all that gossip in front of the entire school," Maddie said, shaking her head. "But I talked to Sahil, and he said not to worry. Apparently, he's going to make sure it gets cleaned up in the editing process or something." She sighed. "I didn't expect this at all from Twinkle. I always thought she was such a good person. You know?"

I wanted to run in there and say, *Sahil's wrong. This isn't going to get edited. That's what you all expect, isn't it, for someone to come up behind you and clean up your messes? Someone to edit away all your mistakes so you can seem as glossy as ever? But that's not my job as a filmmaker. I'm here for the brutal truth of it all.*

But before I could step in and say any of that, Hannah said, "Sometimes the friendships we make when we're little can be hard to see honestly."

"Yeah. Ugh. Thanks for being here for me, though, Han. I'm sorry to bring all this up at your party."

"You're way more important to me than my party, M," Hannah said, reaching over to hug Maddie. "We're sisters."

"Sisters," Maddie agreed, smiling.

My words withered away to dust as I watched them. Everything turned shimmery and blurry; I realized tears, hot and furious, were rolling down my cheeks. Before they could see me, I grabbed my camera bag and ran out of the door.

Nothing makes sense anymore. Does Maddie really think I'm not a good person simply because I want to tell the truth? My mind is reeling at how she agreed with Hannah, that it's hard to see our friendship in the right light.

We used to be sisters; something bigger and deeper than blood bonded us. Maddie used to be able to see right into my soul. So . . . is *she* wrong about who I am now? Or am I?

Love,

Twinkle

Sunday, June 21, but just barely
My room

Dear Mira Nair,

It got worse.

Sahil dropped me off at around three this morning. I crept into the house, shut the door behind me, and took one step—before the lights in the living room flared on.

Mummy, Papa, and Dadi all stared at me.

Crap. That's the only thing my paralyzed brain could think. *Crap, crap, crappity crap.*

"Where have you been?" This was Papa, his voice dangerously low.

"I . . ." I cleared my throat. "I had to get some extra footage for the film."

"In the middle of the night. At a party where the parents weren't home."

I stared at Mummy, my eyebrows knitting together. "What? How do you know that?"

"Maddie *ka* phone *tha*," Dadi said, her eyes wide and sad.

Maddie?? Maddie *told* on me?? I balled my fists by my sides. "I don't know what she told you, but I was there to *work*."

"You know the rules!" Papa thundered. "You cannot leave the house at night without telling us, and you cannot go to parties unless there are parents present!"

"How would I have even told you?" I asked, my own voice rising. "When I left, none of you were home!"

"*Chup karo yeh badmaashi!*" Papa's voice sliced across my own. "That is not how you speak to your elders!"

245

"*Izzat se bolo,* Twinkle," Dadi added. "These are your parents."

That was it. I couldn't take it anymore, their irritation with me, their expectation that I should just be meek and accept it. Something inside me boiled over.

"Well, I don't think they're showing *me* any respect!" I yelled. "Do you know I'm the only person in my entire school who doesn't have her own cell phone? It's a basic necessity nowadays. And I'm *tired* of being the only junior who doesn't drive, either. I don't ever complain about those things, but I don't hear you thanking me. You just expect me to do anything you tell me to do, whether you're here or not. Maybe you think I sneaked out of the house when I had no right to, but maybe you should consider that I left because no one gives a *crap* about me. No one cares whether I'm here or not!"

They all stared at me like I was some teenaged monster species they'd only read about in horror novels and had no idea were in existence. I spun and rushed out of the room before they could say anything, slamming the door to my room behind me. I flung myself on the bed and began to sob, clutching Mr. Bandar, my childhood monkey pal, to my chest. He was in pieces and falling apart, but I was too attached to give him up.

When my eyes were all swollen and my nose was completely stopped up, I heard my door open. I rolled my puffy eyes. Maybe knocking on doors was a silly Western rule that had no place in our house, but right then I'd kill for some privacy. "Please, Dadi," I said, without turning over. "I don't want to talk. There's nothing to say anyway. They don't care about me, and you know it."

A big hand was on my back. "We do care about you, *beta.*"

I sat up and saw Papa sitting on the edge of my bed, his face full of concern. I leaned against my headboard. "It doesn't feel like it sometimes."

Papa put his hand on my shin and took a deep breath. "I'm sorry," he said, and I knew that was a huge thing for him to say. We never apologized to each other. It's just not something *Desi* families are big on. "Sometimes I forget that *you* need me just as much as those kids at the youth house. But when I'm here, in our home, with a warm bed and hot food, it feels . . . wrong. They have no one to care about them. If I am not working every minute I can, I feel that I am failing them."

I watched Papa's hands as he talked about his work, and I realized something: He cared about his at-risk youth just as much as Sahil's mom and dad cared about the state of higher education in our country. The difference was, because of their education and fancy degrees, they could afford to pay money to contribute to their cause. Papa's work had to be in person; his donation was his time, his family, and himself.

"It's good that they have you, then," I said, putting my arms around my legs and resting my chin on top of my knees.

"But that doesn't mean I don't care about you," Papa said, smiling. He touched my cheek. "You make my work worthwhile."

I sighed. "I never thought *you* didn't care, Papa." It was true. Papa wasn't the most involved parent, but at least he asked about me now and then. At least he sometimes checked whether or not I needed lunch money or what I was up to on the weekends.

"Mummy cares deeply about you, too, *beta*," Papa said, squeezing my leg.

I looked away. "Ever since Nani died, Mummy's been . . . different. Like she blames me or something."

"You remember that? When Nani died?"

I nodded. "Yeah. I remember we couldn't afford to fly back to Mumbai. And then Mummy threw away all her art supplies. She changed."

Papa breathed out, this slow, heavy thing loosed from the bottom of his soul. "*Haan.* Your mummy . . . she doesn't blame you, Twinkle. But she does blame herself. She will never forgive herself for Nani dying alone."

"But it wasn't her fault!" I said, my eyes filling with tears. What I really wanted to say was, it wasn't *my* fault. There wasn't anything any of us could've done.

"I know, *beta.* But Mummy can't seem to grasp that. All we can do is remember that she is ours no matter what. No matter how broken her heart is."

After a moment, he got up and left, closing the door softly behind him.

Love,
Twinkle

INVITATION

To: Twinkle Mehra

From: Victoria Lyons

What: Bonfire Party

Why: Celebrate Wrapping Up Dracula!

(AND the return of Neil Roy from swim camp! AND the end of the school year!)

Where: Banner Lake
When: Thursday, June 25, 7 p.m.
Ve Vant to Wrap It Up!

June 22
The Reel Deal Blog
Posted by: Rolls ROYce

My brother, the prodigal athlete genius girl magnet, will return to school from . . . let's say baseball camp . . . in a couple of days. I'm not gonna lie. I've kinda enjoyed being out of his shadow for a while. Almost like one of those flowering plants that's overpowered by a thorny weed. And then the gardener plucks the weed and the flowering plant can fill the world with its brilliance and explosive color. That's me. I'm brilliant and explosive.

It's been so fulfilling. I feel like I've come into my element.

Sparkle has been able to see the real *me*, the one I am when I'm not just Teal's brother, the also-ran, the slightly washed-out twin. And guess what? She likes *me*. One of the most important people in my life likes me for me. She doesn't even *register* Teal on her Sparkle-dar. Her smiles, her laughter, her kisses, her jokes—those are all just for me.

It's been a couple of days since the birthday party

now. I was pretty worried about how she acted there, but the more I think about it, the more confident I am that Sparkle will figure things out. She's finding her footing right now and things are hard, but that's temporary, I'm sure. She's . . . a pretty special person. I have all the confidence that she won't lose herself—or us—because of this hiccup. That's the other thing I realized at the party: Sparkle really, really likes me, too. Once we're done with the movie, I know she and I are going to be together. And man, it feels *so* crazy good to say that.

So let Teal come home, I say. Let him come home because I've already got everything I need. I know exactly who I am and what I'm capable of thanks to the movie Sparkle and I made together. For that, I don't think I'll ever be able to thank her fully.

Tuesday, June 23
4 days till Midsummer Night
My room

Dear Sofia Coppola,

Since early Sunday, my nights have been dark, the days darker still. The only pinpricks of joy in the vast, empty desert of my existence are the few remaining days of editing the movie I have made.

Do you think I'm being melodramatic? Okay, let's take stock of all the people I'm avoiding and/or can't look in the eye right now and why, shall we?

1. Person: Maddie. Reason: We've been fighting nonstop. She *ratted* me out to my parents. She called me a *loser*. She's sisters with Hannah now, not me.

2. Person: Sahil. Reason: We've kissed (multiple times). And I still haven't told him about my e-mail relationship with my secret admirer, who may or may not be his identical twin brother, who is also the one who stood me up.

3. Person: Mummy. Reason: Losing it on her after sneaking out to a party. (Dadi and I are simpatico again. All it took was a simple apology for her to hug me and make me reconciliatory coconut *burfi*.)

4. Persons: Hannah, Francesca, Taylor, etc., etc. Reason: I don't want them to second-guess the interviews they did and ask me to delete them, which I will not for reasons of artistic integrity.

5. Persons: Aaron and Matthew. Reason: They are now officially going out and are always all lovey-dovey at the lunch table, which only forces me to remember what a train wreck my own love life (and life at large) is. Therefore, I have spent my last two lunch periods either in the bathroom or in the library and am savage with hunger by the end of the day.

So? *Now* do you think I'm being melodramatic?? I didn't think so. The thing is, I feel a little bit on shaky ground with most of these people. My brain keeps trying to convince me I'm right, but my heart keeps whispering that I've made some pretty major mistakes. That, like Sahil said, maybe I'm losing my sense of who I am.

Whoa. Mummy just popped her head in here and asked me to come to her room. Avoiding her is out of the question since her room is right across the hall from me and she'd see me running away.

Love,

Twinkle

Nineteen

Tuesday, June 23
My room, redux

Dear Aurora Guerrero,

You know those times in your life when you feel like you're watching everything go down in a movie rather than in real life? People seem to be actors and the lines seem to be scripted and you just stand there with your mouth hanging open, wondering if you look as stupid as you feel?

Yeah, that.

So, Mummy called me into her room. I don't think she's ever asked to "see me" before. I went in there, my hands in the pockets of my KEEP CALM AND MAKE MOVIES hoodie, trying to look like I didn't care. Like I wasn't dying of curiosity and also awkwardness because we hadn't talked at all about the stuff I said to her when I yelled that night after the party.

She had this small cardboard box, the size of a shoe box, open on her bed. She sat down beside it and patted the bed on the other side, so I sat, too. Silently, she pulled out a bunch of papers and set them between us. Some of them were letters written in Hindi. I don't read it, but I can recognize the script. The letters at the top were written in this careful, slow hand, but some of the ones at the back of the pile were in shaky writing. I sifted through them, and then got to some black-and-white pictures. There was one of a little girl around five years old, with short, curly hair and these solemn eyes staring straight into the camera without smiling. Her dress was too small for her, and she was barefoot on a dirt road, standing in front of a little hut.

"Is that you?" I said, peering closer. Those black eyes . . . I'd recognize them anywhere.

"Yes," Mummy said. "I was six years old. You can see the house where I lived behind me there."

Wow. I mean, I knew Mummy had been poor in India, way poorer than we were. But I'd never *seen* evidence of it before. My cheeks got hot when I remembered how I'd shouted at them for not having a cell phone. Mummy didn't even have shoes.

Mummy picked up one of the pictures. This one was of a young couple sitting on a cot with a baby in the woman's arms. "Nani and Nana. You know, they weren't much older than you when they had me. She was seventeen and Nana was twenty. He worked in a factory all his life, but he died when I was ten because of all the fumes he was inhaling there every day. A lot of men in the neighborhood died from that. Nani kept working as a *dhobin*— she washed people's clothes from the apartment complexes nearby. She wanted to be able to afford my school fees. She was determined that I would finish twelfth grade; she never finished fourth. When your Papa came to ask for my hand in marriage, she immediately said yes. She wanted something better for me and he had a job as a bank clerk. It was stable." She smiled and squeezed my arm. "When I got pregnant with you, Papa's friend told us he had a connection to a US company. He said he could get Papa a job here. I wasn't sure. I wanted to have my baby at home, where my mother could help me raise her. I had always imagined that—you growing up near Nani. And I knew that was her dream, too. She was so ecstatic at the thought of being a grandmother. Of spoiling you. But when she heard we could give you a start in the States . . ." Mummy shook her head, and a tear rolled down her cheek. "She told me to go. She made me promise to send her pictures of you as you grew, and she asked that we name you Twinkle if you were a girl, after the daughter of one of her favorite actresses."

"Did she . . . did she get to come visit when I was born?"

"No." Mummy swallowed. "We couldn't afford her visa or her ticket. We sent her a lot of photos and letters. She wrote all the time. She wanted to know what you wore for Diwali, what your favorite sweets were, whether you had the same curl to your lip when you were angry that I did. She was trying, I think, to be as much a part of your life as an eight-thousand-mile separation would allow." Mummy took a breath. "And then . . . she got sick. I would ask about it, but she said she was fine. It was just arthritis." She picked up one of the shakily written letters. "Just a part of getting older, she said. I had no idea how sick she was until she was . . . gone. She never asked for a single thing, even though we sent her money whenever we could. She was making do without so we could live well." A tear dripped off the end of her nose and made a dark blue circle on the sheet. I put my hand on Mummy's. My mind was reeling. I had no idea at all about any of this. What Mummy had been through, what Nani had wanted for me . . . I had no idea.

After a moment, she went on. "When Nani died, something inside me . . . broke. There's no other way to say it. And I'm sorry, Twinkle, that it's affected you. I am sorry it's made you feel like we don't care about you. The truth is, you're the center of our family."

An apology from Papa and Mummy in the space of a few days. It was like being in a Magritte painting. So surreal. Speaking of paintings . . . "You stopped doing your art when Nani died."

"Yes. The world seemed washed of color. It felt pointless." Mummy's eyes held mine. "The only thing that had any point anymore was you, Twinkle."

I shook my head. "That's not how it feels to me," I said, my voice cracking. "It feels like . . . like you blame me for Nani dying alone. If it weren't for me, you never would've come to the States. And you could've stayed there, with her."

Mummy sighed and smoothed my hair back from my forehead. "Twinkle, I don't blame you. For anything. If anything, I'm the one who . . ." She trailed off and started again. "Have you ever done something you were ashamed of, but found yourself powerless to stop?"

I thought back to the time I'd exploded at Lewis. What I'd said to Maddie about her dress. How I'd felt bad but hadn't been able to stop myself from acting out. "Yeah. But . . . how *do* you get yourself to stop?"

Mummy shrugged and smiled a small, sad smile. "I don't

know, *beta*. I'm still trying to work that out. I suppose all we can do is try, hmm? Perhaps life is about doing things in small steps to set things right again."

I looked into her teary black eyes and, for once, saw only love. There was no guardedness, no defensive wall, no spacey/absent look. My mom would never tell me she loved me in so many words. But this was the closest she'd ever come. I put my head on her shoulder and closed my eyes.

So maybe I need to take a step toward making things right again. Maybe it's time to whittle down the "people I'm avoiding" list. I can start at the bonfire party Thursday night.

Love,
Twinkle

From: twinkiefilmfan@urmail.com
To: binadmiringyou@urmail.com
Subject: Bonfire party
Dear N,
I know you couldn't show up at Perk. But I'm done wondering about your identity and if you're ever going to come say hi. So I'm going to find you at the bonfire party, okay? I'm pretty sure I know who you are anyway.
—Twinkle

Wednesday, June 24
My room
Dear Ava DuVernay,

I'm sitting here, thinking about the mistakes I've made. Blowing up at Lewis? That was a huge mistake. Yelling at Maddie? Ditto. Being spiteful and threatening to cancel the movie so everyone's work would've been for nothing? Tritto. But something both Sahil and Maddie have challenged me on just doesn't ring true: the behind-the-scenes interview footage.

I've been watching it for the last hour. When I get to the end, I just go back to the beginning and play again. Sahil and Maddie think this footage is about cold, hard revenge. And you know? Maybe it was, for a little bit at the party. I was furious, and I wanted to lash out in the only way I knew how.

But now? Now I see all the ways in which airing this would be the biggest truth I could ever tell. Unless people are forced to confront their lies, their brutality, their *wrongness,* how are they supposed to put things right? How are they supposed to grow? Yes, I've come to care for many of the people I made *Dracula* with. And that's precisely why I *have* to air these interviews.

They're a game changer, not just for all those involved, but for others watching, too. This is a statement about the way humans can be so ruthless, so cunning, so savage that we're no better than wild animals when you get down to it. This is *art.*

And so, yes, I *am* sorry about how I treated people that day I yelled at Lewis. But I'm *not* sorry about this. This is the most honest thing I've ever dared to create, and this is going to help a lot of people.

Love,

Twinkle

Thursday, June 25
2 days until Midsummer Night
Banner Lake

Dear DeMane Davis,

"Take steps to make things right," she said. "It'll all be okay," she said. Yeah, right.

So, first, I thought I did a decent thing. When Sahil asked me if I wanted a ride to the bonfire party, I said no. Since I was going to be talking to Neil there, I didn't want it to be awkward between us or for him to feel like I was lying to him by not telling him the entire ride there. So I took a Lyft there even though it cost me a good chunk of some birthday money I had left over. So, Universe? A few karma points for that would've been nice.

The entire ride there, I thought about what Mummy and I had talked about. How she'd said the way to make something right again was to take a small step in the right direction. As soon as the driver pulled up, I hopped out and looked at all the people clustered around the giant bonfire, which was already roaring. Off to the left, Banner Lake was as still and dark as a piece of black glass, and a cool wind was whipping across the clearing where the party was, making people shriek and huddle into each other. I pulled my hoodie closer around me and walked up to Sahil, who was talking to Skid off to the side.

His eyes lit up even brighter than the bonfire when he saw me. He looked heartbreakingly handsome in a black skull hoodie and jeans, his hair all tousled from the wind. "Hey, T!" He leaned over and gave me a hug, and I closed my eyes, just relishing it.

When Sahil held me, he blocked out the cutting wind, and it felt like everything would be okay.

Skid gave me a fist bump. "Yo, T," he said, grinning. "Guess what? I finally talked to Portia. Told her about Midsummer Night like you said?"

"Yeah? And?" I crossed my fingers without even thinking about it.

He nodded, a smug grin on his face. "She was into it. She'll be there Saturday."

"Oh my God, I knew it!" I clapped, and then hugged him. "Congrats, Skid. Now all you have to do is be your charming self and it's in the bag, dude."

Sahil snorted. "This guy? Charming?"

Skid glared at him. "Don't be jealous, Sahil. Green isn't your color." Then, laughing, he swaggered off to get another hot chocolate. In the distance, I saw Aaron and Matthew huddled together under a tree, their arms wrapped around each other. I felt this warmth in my chest. I was happy for my friends. Extremely happy. But I wanted to be in that lovestruck, gooey place too. I glanced at Sahil and amended silently, *In a guilt-free way*.

"It's finally here," Sahil said, smiling at me and spreading his arms wide. "The wrap party. We're almost done."

I sighed happily. "I know." Then I looked around again, searching.

"You okay?"

"Hmm?" Looking back at Sahil, I saw him frowning at me. "Oh, yeah." I stuck my hands in my hoodie pockets and scuffed my sneaker on the ground. "I just . . . I want to set things right. You know, for how I acted that day with Lewis and all of them."

Sahil's frown morphed into a small smile. "Yeah?"

"Yeah. I don't know what happened. . . . I lost my head or something. Anyway." I looked him in the eye. "I'm sorry I acted like that."

"'S'okay, T," he said, gently bumping my shoulder with his. "I hear it happens to all the greats now and again."

I rolled my eyes. "Maybe my problem is that I was starting to think of myself as one of the 'greats,'" I said. "A little humility never hurt anyone."

Sahil smiled fondly at me. "Yeah."

I caught sight of Francesca and Brij, standing off to one side talking. That was one of the coolest things the movie had done. It had brought together the groundlings and the silk feathered hats for the first time in the history of PPC's existence. (Okay, there was no way for me to prove that, but it was my claim to fame and I was sticking with it.) "Oh, hey, there's someone now. I'll be back in a bit, okay?"

Sahil nodded and I rushed off. "Hey, Francesca! Brij!"

Francesca turned to me, her hands around a thermos, a plaid scarf around her neck. Only in the mountains would you need a scarf when it was almost July. "Oh, hey, Twinkle." Brij just waved. He looked a little thunderstruck, his eyes all wide, like he was having trouble believing he was here. Ha. I so got that.

"Listen," I said to both of them. "I just wanted to say sorry. For the other day, when we were filming that scene? I pitched a hissy fit with you guys and Lewis and it wasn't cool at all."

Francesca smiled and waved a hand. "Ah, it's not a big deal. Lewis should've learned his lines."

"Oh yeah," Brij agreed, huddling into his camo jacket as the wind picked up. "It wasn't just you."

"Maybe. But I shouldn't have said all that stuff and acted like a giant brat. That was wrong. So, I'm sorry, again."

"Apology accepted," Brij said.

Francesca grinned. "You and Skid just make me look unbelievably gorgeous in the final version and I'll never mention it again."

I laughed just as Victoria walked up, her thick red mane blowing in the wind. "It's a deal."

"Twinkle!" Victoria screeched, throwing her arm around my neck. "How's my fave director?"

"Good!" I smiled at her. "How's my fave, uh, Victoria?"

She grinned. "I'm fantastic. Listen, come with me." Before I could protest, she grabbed my hand with her leather-gloved one and pulled me toward the bonfire, where most of the people were clustered. "People!" she said, her voice like a bell in the night. "People, listen up!"

Everyone gradually got quiet. "Victoria," I said nervously. "What are you doing?"

She ignored me. "I want you all to listen up! Because our very fearless and very talented director is about to make a speech!"

Everyone began to cheer and clap. I held up my hands. "No, no," I said. "I'm not so great with speeches. How about Sahil instead? He's the producer, and this entire thing was his idea anyway!"

I pointed to him, where he stood a few yards away, but he laughed and held up his hand. "No way," he said. "The producer's meant to just blend into the background."

"Speech, Twinkle!" Victoria said again, and soon everyone was chanting, "Speech! Speech!" in that embarrassing way and staring at me. So I threw my hands up in the air.

"Okay, okay, settle down!" There was a titter through the crowd, but they did settle. I looked around at all their faces, glowing in the crackling firelight. Across from me, Maddie and Lewis were standing together, with Brij off to Maddie's side. Brij was watching them glumly, though she didn't know because she was watching *me*, her face serious, her eyes steady.

I took a deep breath. "You know, I've always wanted to be a filmmaker. Some of my earliest, most favorite memories are of me making videos with . . . a friend." She blinked but didn't look away. "I'd video her doing something silly like riding her bike or baking a mud pie or something, but it always felt so vital to me. Like I was recording a piece of history." I looked around at the cast. "I knew from when I was little that filmmaking was what I wanted to do when I grew up. But this was the first time I've ever had a chance to do something even vaguely on a professional level, and I wouldn't have been able to do it without all of you. So thank you. Sincerely. You've all shown up, every time, and you've all been so fun to work with." There was no need to mention all the times Lewis forgot his lines or Victoria took too long redoing her makeup or Francesca showed up fifteen minutes late because she had to stop at Starbucks to get her cappuccino. "May this movie be the ticket to your Ivy League futures. You're all A-list in my eyes."

Everyone laughed and clapped, and Sahil put an arm around me and pulled me close. "That was a nice speech," he said quietly.

I smiled, a little embarrassed, and shrugged. "It was honest. Everyone's been awesome. I feel like . . ." I looked around. "I feel like they're my friends now. Sort of. Pseudo. Maybe."

Sahil laughed. "A few qualifiers, but still. That's cool."

"Yeah." I spotted Maddie and Lewis then, walking away quickly toward a grove of trees on the far right, under which was parked Lewis's Range Rover. "Hey, I've got to go talk to Maddie before she leaves. I'll catch up with you later, okay?"

"Sure."

I hurried off, trying not to trip on the tree roots and rocks. "Maddie! Lewis! Wait up!"

I saw them glance back at me, whisper something to each other, and then stop. They had this tense look about them, like they were in a hurry and I'd caught them at a bad time. Breathing hard, I came to a stop in front of them. "Hey," I said, smiling at both of them. Lewis smiled back; Maddie didn't. "Listen. I just wanted to say . . . I'm sorry for the other day when we were shooting that scene. Lewis, I shouldn't have said all those things to you. It was absolutely uncalled for and totally uncool."

Lewis jerked his head so his blond hair flopped out of his blue eyes. "It's okay. I shouldn't have been a jerk to you either, and I should've learned my lines. You'd only told me a hundred times. So I'm sorry, too."

I smiled. "It's okay. Thanks for the apology."

I looked at Maddie, who still wasn't smiling. Her gold chandelier earrings glinted in the muted light from the bonfire. "I'm sorry to you too," I said softly.

She crossed her arms, her puffy green vest crinkling. "For?"

Lewis cleared his throat. "I'm just going to, uh . . . make a phone call." And he loped off toward his car.

I looked back at Maddie. "For the way I acted. When we were filming."

Maddie nodded. "Right. And that's it."

I shook my head slowly. "What are you talking about?"

"You've been acting like a jerk for a lot longer than just that day," she said, her eyes flashing. "Are you still going to show the footage that you took at Hannah's party?"

I straightened my shoulders. This was my whole purpose in being a filmmaker. I wanted to show the world as it was, and this was my chance. "Everyone spoke to me on their own, Maddie. I didn't trick anyone."

"Right. So yes, you *are* still going to show it."

I forced a laugh. "I don't know what you're getting so high and mighty for," I said, throwing up my hands. "Speaking of being a jerk, how about the fact that you told me I shouldn't even go to Hannah's party because I'm too much of a loser? Or the fact that you ratted me out to my parents so I'd get in trouble?"

Maddie stared at me, her eyes wide. "I said you shouldn't go to Hannah's party for your own protection! Okay? Because I didn't want you to get made fun of!"

I felt like she'd just stabbed me through the heart with her lip liner. "Oh, wow. Thanks for doing this big loser such a big favor, Maddie. Thanks a lot for looking out for me!"

"I *was* looking out for you," she said. "*That's* why I called your parents. Because I was worried about the way you were acting at the party!"

"The way *I* was acting?" I asked. "Are you freaking serious? You've totally forgotten how to be my friend, and *I'm* the one who's acting different? You're off dating Lewis Shore, who you said was too dumb to be dateable because he once said Africa was a country. Remember, Maddie? Or how about how you used to say people who got popular and forgot their friends were the worst? I'm not the one who's changed!"

Maddie opened her mouth and then shut it again. "You know what?" she said. "I'm not going to argue with someone I don't even know anymore." She stalked off.

I stood there, my heart racing, my eyes burning and hot, for a long time after Maddie and Lewis had driven off. And then I walked away, making my way down to Banner Lake. So now I'm just sitting here looking at the black water while the wind makes the tips of my ears go numb.

Why can't Maddie see I'm still me? I'm still Twinkle Mehra, the girl who wants to make movies that'll get the world talking. Everything I'm doing, I'm doing for my art. And isn't that the noblest purpose?

Mummy didn't exactly tell me, but what if the steps you're taking to make things right just make things wronger? What are you supposed to do then?

Huh. I hear footsteps. Wonder who's coming down the path.

Love,

Twinkle

Twenty

Dear Mira Nair,

It makes me laugh now that I thought my life sucked before. Haha, Universe. Joke's on me. I get it.

Where do I even begin with chronicling this train wreck? *Where*?

Oh, yes. The path and the footsteps. It turned out those belonged to none other than Sahil, who came to sit by me on the boulder. I scooted over and wrapped my arms around my waist.

"You cold?" He immediately took off his hoodie and set it around my shoulders.

I protested, but only mildly, because it smelled incredible, like lemon and stars and boy. And it was also very, very warm. I pulled the sleeves over my fingers and moved close to him, so our thighs were touching. "Thanks. You're so warm."

"Sure." Sahil put an arm around me for good measure. He

should hire himself out as a portable heater for outdoor spaces. "Things didn't go so well with Maddie?"

I glanced up at him. "You saw that?"

"A little bit of it, not much."

"Yeah. She wasn't interested in accepting my apology. I'm not who she thought I was or some such."

He pulled me closer, and I let my head fall against his chest. "That doesn't seem very fair. Especially since Maddie has changed so much over the past year."

I looked at him. "Right? That's what I said. It's not just me?"

"*Psh*, no way. I mean, even I could see it, and I rarely speak to Maddie."

"Exactly! And she was all, 'How could you do those interviews with my friends, blah, blah.'"

"Wait, the interviews at the cabin?"

I nodded. "Yeah. You know, the ones you set up?"

"Yeah . . . but we talked about it that night. I thought you decided not to use those."

"No, we're definitely using those. And we're not editing anything out either, even though I know you told Maddie we were." I scrunched up the sleeves of his hoodie in my fists.

"But . . . you wanted to apologize to everyone for the way you acted."

"I did. I do." I shook my head. "That doesn't have anything to do with the interviews, though."

When I saw his face change, I added, "Don't worry, most of them *told* me to air that at the festival. They're—they're vicious, Sahil. They're not like us."

He was still looking at me, and he pursed his lips.

"What?" I asked, getting a little annoyed at the look on his face. Why couldn't he just agree with me?

"Maybe one or two of them have had their unpleasant moments. But for the most part? They've been great at working with us. You just told me you've even begun to consider some of them your friends. I saw you and Victoria out there. I was looking around while you were making your speech. Francesca? Lewis? Taylor? Sherie? They were all so excited and happy for you. I'm pretty sure they all consider you their friend too."

"So just because they consider me their friend I shouldn't tell the truth about them? I should be hypocritical?" I asked, feeling my temper rising. "It's *because* I'm their friend that I have to do this, Sahil. They need to see themselves unmasked. And you know what? After this? I won't be invisible anymore. I won't be that disposable wallflower Twinkle Mehra. Everyone will realize I have important things to say and that they should listen to me."

"I'm not saying you don't have important things to say," Sahil said, his face serious. "And I'm not saying that they haven't done bad things. Some of them are downright jerks. But do you want to stoop to their level? Do you want to risk all the friendships you *have* made, all the minds you *have* changed? Is this the type of art you want to create? Because when we first talked, T, you were all about empowering people. About breaking glass ceilings to champion the underdogs, about speaking pure truths." He shrugged. "So maybe this isn't about revenge anymore. Maybe this *is* about speaking the truth. But still. It . . . it doesn't feel pure. It doesn't feel like *you*."

I stared at him, arguments dying in my head. Was he . . . right? Had I completely lost sight of my art, of why I was doing all of this to begin with? What would I achieve by showing people at their worst? If I wanted to empower people, to make them feel included and seen, this definitely wasn't the right way.

So maybe . . . maybe Maddie was right too. Just because those people had lost their heads at the party, just because they'd gotten mad at each other, didn't mean I should air their secrets and grudges publicly. I thought about all the fights and arguments Maddie and I have had, all the things I'd said about her to other people like Dadi and Sahil and Skid and Aaron. What if someone recorded those and then aired them at the festival for everyone else to see? For Maddie to see? How would I feel?

I put a hand to my mouth. "Oh my God," I said softly. How had I turned into such a *monster*? How had I become this person who couldn't even see what she was doing was so blatantly wrong? And after I'd apologized to Lewis and the others, too.

Sahil smiled softly down at me. "It's okay, T," he said. "We all make mistakes."

"I can't believe I . . . I couldn't even see it, though." I blew out a breath and looked at the stars glittering in the lake. "I think I was beginning to lose myself there, Sahil."

"That's okay," Sahil said gently. "Because I'll always be here to find you."

I looked back at him. At his deep, kind brown eyes. Those bushy eyebrows. That strong, stubble-dotted jaw. "Why are you so nice to me?" I asked, my heart racing. I brought one hand up to stroke his jaw, his chin, his chest and, without even thinking about it, moved even closer to him.

"Because, in case you haven't figured it out," he murmured, cupping my face with one big hand. He brought his face closer; his lips brushed mine. "I'm a total fool for you."

In the distance, I heard, "Yo, Neil! You made it!"

I jumped back. Sahil stared at me, his hand now cupping empty air instead of my face. "Are you okay?"

"Fine!" I said, smiling brightly. "I just . . . I have to go do something."

"Right . . . right now?" His eyebrows were raised all disbelievingly.

"Yes. But! We'll pick up where we left off, okay? I promise. Sahil, I'm ready now. To take things forward between us." I held his gaze.

A slow smile spread across his face. "Really?" he asked, his voice hoarse.

"Really." I took a deep breath, got up, and handed his hoodie back to him. Going up to Neil wearing his brother's hoodie just felt wrong.

It was time. It was time to end this whole N thing once and for all. I had made my decision. Part of the shiny, future Twinkle dream or not, Neil wasn't someone I wanted to be with. He was something I'd thought I desperately needed for a while. I'd needed to believe I was meant for bigger, better things, and the only way I'd known how to do that was to invent this love interest for myself who was bigger and better than me. But now I saw it: Neil *wasn't* bigger and better than me. He wasn't bigger and better than Sahil. He was just him, and we were just us. Sahil was the one for me. Sahil was the only one who made sense.

I had taken only a few steps when I heard crunching footsteps and then Brij was suddenly in front of me. I glanced at Sahil in confusion to find him watching us curiously. "Uh, hey, Brij," I said. "I'm in a little bit of a hurry now, but we'll talk later—"

"Twinkle, wait." He was looking at me weirdly, his almost-black eyes bright and intense. He licked his lips and tucked his hands into his camo jacket. "I have to tell you something." He glanced at Sahil. "Hey, Sahil."

"Hey, Nath."

Brij looked at me again. "Can we just . . . ? Do we have to talk here?"

I sighed and tried not to let my impatience show. This was either about Maddie leaving with Lewis or the film, neither of which were high on my list at the moment. "Look, Brij, whatever you want to say, you can say it in front of Sahil. Just . . . can you please make it quick? I have to go do something."

He stared at me for another long moment in silence. I waited, my eyebrows up, and then sighed as I tried to push past him. "Okay, well, if you aren't going to say anything, I'm just gonna—"

"I'm N."

I stopped breathing. To be more accurate, it felt like the entire world stopped breathing. The wind kept whistling and pushing, but the rest of it—the stars, Sahil, the lake, the earth—everything stilled. After a while, I realized I was shaking my head and forced myself to speak. My voice came out like a croak, so I cleared my throat and tried again. "Wait. What?" I stutter-laughed. "That doesn't make any sense. Your . . . Your name is *Brij*."

"You're the only one who calls me that," he said quietly, digging the toe of his shoe into the dirt.

"Right." I heard the blood whoosh through my ears. "Because everyone else calls you Nath." Nath. *N.* How had I not seen that? "And your middle name is . . ."

"Indresh."

BINadmiringyou. Brij Indresh Nath. I nodded and swallowed. "You . . . you *like* me?"

"Yes. No. I mean, I did at first." He glanced down at his shoes. "But then . . ."

"Maddie," I said. It wasn't a question. It was pretty clear to see that he liked her. That she liked him, too, even though she had temporarily lost the plot and was going after Lewis Shore for some reason.

He nodded. "I kept trying to make things work with you, *wanting* them to work because I'd already e-mailed you and you'd e-mailed back and everything. But the more I spent time with her . . ." He shrugged.

"That's why you canceled our meet-up at the Perk. And why you sounded so unenthusiastic."

"Yeah. Sorry."

I shook my head. "No, it's okay. I was . . . I was about to tell, um, *N* tonight that I wasn't interested. That's where I was going."

"Right." Brij frowned. "But you didn't know it was me. So . . . who did you think it was?"

I glanced up the path, where Neil and his swim-team buddies were hanging out, laughing.

"*Neil Roy?*" Brij's face was alit with disbelief. "You thought Neil Roy was e-mailing you?"

I glared at him, offended. "You don't have to sound so surprised. It could happen."

"Wait." Sahil was suddenly standing beside us. *Ohhhhhh crap.* I'd forgotten for a moment that he was listening to everything. *Oh, no, no, no.* "You had a secret e-mail admirer who you were e-mailing back and forth with, and you thought it was my brother?"

Brij shifted. I saw him in my peripheral vision as Sahil and I stared at each other. "Um, guys? I'm gonna . . . just . . . yeah. Okay." He hurried off.

My heart was sinking, but I rallied. This was bad, but not unsalvageable. I mean, I could just explain. He had to understand. "I did think it was Neil. But I was going to tell him tonight that—"

"You know what?" Sahil scoffed, putting his hands in his hoodie pockets. "I am *such* an idiot."

"What?" I frowned and reached for him, but he stepped back. "No, you're not. Don't say that."

"No, I am, actually." His eyes were full of a brilliant, burning hurt. "Because I thought that for once in my life someone important to me was appreciating me for who I was. I thought you were falling for *me*, that you saw me just for me, outside of my brother."

"I did," I said, my heart breaking at the pain in his voice, on his face.

"No, you didn't! The entire time, you were comparing me to Neil. The entire time I was falling for you, Twinkle, you were falling for who you thought was my brother. You were weighing your options. That's why you wouldn't fully commit to me. You wanted to see if my brother would be better boyfriend material. That's what it was all about. But don't you know by now? In the comparison between Neil and Sahil Roy, Neil Roy will always come out on top. He's smarter, more athletically gifted, Harvard bound. He's the golden boy. I could've saved you a lot of time if you'd just asked me." He laughed mirthlessly and kicked a rock.

"Stop," I said, tears filling my eyes. "That's not what I was doing at all; I wasn't weighing you against him! Sahil, I was falling for you, too. That's the realization I was coming to this whole time. That I liked *you*. I had this idealized, fantasy version of Neil in my head. But my fantasy wasn't about Neil at all. Okay? It was about *me*, my need to be more than just some wallflower!"

"But Neil was the one you wanted. I'm not even surprised." He looked away, out at the lake.

I grabbed his upper arm and he looked back at me. "So what? So what that I thought I wanted Neil? I've fallen for *you*, Sahil. That's what I was going to do tonight—to tell Neil I didn't have feelings for him. Because *you're* the one I want."

Shaking his head, he pulled his arm from my hand. "It's too late, Twinkle," he said, thrusting a shaky hand through his hair. "We can't be together now without me *constantly* wondering if I'm just some—some sloppy seconds. Your e-mail admirer wasn't my brother. Your feelings for him are still unrequited.

That will always, *always* be between us, like a shadow of him there. You never just CHOSE ME!"

"I'm choosing you now! And my feelings *aren't* unrequited." I tried not to yell, but I was getting desperate. This couldn't be it. It just couldn't. Sahil *had* to understand. "My feelings were never for him, Sahil. They were *always* for you."

Sahil shoved his hands in the pockets of his hoodie and began to walk backward, away from me. "Well, I wish you would've realized that sooner."

"Wait, Sahil—"

He turned and was gone.

Victoria tried to rope me into staying late, but I literally felt like my entire body was numb. I could barely talk. So she gave me a ride home instead. She asked me a few times what was wrong, but when I just kept shaking my head, she left me alone and told me to call her if I wanted to talk to her later.

I don't want to talk later. I don't want to talk to anyone. I'm a horrible person. I deserve to live out the rest of my days under-ground, like the naked mole rat that's absolutely revolting to look at and lives forever in darkness and isolation.

—Twinkle

From: twinkiefilmfan@urmail.com
To: skidtheman@urmail.com
Subject: Behind-the-scenes footage
Skid,
I'm sorry to change this so late in the game. But I think I

want to go in a different direction for the end footage than
what I was originally thinking. Can you just do the best you
can with this (attached)?

—Twinkle

From: skidtheman@urmail.com
To: twinkiefilmfan@urmail.com
Subject: Re: Behind-the-scenes footage
You sure? This is . . . pretty different.

From: twinkiefilmfan@urmail.com
To: skidtheman@urmail.com
Subject: Re: Behind-the-scenes footage
I'm sure. Just do your best, okay? Thanks, Skid.

Twenty-One

Friday, June 26
1 day until Midsummer Night
Backyard

Dear Jane Campion,

Today I was moping around after school. Mummy was substitute teaching again (sometimes she likes to stay late to help grade tests) and Papa was at the youth home, where he'd be all weekend. I'd hidden in the library at lunch again and had pretty much avoided or been avoided by all the people I didn't want to see. Once I caught sight of Sahil coming down the hallway and leaped into the janitor's closet. Does that surprise you? I think it's pretty clear by now that I don't always make the best choices.

Anyway, I was sitting on the couch, watching some show about a police dog who was getting a medal for bravery (why does everyone else's life have to be so full of colorful, interesting things?) when Dadi came to sit beside me. She just sat there and watched with me for a while, but I could tell from the way she kept shifting around and drumming her fingers on her sari-clad thigh that she was bubbling with something. There should've been steam coming out of her ears and nose like a pressure cooker.

Finally, during a commercial break, I muted the TV. "*Kya hua,* Dadi? I can tell you want to ask me something."

"*Beta,*" she said. "I require your assistance in a most urgent task."

Uh-oh. Dadi only talked like that, all formal and stuff, when she was cooking up some cockamamie plan that would usually end up with something valuable broken. (Once it was her little toe.)

"Uh-huh," I said, waiting.

"Twinkle, Chandrashekhar has informed me that all is not well within your soul."

I glanced at Oso, who side-eyed me suspiciously from his dog bed and then put his head back down with a snuffle.

"He did?"

"Yes. And I feel that in order for you to feel more peaceful, we must look into your future."

I studied Dadi's clear, eager eyes. "My future?"

"Yes. Perhaps if we find some answers, you'll be able to rest more easily, hmm?"

"I guess. I mean, I do have Midsummer Night tomorrow, and . . ." I stopped before I could tell her the entire saga with Maddie and Sahil and everything. A girl needed to preserve some mystery, even from her omniscient Dadi.

"Exactly." Dadi beamed, patted my thigh, and then stood. "Come on," she said, bustling off.

With a sigh, I stood and followed her to her room.

Dadi's laundry closet/room was just big enough for a cot and a table. On that table, I saw, was a gigantic wooden bowl full of water.

"Help me, *beta*," she said, and then proceeded to lift the wooden bowl. It looked heavier than Dadi; I didn't see this ending well. Between the two of us, we managed to lift the thing up and then Dadi began to guide me out into the hallway again.

"Where are we going?" I grunted, walking backward. My arm muscles were already aching with the effort of carrying the bowl and we'd gone maybe four steps. I should start doing push-ups in my room after school or something.

Dadi smiled. She looked like she was carrying a ball of cotton candy the way she was beaming. "Just to the kitchen table."

Great. I tried to keep my face neutral as I walked down the hallway through the living room and to the kitchen, all backward. It was the first time I was happy we had such a tiny house.

I helped Dadi set the bowl on the table, and then we both sat in chairs across from each other. Oso took his spot by Dadi's feet. I looked at her over the top of the bowl, massaging my biceps. "So, now what?"

Dadi reached for a small white candle and a box of matches, which she'd already set on the table. "Now we scry." She held them out to me.

"Light it?" I asked, curious in spite of myself. Whatever you thought of Dadi's "experiments," they were never boring.

She nodded. I lit the match and it sizzled to life, the burnt sulfur smell singeing my nostrils. I lit the candle next; the flame danced in Dadi's brown eyes. A twinging excitement worked its way into my belly. There was so much in my life I wanted to know the endings to right now.

"Now turn the candle sideways so the wick is directly above the water, *beta*. Then let the drops of wax fall into the water until you feel like stopping."

"Okay." Biting my lip, I pivoted the candle gingerly on its side and watched as one drop of wax after another plopped onto the surface. The wax hardened immediately, floating on the surface. I kept going until a big wax piece had coalesced in the center of the bowl. I blew out the candle and looked at Dadi.

She nodded, her face solemn. "Now, pick up that big chunk and look at it. Tell me what you see."

I did as she asked, the cold water dripping off the tips of my fingers and running down my wrist. The wax was thin and cold, and I flipped it over and over in my hand, thinking. "It looks like an archipelago: lots of islands clustered together, almost holding hands." I tilted my head and squinted. "And there's a heart shape here in the center, but it's got little fissures in it." Looking back up at Dadi, I smiled, feeling a tad embarrassed. "How'd I do?"

Her answering smile was soft and loving. "Beautifully, *munni*. Just beautifully."

I set the wax piece down carefully on the table and wiped my hands on my jeans. "So . . . what does it mean that I saw those things?" My heart pounded; I was more nervous than I had thought I'd be. I didn't really believe that Dadi could see the future . . . but I didn't really *not* believe it either.

Dadi put a finger to her chin. "Hmm . . . The archipelago makes me think of travel. Perhaps you'll be seeing the world soon. And the heart with little cracks in it . . . Perhaps you feel you're giving away pieces of your heart?"

"But if this is telling the future, does it mean that I'm going to have my heart broken?" My mouth went a little dry at the thought. I mean, my heart was already pretty much in smithereens. How much worse could it get? Actually, Universe, forget I asked that question. Okay? I do *not* want to know.

"Only time will tell," Dadi said, looking steadily at me. "We must embrace the good with the bad."

So there you have it: I'll travel and have my already-broken heart pulverized, maybe. Or maybe this is all just crap. Who can say?

Oh God. Why did I even agree to do the stupid film in the first place? I am so not in a film-festival mood right now. I just want to burrow under the covers on my bed and stay there until the new millennium. Is that too much to ask?

Love,

Twinkle

Friday, June 26
Vic's car

Dear Haifaa al-Mansour,

The burrowing plan didn't last too long. I was ensconced in my covers and had just unwrapped the first Peanut Butter Cup I'd pilfered from the kitchen when I heard the doorbell ring. I poked my head out from under the covers, my heart thundering. Was it

Sahil? Maddie? But then Dadi walked in and told me it was "that girl who looks like her head's on fire."

Victoria Lyons.

I scrambled out of bed, wiped the chocolate off my hands, finger-combed my hair (I mean, I *am* still her director, come on), and walked out. Sure enough, Victoria stood there, all statuesque and tall, her big red hair looking especially shiny. She noticed me staring. "You like?" she asked, patting the crown of her head. "I asked my stylist to use this new snail slime treatment I read about in *Vogue*. They only use it in Japan right now, but . . ."

"Snail . . . slime?"

"Yeah." Her green eyes were humorless. "It's great for your hair. And supposedly it's good for your pores, too."

"Right." I folded my arms across my chest. I didn't need snail slime in my hair; I already had it smeared across my life. "So. What's, um, up?"

She shrugged and walked over to my couch, where she sat down in a flounce of her retro circle skirt, putting her wedge-clad feet on my coffee table. "I was worried about you. You left the party all weird yesterday, and I saw you moping around at school today looking pathetic. What's going on? Does this have to do with the mysterious boy you were getting all vamped up to see that one night?"

I saw Dadi straighten at her cutting board in the kitchen. She was stress cooking because she knew I was upset and wouldn't talk to her about it. "Um, do you want to go to my room?" I asked Victoria, nodding my head at Dadi's back.

"Oh, sure." She stood up and walked off, like she owned the place.

Sighing, I followed her.

Once we were safely ensconced in my room (Victoria sat on my wobbly computer chair and squealed, "I love how authentically rickety things are in your house!" which I'm pretty sure she meant as a compliment?), I grabbed a pillow to my chest. "Thanks for coming over to check on me. That's so nice of you."

"Duh," Victoria said, picking up my change jar and looking at it interestedly. She probably had never seen pennies before, having dealt only in Benjamins. "It's what friends do. So, tell me what happened at the party last night."

I blew out a breath. "Ugh. Where do I even start? Okay, so Maddie and I had a fight. I mean, I tried to apologize to her for blowing up at your house that one night. When I yelled at Lewis and everyone?"

Victoria nodded. I'd already apologized to her in her car yesterday.

"So, she just refused to accept my apology. Which, okay, after I talked to Sahil, I kinda get why she was mad." Glancing at Vic, I shook my head. "I was making some bad choices, and Maddie was right to call me out on it. But at the same time, she isn't blame-free. She's been pulling away from me and blowing me off for Hannah and her other friends for a long time. She's changed so much about herself, but somehow it's all my fault for how *I've* changed? I told you, right, how she didn't even want me to come to Hannah's party?" It stung to talk about it, and I rubbed my chin and looked away, at my twinkle-light photo wall. I'd put up more pictures of me and Sahil, Skid, Aaron, and the others who were in the film. Maddie's and my pictures were off to the sides now, no longer the main focus of my life.

Victoria leaned back in my squeaky chair and picked up one of my pens. Tapping it against the palm of her other hand, she said, "Hmm. Okay, so first, Maddie pulling away from you? Totally sucks. She didn't handle that well at all. I even told her a couple of times that she should invite you to my place to hang out. But then Hannah would just say, 'Twinkle's just going to be out of place here. She doesn't know all the people we know, so it's better for her if we just leave her out.'"

"Great."

"And Maddie went along with it. But here's the thing—I don't think Maddie wanted to leave you out. It was more like . . . she didn't know how to integrate you into her new life. Especially with the loudest, most convincing one among us—Hannah—telling her it was for your own good."

"So it's not Maddie's fault at all? It's all Hannah's fault?" I shook my head. "I can't accept that."

"No, that's not what I'm saying." Victoria frowned. "Like I said, Maddie didn't handle it well. I'm just trying to help you understand from my perspective what went down. Anyway, I don't even think it's Hannah's fault, exactly. I mean, sure, she's constantly worked to keep you excluded, saying someone like you would just feel uncomfortable with people like us."

"Stop trying to cheer me up," I mumbled.

"But," Victoria said, holding up one pointy finger, "I think that has to do more with Hannah's insecurities than about you. She's . . . super jealous."

I jerked my head up. "Wait, what? You think she's jealous . . . of *me*? Are you drunk?"

Vic threw her arms up and grinned. "On youth and beauty!" Then, seeing my raised eyebrow, she lowered her arms and got serious. "Look, Hannah's BFF is Maddie, okay? But Maddie's BFF, no question, has always been you. Even when she hangs out with us, she used to bring you up in every other conversation. 'Oh, Twinkle had me watch that movie once. I didn't get it, but she was talking about the symbolism and structure. She's such a genius.' 'This one time, Twinkle and I made these peanut butter brownies, but we ended up almost burning down the kitchen and then her *dadi* tried to do a spell or something to get rid of the bad juju we'd invited into the house. Her parents were soooo mad. It was hilarious! I've never laughed so hard in my life!'" Victoria looked at me. "And you're always so sharp in AP English with all your comments and questions, and Maddie just about burst with pride when you won that essay competition. You see what I'm saying?"

I bit my lip, still not convinced. "I think so. . . ."

"Hannah just can't compete. So she reacts the only way she knows how: by trying to keep the two of you apart. Han's never been super good at managing her negative emotions. She's so used to everyone loving her best. It's not easy for her. I tried to suggest including you more, so she could get to know you too, but she was not on board for that. It's scary for her." Victoria shrugged. "I mean, it's not an excuse and she's spoiled, no question. But maybe it'll help for you to see *why* she's like that."

I couldn't believe it. Hannah, with her cool palindrome of

a name and her shiny, purple VW Bug, was jealous of *me*? Of how much Maddie loved *me*? The entire time I thought I was an invisible wallflower, I was intimidating to *Hannah Macintosh*? It made me feel bad for her. Maddie's such a cool person. I know how much it sucks to lose her as a friend. But what if I'd never had the opportunity to be her best friend at all? What if I'd always known that there was someone else she liked more? What if I had to be relegated to second place all the time? That would suck even worse.

"Wow," I breathed after a moment.

"Yeah. Case in point . . ." Vic pulled something out of the pocket of her skirt and held it out, her fist closed around it.

"What is it?" I asked, automatically extending my hand, palm open, so she could drop it in.

"Maddie wanted you to have that."

I looked at the shiny metal in my palm. It was a silver charm bracelet with two charms on it. One was a video camera, and the other was half a broken heart with the words "Twinkle Mehra, Director" engraved on it. I looked up at Vic, blinking.

"She's got the other half of that heart charm," she said. "Hers says 'Lead Actress, Maddie Tanaka' on it. She told me she ordered it when you first cast her; it just came in."

I was one of her charm bracelet buddies now. Was that Maddie's way of telling me I was just as important to her as the rest of them? I closed my fist around the bracelet. "She gave it to you, not me," I said, my voice thick.

"Yeah." Victoria sighed. "She wanted you to have it, but . . ."

"But she didn't want to see me or talk to me." I swallowed the lump in my throat, not surprised that Maddie still had so much power over me.

"She's pretty mad," Vic explained.

We sat in silence. There wasn't much to say about that.

After a few moments, Vic said, "It's Sahil, right?"

Startled, I looked at her. "What?"

"You know." She waved my pen around in the air. "The one you're pining after. The one you dressed up for that one night. The one you're so completely in love with."

I shrugged.

"Mm-hmm." She tossed my pen back on my desk and hopped up. "Come on."

I frowned. "Where are we going?"

"Perk—we need some caffeine and sugar. I can't have you Eeyoring it up tomorrow at Midsummer Night, Miss Director. So we're going to flush this whatever-it-is out of your system. Let's go."

What choice did I have? Vic's like a gale-force wind, sweeping people up in her wake like helpless little leaves. Setting the charm bracelet down on my desk, I followed her, and now we're hurtling toward Perk. More soon; she's trying to peek into this diary while also incessantly asking me questions.

Love,

Twinkle

Twenty-Two

Friday, June 26

Perk

Dear Sofia Coppola,

Maybe I'm stuck in one of those repeating wormholes or something (is that a thing? Neil, the future astrophysicist, would know) where time loops infinitely and I'm forced to just repeat a sucky time in my life forever. Like that old movie? What's it called? *Warthog Day* or something?

So I'm standing in line at Perk, about to order a caramel frap for myself and a skinny soy latte for Vic (she was in the bathroom) when the door *ding*s and someone comes in. I look up to see Sahil, who sees me at the same time. And we both just sort of . . . stop. It was like the entire buzzy, loud chatter of the other people in there went silent. I stared at him; he stared at me.

Finally, his paralysis broke and he forced himself to trudge toward me. It killed me a little to see that, the forcing and the trudging, both. It was like he couldn't even stand to wait in line with me anymore.

"Hey," I said, smiling a little.

He just nodded, his hands deep in his jeans pockets. He barely looked at me. His hair was adorably mussed, his vintage *Poltergeist* T-shirt hugging his frame nicely. I missed him so much. I just wanted to throw my arms around his neck, snuggle into his chest, and smell him. But I didn't. I forced myself to keep my distance.

"Can I help you?" Stan and his apathetic skinny mustache were waiting for me.

"Um, a caramel frap, a fat-free soy latte, and . . ." I turned to Sahil. "What can I get you?"

His brown eyes widened. "Oh, uh, nothing. You don't have to do that."

I just kept looking at him. At his complete lack of desire to cross paths with me in any shape or form. I fought against the painful tightening in my throat. "I know I don't have to, Sahil," I said quietly. "But I want to. Please let me?"

He opened his mouth to argue, then studied my expression and closed it again. "Okay. I'll have an iced mocha." He cleared his throat. "Thanks."

I nodded and spoke to Stan to finish the order. We stood off to the side while he made them, and I looked up at Sahil, who was staring at some poster on the wall. "So," I said, and he turned somewhat reluctantly to look at me. I forced a smile. "Are you ready? For Midsummer Night, I mean."

"I am," he said. "But as the producer, I don't have to do anything. You're the one who gets all the glory."

I took a deep breath. "Or all the flak."

Victoria came out of the bathroom, headed toward me, and then, seeing who I was talking to, made an abrupt right turn and went off to find us a table.

"Are you nervous?" Sahil asked, his face showing genuine concern.

My heart melted a little. Maybe he still cared? Way, way deep down somewhere? Maybe he knew in some small part of him that I wasn't the crappy, horrible, mean girl he thought I was, the one who weighed him against his brother like everyone else. "Not exactly, funnily enough," I said, looking right into those soft brown eyes. "I think I'm just going to be honest and hope people see where I'm coming from. Who I really am."

After a long pause, he nodded and looked away, like he knew I wasn't just talking about the movie.

"Sahil—" I began, just as Stan called our names.

"Twinkle. Nothing's changed. I don't know if you fully appreciate how much it hurts, just seeing you here. Talking to you. So . . . please. If you care about me at all, just . . ." He swallowed, and a muscle in his jaw twitched as he looked at some spot above my head. Then, meeting my eye again, he said, "Please just give me some space to get over this. Okay?"

"Okay." I mouthed the word; my voice had disappeared.

With one long look at me, Sahil grabbed his drink and headed out the door.

Victoria was staring at me as I sat down with our drinks. "That looked . . . brutal."

I slid her latte over. "Yeah. It was even worse up close."

She made a face and patted my hand. "That sucks. Want to talk about it?"

I looked at her pretty face, her perfect makeup, her gorgeous hair. She could've been any number of glamorous places—it was Friday night—but she had chosen to come to my authentically rickety house instead. I took a sip of my frap and nodded. "Settle in," I said. "Because it's kind of a long story."

Starting with our meeting here in Perk under Stan's mustache, I filled her in on my future Twinkle fantasy and my secret admirer and how I'd fallen for Sahil. Our first kiss at the cabin, hanging out at the Ferris wheel at the carnival. How Brij had confessed to being N at Banner Lake and how Sahil had heard everything. How heartbroken he was now, how he couldn't even bear to look at me anymore. "I totally blew it," I said, shaking my head. "I had everything, you know? I'm such a fool."

"Mm," Victoria said. "And a bit of a tool."

I raised an eyebrow. "Gee, thanks." In spite of Vic's brutal honesty, it felt great to finally unburden all of this on someone. Part of me was sad it wasn't Maddie—I'd always told her everything—but another part of me was so grateful for this new friendship.

"I'm just saying! You should've been honest with Sahil about the secret admirer thing."

"I can see that now. But also . . . if I had, would he even have given me the time of day? I mean, look at how he's completely disengaged now. Just mentioning his brother was an anti-Sahil talisman."

Vic took another sip of her latte and tapped her long fingers on the table. "Yeah. It's always been like that with them, for as long as I can remember."

"That doesn't surprise me. I just hate that I hurt him because Sahil's a good person. Genuine and nice. But he's always behind the scenes. It's hard to notice him when Neil's sort of like this brilliant sun or something, and Sahil's just gentle and less in your face. Like the moon, I guess."

"The sun and the moon. Huh. That's a pretty good analogy for them, actually." She drank the rest of her latte.

"Yeah. It sucks, but I figured it out too late. I think I'm more of a moonlight kind of girl." I bit my lip and looked away, trying not to cry.

Victoria squeezed my hand and stood. "I'm sorry, Twinkle. I can't give you Sahil, but I can give you more sugar. I'm gonna get us another round."

Now I'm just sitting here at our table alone, beginning to realize just how deeply I cut Sahil. How do you come to terms with the fact that you can't set something right? How do you begin to let go of the moon?

Love,
Twinkle

Saturday, June 27
0 days until Midsummer Night
Backyard

Dear Ava DuVernay,

This is the day. In roughly eight hours, I will be sitting in an auditorium full of people who will be watching a movie I made.

You know that shirt you have that says, "I am my ancestor's wildest dream"? *That's* what I'm trying to do here; I'm changing the narrative. I so badly want to earn the right to wear that T-shirt one day.

Oh, God. I don't think I'm equipped to deal with this. I don't know whether to be terrified or exhilarated or excited or bawl like a baby. I went downstairs at the crack of dawn this morning and saw Dadi in the kitchen, stress cooking and baking.

"*Beta!*" she said when she saw me. She was wearing this ridiculous apron with squirrels all over it, and Oso sat at her feet, waiting for scraps. "I am making *kaju pista* biscuits. And *idli* and chutney is ready for you. Oh, and next on the list is *gajar ka halwa.*"

My nervy stomach churned at the mention of all the food and desserts. But I knew if I didn't eat anything, Dadi would take it as a personal insult. "*Idli* sounds delicious," I lied, going to get a plate. "Dadi, how long have you been awake?"

"Only since three a.m.," she said. "There is no better utilization of nervous energy than into ingredients that can make the stomach happy. Isn't that right, Chandrashekhar?" she said to Oso, and dropped a piece of *idli* for him to eat. He struck like a cobra; the food was gone before it even touched the floor.

"*Three a.m.?*" I sat down with my food and milk. "And I thought I was anxious."

Dadi smiled at me as she grated carrots with lightning speed. "There is no reason to be anxious, *beta*," she said. "Your movies are of Oscar quality!"

I groaned. "Dadi, I don't think you're the most reliable judge of that," I said. "But I appreciate it." Swallowing my mouthful of *idli,* I asked, "So . . . are you coming tonight?"

"Of course I am!" Dadi said, looking mortally offended. "I have already reserved my taxi!" Then, seeing my face, she said, "Oh. But you're not really asking about me, are you, *munni*?"

Dang. Sometimes I wish Dadi didn't know me *quite* so well.

She came to sit across from me at the kitchen table and put her hand on mine. "You're asking about Mummy."

I shrugged. "I mean, it's Saturday, so I know Papa's going to be at work. But . . ." I didn't have to complete the rest. Mummy always dutifully showed up at any school-sanctioned, required events like plays or choir recitals. But when it came to my film-making, something that made up three-quarters of my soul, she wasn't there. It was like she had this quota to fill in order to not be a crappy mother, and my filmmaking was above and beyond the call of duty.

Dadi didn't try to lie and tell me of course Mummy would be there, of course she wouldn't want to miss this momentous event in her only daughter's life. Which both made me feel bet-ter and worse. "It will be what it will be," she said instead, smil-ing sadly. "Sometimes one must be strong enough for two."

I nodded and pushed my plate away with my free hand. I knew I had to be strong for Mummy. She'd been through a lot in her life, things I could never even imagine going through. But sometimes? I just get tired of being strong.

"But I have a feeling this moroseness is not only about Mummy, hmm?" Dadi said, stroking my hand. Her brown eyes looked right into me, like she was taking an X-ray of my thoughts. Am I that easy to read? "I have noticed that Sahil and Maddie haven't been calling here."

I looked away and swallowed the lump in my throat. "The movie's over, so . . . there's no reason for us to talk anymore."

When Dadi didn't say anything, I looked back at her to see her gazing sadly at me. Then she suddenly patted my hand, stood up, and went back to the kitchen.

"Okay, good talk," I mumbled, feeling even more pathetic than ever. Even Dadi didn't want to hear about my love/ friendship life.

Dadi chuckled. "Just a minute, *beta*," she said. "I am getting something. . . . Just one minute. . . ." I heard her clattering around the kitchen, but I just stared straight ahead, feeling extra morose. Morose. I like that word. Maybe it'll be my new band name, if I ever pick up a musical instrument or suddenly learn how to sing, like that super-average American guy who hit his head and woke up speaking in the most perfectly posh English accent.

Dadi was at the table a minute or two later, holding a silver container with an ornate lid. She kept running her hands over the domed top, and finally I glanced at her.

"What is that?" I asked, recognizing that my voice sounded muffled and bland. I was slumped over the table, like a gloomy carcass.

"Oh, this?" Dadi looked at me in surprise, as if she had forgotten I was there, and opened the lid. The inside of the container held two small bowls, each full of a powder. One was a deep, vivid red and the other a brilliant orangey-yellow. "This is *sambandh* powder."

I frowned and sat up, curious in spite of myself. "*Sambandh*? Meaning . . . relationship? What do the powders have to do with relationships?"

"We humans think we exist like this." Dadi gestured to the powders in their individual bowls. "Apart. Single. Beautiful and vivid, but alone." She looked calculatingly at me. "But on the other side, on Dada's side, he can see that we are like this in reality." She upended the two bowls into the center of the larger container, and the powders came together. They were mixed somewhat, but still in their separate piles for the most part— red on the left and orange on the right. "Then," Dadi continued, "with each interaction with another soul, we begin to change." She put a finger into the pile of powders and began to stir gently. The powders mixed more the longer she stirred, red mingling with orange, losing its distinct form. "We take pieces of them, and they take pieces of us. It's not bad. It's not good. It just is." By now the powders were completely mixed together, indistinguishable from each other. "Our best friends, the ones we love the most, are the ones who can hurt us the most. Because look." She pointed down to the powders. "We have had so many interactions with them, deep, meaningful interactions, that we cannot separate their pieces from ours. And if we try, we would only be getting rid of some of the best parts of ourselves." She brushed off her fingers and put one hand under my chin. Her soft brown eyes bored into mine. The X-ray again.

"This is how it was with you and Maddie . . . and Sahil?"

I nodded. "Yeah. You could say that." She'd put it so well. We were exactly like the powders. My connections with Maddie and

Sahil were so different, but equally strong. They'd totally mixed up their powders into mine. And what was I supposed to do now that they'd decided I wasn't worth their time anymore? "Ugh, Dadi, why'd you have to put it like that? You just made me even more depressed."

She laughed and came around the table to hug me. "Oh, *beta*," she said. "Don't you see? Each powder has been mixed. So they feel the same way that you do. They feel the same pain."

I looked at her, my chest squeezing with hope. Could it be? Are Sahil and Maddie just as miserable without me as I am without them?

But now that I'm out here in the backyard by myself, I don't think so. Those powders wouldn't be so mixed up if they had other powder friends to mix with.

Okay, that is easily the weirdest sentence I have ever written.

Can't I escape visions of my loss and utter failure *anywhere*, at least in my own freaking backyard? Maggie and Oso are having an epic love meeting at the fence right in front of me. I wish my love life was at least better than, you know, my dog's.

Sigh.

I miss him. I miss him so much. It's sort of like this numb, weird feeling under my skin all the time.

Love,

Twinkle

Twenty-Three

Saturday, June 27

PPC Auditorium

Dear Mira Nair,

I am writing this as a newly minted director who's shown her work to an audience of . . . I don't know, a thousand people? Pretty much every single PPC student was there, plus their parents. The auditorium was *full*.

But wait, let me back up. Because this evening wasn't all roses and clapping and happy singing.

So I took the public bus to school because, of course, Papa was at work with our car. Mummy was ensconced in her bedroom, sleeping off a headache according to Dadi, but Dadi gave me multiple kisses and even a bracelet she'd woven from an old sari that she said "Chandrashekhar has put his blessings on." I don't think I need to know the details. I rubbed my finger over it the entire bus ride, my stomach bubbling over with nerves. I thought I'd get car sick (bus sick?) for the first time in my life.

I got off the bus and walked the half mile to school, and right when I was about to climb up the steps of the auditorium, Sahil was coming down. We stared at each other. I smiled a little and then tried to walk past because I was trying to respect his space and everything, when he put a hand on my arm. It was like grabbing an exposed wire with your wet hand (which, if it wasn't clear, is a super-bad idea and you should *never* do) but less lethal. I tried not to gasp audibly.

"Hey," he said, his eyes gentle as always. He was dressed in a green and blue striped button-down shirt with the sleeves rolled up, and black jeans. His hair was spiked and he was clean-shaven. It was a punch to the gut, a forcible reminder of all those times he'd taken me in his arms, all the times we'd kissed, all the sweet words he'd whispered that were now scattered to the winds. "You ready for this?"

Taking a deep breath, I patted my lucky film-reel hair sticks. The charm bracelet Maddie had given me clinked on my wrist. I was also wearing my lucky film-reel toe socks, but he didn't need to know that. "I think so. I mean, can you ever be ready for your first-ever film screening?"

He smiled, but there was a distance that had never been there before. "I guess not. I heard it's going to be a full house tonight too." He must've seen the utter panic on my face, because he added quickly, "It's going to be great. You're a gifted director, and we've worked hard on the movie. People are gonna love it."

I realized how . . . professionally aloof his words were. He was purposely holding me at arm's length, afraid to let me get too close. "Thanks, Sahil," I said, wondering if he could hear the tears threatening, the pain and regret behind every syllable.

I wanted to say all the things I was holding back. I wanted to play our road trip game again.

Did you hear I've tossed and turned without you since you walked away from me?

Did you hear I'm wondering if you'll ever stop hating me?

Did you hear I don't care about your brother beyond the fact that he's your brother?

Did you hear I'm falling in love with you?

But I didn't say any of the above.

"Well . . . ," Sahil said, rubbing a hand along his jaw. "I should, um . . . go get the props from the SUV. Skid and Aaron are waiting for me in the parking lot."

"Okay." I watched him walk away. I waited for him to look at me at some point before he disappeared. But he never did.

Our movie was scheduled to play last. I sat backstage through all the acts before ours—including the pineapple chopping by CC and his friends which, miraculously, didn't end with anyone having to go to urgent care—with a pounding heart and a completely dry mouth.

When it was time for the festival to begin and I'd given the tech person the thumb drive with our movie and the bonus footage on it, I walked back out to the audience. All the *Dracula* actors and stagehands were sitting together, toward the front. Someone had saved me a seat in the middle, with a sign on the back that said DRACULA DIRECTOR—RESERVED. I grinned as I sat, with Sahil on one side of me and Maddie on the other. They both sat stiffly, making sure not to get in my personal space at all, but I was too distracted to be distraught.

I'd already seen the movie, naturally, so while it played, I kept my eye on the audience. I think it's an epic compliment that the entire auditorium of about one thousand people was *completely* silent while the movie played. The actors and actresses beside me were all wide-eyed. I realized that for most of them, this was the first time they were experiencing the absolute magic of seeing themselves transformed by a story. Maddie kept beaming at various scenes, her eyes shining in the darkness, like she was so utterly proud. I was incredibly happy for her in those moments, I can't even tell you.

And then . . . then the behind-the-scenes footage began to play. As the last scene faded and the segue music played, my heart started to thunder. Skid and I looked at each other, and he gave me a tiny thumbs-up. I felt Maddie stiffen beside me. The other actors and actresses all shifted around and looked uncomfortable, probably remembering all the awful things they'd said and wondering how I'd portray them and their secrets on-screen.

The first candid scene began.

It was a shot of Sherie Williams at the Aspen cabin, talking about how she'd been failing a bunch of classes. The cheer coach had told her she couldn't be on the team anymore unless she brought her GPA up, so all the other cheerleaders had taken turns tutoring her after school every day in the classes they were best at. Sherie had managed to bring her GPA up to a 3.0 and stayed on the team.

The scene faded into a shot of Francesca Roberts talking about how her friends, all of whom she'd known since kindergarten, had "kidnapped" her from school on her sixteenth birthday and taken her to Six Flags, her favorite place in the world.

Vic, Lewis, and Taylor were next. I watched people leaning forward, to take in each story, their faces shining, laughing with the people on-screen. I watched people looking at one another, their eyes busy with memories, *connecting* because of my movie. I saw parents put their arms around their children, best friends hug.

And it hit me fully: I wanted to make movies that would bring people together, not ones that would tear them apart. And if that meant I had to be penniless and unsung all my life, then that was okay with me. Some things were more important than fame and money.

As the footage wound to a close, Sahil took my hand. Just for a second. I was so shocked, I didn't even close my fingers around his before the audience broke out into thunderous applause, many of them even giving us a *standing ovation*, and by then Sahil had already pulled away. I stood too, and clapped for everyone around me, all the actors, actresses, the stagehands, the technicians, my producer. Sahil, Maddie, and I were grinning and cheering and happy. Just for that second.

Afterward, I hugged Skid, who was standing there with Portia, who was absolutely as stunning as he'd said she was. "Thank you," I said to him, squeezing his arm. "You did a fantastic job with the footage. I know I didn't give you much time."

"Ah, you made it easy," he said, waving a hand. "Your shots were all clean."

I looked at Portia and shook my head. "He's being overly humble right now. He's basically a genius."

"Oh, I know." She smiled down at Skid (she had about six inches of height on him) in this adoring way. I knew then he was definitely going to have a serious girlfriend by the end of the summer. They waved to me and strolled off together. I sniffed. Wow. Skid hadn't skimped on deodorant tonight.

Sahil came up to me. "Hey," he said. "That was"—his eyes searched mine—"incredible."

I smiled. "Thanks. I couldn't have done it without you."

There was a pause that stretched on as we stared at each other. "So," I began.

"I have to go," he said, scratching his jaw. "I came over to tell you there are a cluster of reporters and radio hosts from various places over there." He waved to the back of the auditorium, where a group of people stood. "They want to talk to you."

I stared at him, my mouth open. "Are you serious? The media people want to talk to *me*?"

He nodded, a small half smile playing at his lips. "You're a star." He leaned down and gave me a hug, and my eyes slipped shut as I felt his hard planes against my soft curves. "Good-bye, Twinkle," he whispered, and then he walked away. My heart broke at the finality of his tone. He wasn't just saying good-bye for tonight. He was saying good-bye forever.

Somehow, despite feeling like the moon had just crashed into the ocean and been swallowed, I managed to give the reporters what they wanted. They were all smiling and nodding; that's how I know. When they left, Dadi came up to me. She hugged me and told me she was proud of me and that she loved my movie, like, a zillion times. And when she moved aside, I saw Mummy behind her, staring at me like she couldn't believe it: *Dracula*, this creation, had come out of *her* creation.

I sat back after a while and just watched people. Neil, with some blond girl who didn't go to our school, their arms around each other's waists. I felt absolutely nothing. Matthew and Aaron, holding hands and walking out into the night. Lewis Shore and his dad talking to Maddie. Then she walked up to Brij and *they* began to talk, their heads close together. Victoria flirting with some big muscular dude wearing a Yankees jersey, who looked to be Francesca's cousin.

I was happy for everyone. But all the celebrating felt like a distant world I couldn't fully be a part of because of the gaping hole where my heart used to be. Dadi was right. It had gone from broken to pulverized.

Slowly, the auditorium began to empty out. And now I'm just sitting here, among all the empty chairs. I have no best friend and the guy I love doesn't love me back anymore. The minute I leave, real life will begin again. All the magic will be over. So maybe I'll just sit here writing in this journal until someone forces me out.

Which might be now, actually. I hear footsteps walking up behind me. Probably that spiteful-looking security guard with the patchy goatee I saw before. Sigh.

Love,
Twinkle

Saturday, June 27
Maddie's car

Dear Sofia Coppola,

It wasn't the security guard. It was Maddie. And Hannah.

Maddie came and sat by me, sweeping her fuchsia maxi dress under her. Reaching into her bag, she pulled out two Twizzlers and handed me one. "Here."

"Oh. Thanks." I took it and looked from her to Hannah, who was fabulous as usual in a bright yellow dress and a turquoise bib necklace. I sat silently, waiting for someone to explain what was going on. Hannah's cheeks were faintly pink, and she kept looking at me and then away, fiddling with the strap of her purse.

Finally, Maddie cleared her throat and looked at Hannah, who walked forward and perched on the armrest of one of the theater chairs near mine. "Twinkle," she said, "I'm so sorry."

I dropped my Twizzler. "Um. What?" Maddie pressed another one into my hand, but I barely felt it.

"I've treated you pretty badly," Hannah said, her clear blue eyes focused on mine. "And I'm sorry for that. I want you to know that it wasn't about you at all." She took a breath. "Maddie and I have had a chance to talk, and . . . I realized I was just, um, jealous. And scared. I didn't want to lose Maddie to you, and it brought out this bad side of me." She looked down at her hands in her lap, at the many rings on her fingers. "I know you're really Maddie's best friend. I never had a chance at all, and that bothered me. A lot. I shouldn't have lashed out at you, though. I hope you'll accept my apology."

I glanced at Maddie, who was playing with a Twizzler and looking intently at me. "It's okay," I began to say to the both of them. "Well, maybe it's not okay. But I . . . I understand. I know losing Maddie as my best friend hurt." I smiled a little. "I let that hurt change me, too. But someone recently told me that if you can take steps to correct your mistakes, it makes a world of difference. And I respect that you're doing that, Hannah."

She smiled. "So . . . you forgive me?"

"Yeah. I do. And, you know. We can all still hang out, if you want."

Her smile brightened. "Thanks. I'd like that."

Maddie nodded.

"Anyway, I think you guys have some talking to do, so I'm gonna head out. Thanks for listening, Twinkle."

"Thanks for apologizing," I said, waving as she tip-tapped her way to the exit. Wow. Talk about blurring the line that separates us, Sofia. It was like a scene right out of one of your movies.

I took a breath and turned to Maddie. She took a big bite of her Twizzler and chewed. "I like your bracelet," she said, shaking her wrist. I saw the other half of the heart charm there, and felt a lump in my throat.

"Thank you for getting it for me. It's perfect."

She smiled a little and shrugged. "I got it a long time ago."

I cleared my throat. "I . . . I thought you left. After the movie."

"No. After Hannah and I spoke, I was outside, in Brij's car. We were . . . talking." I raised an eyebrow and her cheeks stained a light pink. "Yeah . . . he's . . . nice." One corner of her mouth lifted up. "Really nice."

"Oh." Grinning, I took a bite of my Twizzler. So my matchmaking *had* paid off, after all. "And Lewis?"

Maddie shook her head and tucked a loose strand of hair behind one ear. "Lewis and I aren't . . . He was talking to his dad for me. You know his dad's on the boards of a few hospitals?" I nodded. "So, there's this big internship over the summer on the Johns Hopkins campus he thinks he can put in a good word for me for. Only three people from the entire country are chosen for it, and every single person who's been chosen has been accepted to Johns Hopkins." She grinned suddenly.

"Oh my God," I said, staring at her. "That's everything you've ever wanted since you were, like, six, Maddie."

"I know." Her eyes shone. "I'm just . . . I have my fingers crossed. I'll hear in two weeks if I got in or not."

"You'll get in. I know you will."

Maddie smiled. "Thank you." She was wearing a side ponytail, big chandelier earrings, and winged eyeliner. She looked like a professional actress at her first-ever premiere. Some people just naturally have that glam gene. I am so not one of them. I could tell my hair was frizzing, and my purple tutu skirt was completely rumpled. My lip gloss was probably all over my teeth. "So. You didn't show the footage," Maddie said quietly.

I let out a breath. "No, I didn't."

She nodded and kept chewing. "Why not?"

Sighing, I took another bite of my Twizzler. "I don't know. Maybe I learned that spreading gossip for popularity is a douche-heady move, even if I thought showing people the truth would be doing them a favor. In the end, I realized that we all make mistakes, but that doesn't mean we deserve to have those mistakes plastered on the wall in an auditorium. Besides, every action I take is a brick in my character. Do I want to be the sort of person who spreads misery and unhappiness with my art?" I looked at her. "You were right. I'm sorry I didn't see it then."

She smiled at me. "You fixed the problem. That's all that matters."

I nodded and looked away. "I guess so." I wondered if Mummy showing up tonight had been her way of trying to fix something too.

"Twinkie."

I looked back at her, my heart squeezing at the sound of her childhood nickname for me.

"You were right too. I *have* been bad at trying to balance my new friendships with my old ones." She grabbed my hand. "I'm so, so sorry. It's been horrible for you, hasn't it?"

"It's . . . yeah." I shrugged. "It was pretty awful at first. But recently, with the movie and everything . . . I had Sahil, and Skid, and Aaron, and Victoria. They helped me feel not so alone. Besides, it wasn't all you. I had a hard time coming to terms with you making new friends too. I . . . It exposed all my insecurities, like a raw nerve, and you saw what happened. I went ballistic."

"Maybe a little." After a pause, she added, "Hey, so, Brij told me about the whole secret admirer thing."

I glanced at her, surprised. "He did? Did it bother you?"

She laughed. "No. I told him it was obvious why he had a crush on you. You're adorable."

I rolled my eyes and smiled. "Right. And anyway, he stopped having a crush on me because he realized *you* were the truly adorable one."

She waved me off, but her cheeks turned a bright pink, and I knew she was happy. "But tell me something. Are you and Sahil . . . ?"

I smiled a little at her expression, but my heart hurt at the truth. "It's a long story, but . . . no. Not anymore."

She tugged on my fingers. "Hey. I've got time."

I watched her, trying to figure out if she was just saying that to be nice. But all I saw was love and friendship. So I filled her in on everything that had happened, with me thinking Brij was Neil, with how Sahil and I had fallen for each other, and how he wanted nothing at all to do with me anymore because of the whole Neil thing. How it was so much bigger than sibling rivalry, like I'd thought at first.

Maddie tapped her fingers against the armrest as I spoke. "You know, that makes sense," she said when I finished. "Remember when you had bronchitis and were too sick to go to that skit a bunch of us put on in second grade?"

"Vaguely . . ."

"It was that talent show thing for our parents one summer. I think we set up the fake stage on Skid's deck. Anyway, Neil and Sahil were a joint act, and they decided to do a bit from a Frog and Toad book. So, they got up there and Neil delivered his lines perfectly. And when it was Sahil's turn, he just . . . shut down."

"What do you mean, shut down? What did he do?"

"Nothing. That's the thing." Maddie sighed. "He just stood there, staring at all the parents and us kids, and his mouth opened and then closed again, like a fish."

I winced, feeling humiliated on Sahil's behalf. "Oh my God."

"Yeah. So then Neil stepped forward and seamlessly took over Sahil's part too. He did these two different voices, one for Frog and the other for Toad—which was supposed to be Sahil—and the parents and the other kids *loved* it. Everyone was clapping and laughing and cheering for Neil. And Sahil just . . . faded off into the background. And then he stepped off the stage and no one noticed, because everyone was looking at Neil. I still remember, though. I remember feeling bad for Sahil, but at the same time . . . that's just how it was, even back then. He wasn't meant for the limelight like Neil was."

"Yeah, but . . . what a horrible way to figure that out." My heart was breaking in my chest at the thought of tiny, eight-year-old Sahil realizing people were so much more adoring of his brother. That he just couldn't compete.

"Yeah. And you know what? Now that I think about it, Neil went off with Lewis and the other guys afterward. But Sahil stayed behind and helped clean up. I think that's the summer he, Skid, and Aaron became good friends."

"Sahil's selfless like that, always doing the right thing." And I'd broken his heart. He thought I was the *one* person who wouldn't put him up against Neil, that I wouldn't compare them, and I'd done just that. "I screwed up bad, Maddie," I said, my voice thick with tears. "He took my hand at the end of the movie and I thought maybe he'd be able to forgive me . . . but no. As soon as I said his name, he walked off. Like he said, it hurts too much for him to even look at me. He hates my guts."

"But he took your hand? When the footage played?"

I nodded. "Yeah."

"And he told you it hurts him to be near you?"

"Um, sort of. That's the gist, yeah."

"Twinkie." Maddie looked at me, one eyebrow raised, like I was missing something obvious.

"What?"

"Sahil is madly in love with you."

"What?" I said again, scoffing. "Please. I mean, maybe he *was* falling for me. *At one time.* But I wrecked everything with the whole Neil thing."

Maddie cocked her head. "It's pretty clear from where I sit that Sahil is just in pain. A lot of pain. But if he truly hated your guts, he wouldn't say it *hurt* to be around you. He wouldn't look at you the way I saw him looking at you all night. He wouldn't take your hand. Twinkie . . . the boy loves you. Like, seriously *loves* you."

I stared at her, too afraid to say anything, just in case she changed her mind. "Are you . . . ? Are you sure?"

"One hundred percent." She sat back and pulled another Twizzler out of her bag. "So. Now the question is, what are *you* going to do?"

I knew what I, Miss Wimpy Wallflower Extraordinaire, *wanted* to do: I wanted to go home and go to bed. To just ignore all of this. But on the other hand, I knew what I *needed* to do. What the brave thing to do was in this situation. And if I didn't do it, if I didn't take this chance, I knew I'd regret it forever.

"Maddie," I said, swallowing my fear. "Could you please give me a ride?"

She stuffed the entire Twizzler in her mouth in three bites and hopped up. "Let's go."

And so here I am, in her car, speeding toward either ecstatic love or devastating heartbreak (again). Gulp. Wish me luck.

Love,

Twinkle

Twenty-Four

<text message 11:12 p.m.>
From: Sahil
To: Skid, Aaron
I broke it off with her

<text message 11:12 p.m.>
From: Skid
To: Sahil, Aaron
DUDE WHY

<text message 11:13 p.m.>
From: Sahil
To: Skid, Aaron
I told you man. I can't go out with her after knowing she
wanted to hook up with Neil

<text message 11:14 p.m.>
From: Aaron

To: Sahil, Skid
But dude she explained that

<text message 11:14 p.m.>
From: Sahil
To: Skid, Aaron
I don't want to talk about it

<text message 11:15 p.m.>
From: Skid
To: Sahil, Aaron
i know what you need bro. I got a giant bag of chili cheese
Fritos and Call of Duty ready to go

<text message 11:16 p.m.>
From: Aaron
To: Sahil, Skid
He doesn't need a video game that encourages toxic
masculinity and brainless murder rn. He needs to chill and
listen to music. I just found this new band Piggy's Death
Rattle. Perfect for how he's feeling

<text message 11:17 p.m.>
From: Sahil
To: Skid, Aaron
I welcome both the toxic masculinity and the . . . piggy's
death rattle. But aren't you guys with Portia and Matthew?

From: Skid
To: Sahil, Aaron
bros first

<text message 11:19 p.m.>
From: Sahil
To: Skid, Aaron
Thanks guys. I think I'm just gonna chill in my room for now but I appreciate it

Sunday, June 28, but just barely
My room

Dear Nora Ephron,

I have never been so scared in my life. Maddie pulled over down the street from the Roys' house. (I was afraid Ajit Uncle would see me and insist on making me peanut butter pancakes or something, thus ruining the element of surprise—the only thing I had going for me at that point, let's be honest.) I looked at her, my cold hands gripped tightly in my lap.

"It's going to be fine," she said, smiling. "What's the worst that could happen?"

"I could end up an empty, emotionless husk sitting alone in my authentically rickety house night after night until the leaking roof eventually caves in on me and finally releases me to sweet, merciful death?"

She stared at me for a long minute. "Okaaaay . . ."

I looked down at my lap and then back at her. "I really want this, Maddie. I really want *him*."

"I know you do," she said, leaning over to hug me. Then, holding me by the shoulders, "And he wants you. You just need to show him that his insecurities about his brother are unjustified. That you're crazy about *him* and not Neil. That all of that Neil fantasizing stuff is in your past."

I nodded. "Right. I can do that. I can, I can, I can."

Maddie patted me on the arm. "Get to it, Juliet. Actually, no, wait. Juliet dies at the end, so . . . maybe don't channel Shakespeare for this one."

"Awesome. Thanks for . . . that."

Maddie laughed and, grinning, I hopped out of her car, waved, took a deep breath, and walked toward the back of the Roys' house.

When I was in the almost completely dark backyard, it occurred to me that if any of the neighbors happened to be looking out their window, I'd look very much like a thief. And that might not end so well for me. Before I lost my nerve, I jumped and grabbed the bottom limb of a giant bur oak tree and began to climb up. It had been years since I'd climbed a tree, but I didn't have a choice right then, did I? This was my last-ditch attempt. My Hail Mary pass. My—

Owwww.

A sharp twig had just scratched the crap out of my bare leg. I could feel the blood beading there. I glared at the twig and then kept climbing until I was right outside Sahil's window. The shades were drawn, so I couldn't see in, but there was enough light emanating from behind the shades that I could tell he wasn't asleep.

I held on to a branch with one hand and shakily reached the other hand toward his window. I knocked twice and then put my hand back on the branch. *Do not look down. Do not look down, Twinkle*, I told myself. Why had I neglected to consider my fear of heights?

No one opened the window.

Oh, great. So either (a) Sahil wasn't home or (b) he'd decided, wisely, not to open his second-story window at midnight to any rando who happened to be knocking.

I looked down. Oh my God. I began to hyperventilate until those little black dots swam in front of my eyes. There was no way I was going to climb back down. No. Way. They'd just have to call the fire department whenever Ajit Uncle happened to come outside and find me in their tree. I could fall and break my *neck*. Oh my God. It felt like someone was pushing me out of the tree. My breath came out faster and faster, and the black circles grew. . . .

"Twinkle?"

I snapped my head around to see Sahil leaning out his window, staring at me, his mouth hanging open. "Hey, are you okay?"

There was a ringing in my ears now. "I, um . . ."

Sahil leaned farther out of his window, and then I felt his strong arms around me. "Hey. Come on. Careful . . ." He gently tugged and guided me until I was able to let go of the branch and clamber into his room. Leading me to his chair, he had me sit. "You don't look so good. Would you like some water?"

I put my head down on my lap. "No, I'm okay. . . . I just got a little light-headed looking down at the ground."

The black spots slowly receded, and the ringing in my ears was gone. And then it hit me: I'd been trying to stage a romantic, daring scene and I'd almost passed out and had to be rescued by the object of my affections. I sat up, my cheeks heating up. "Um . . . wow. This is embarrassing. Not how this was supposed to go."

Sahil's mouth twitched, like he was trying not to smile. "What, um, what were you doing in my tree?"

I twisted my fingers together. My face was probably as purple as my idiotic skirt. "I was trying to be . . . you know. Dashing and gallant?" I forced a weak smile.

"Oh." He frowned, apparently not impressed. "Hey. Your leg's bleeding."

I looked down to see the scrape on my shin. Wincing, I blew on it. "Oh, yeah. I scraped it on that stupid tree."

"Wait here." Before I could protest, Sahil had left the room, closing the door behind him.

I sagged back against the chair and looked around his room. Was this a dumb idea? Why had I come here? He'd already asked for space. . . . Would he think I was being disrespectful of his wishes? He wasn't even fully *looking* at me. Besides, did guys even think things like this were romantic?? "Great, Twinkle. Maybe you should've asked yourself these questions *before* you played Tarzan outside his place."

"Hmm?" Sahil asked, bustling back into the room with a bowl of water and bandages.

"N-nothing. Oh, no, you don't have to do that. I'm fine."

"I insist," he said, kneeling before me and setting all of his first aid things on the floor.

We sat in silence as he washed my cut with soapy water and a washcloth, one hand grabbing the back of my ankle to raise my leg up. I tried not to concentrate on the feeling of his breath, light and warm, on my leg, or his fingers pressing on my bare skin. I'd missed his touch. I'd missed . . . just about everything. He put on some anti-bacterial ointment and then a big Band-Aid over the scrape.

"There," he said, lowering my leg gently. "That should feel better."

"Thank you," I mumbled, feeling suddenly like I might cry. I just wanted him to smile at me. I just wanted some hint of the things we'd shared with each other, that was all. I felt physically cold.

"Sure." He set the water on his desk and then went to sit on his bed so he was facing me. He was dressed in this plain white T-shirt and gray sweats, but he still managed to look heart-stoppingly perfect somehow.

"Hi," he said after a moment of silence, the expression in his eyes inscrutable.

I felt suddenly very shy. "Hi."

"You did really well tonight."

"*We* did." I paused, rallying my ever-dwindling reserves of courage. I could do this. I *had* to do this, or I'd kick myself for the rest of my life. "But . . . that's not what I'm here to talk about."

Sahil's face went still. "It's not?"

I shook my head. Taking a deep breath, I went to sit by him on the bed. "Sahil, I . . . I'm so incredibly sorry I hurt you. That was the *last* thing I wanted to do, I promise." I forced myself to keep looking into his eyes even when I wanted to look away because I felt so guilty for how I'd hurt him. "I know I kept the whole N e-mail thing from you, and that was wrong. The thing was . . . I was so confused. I was falling for *you*, but in my head, I'd built up this whole thing of how *Neil* was the one I should be with. How I wanted to give it a shot." Sahil's face fell, and I hurried to continue. "Mostly because I felt like being with someone like Neil would elevate who I was or something. Like it would show the world—and me—that I was finally visible. Make me special for the first time in my life."

Sahil shook his head. "You *are* special, Twinkle. And you've always been visible. You've shined the brightest in any room. To me, anyway."

I smiled and tears blurred everything. By now I knew this was true. Sahil saw me; he'd *always* seen me. "You're one of my best friends, Sahil. When I was with you, I didn't even *think* about Neil. I saw only you, and you were—you were more than enough. I don't want this to end. I feel like we . . . we belong together, and I can't imagine never holding your hand or laughing with you . . . or—or kissing y—"

Sahil's hands were suddenly around my face, his body pressing into my body as he lowered his mouth to mine, his lips devouring my lips hungrily, his stubble scraping against my skin in the most delicious way. I wrapped my arms around him and pressed myself even closer, gripping him tightly, feeling his body heat completely envelop me.

When we finally pulled apart, panting, he smiled down at me, his hand drawing a strand of hair off my face. "You never have to imagine that again. Okay?"

My arms around his waist tightened. "Really?" I asked. "You forgive me?"

He kissed me gently on the eyelids, on the nose, on the earlobe. "Really. After you explained how it all played out for you, it dawned on me that the hang-up was mine, not yours. I was the one who needed to move past Neil's shadow. I was still feeling inferior to him, and . . ." He paused and shook his head. "That's something I need to work on. But you know what?"

I shook my head.

"The movie helped me so much. Seeing all those people in that auditorium, taking in a movie I'd helped with in some way. . . ." He trailed off, his eyes far away. "I have a lot to offer too. I don't need to compare myself to my brother all the time. I may not be talented in all the ways he's talented, and that's okay. We're two different people."

I stroked his cheek lightly. "Yeah. And I adore the person *you* are."

Sahil grinned and pulled me closer. "Good. You're stuck with me now."

"Perfect. Because I have universes I want to explore, Sahil Roy. And I want you to be my partner through all of it."

He looked deep into my soul with those liquid brown eyes of his. "Twinkle Mehra, it would be my privilege."

And then we kissed again.

June 28, 5:13 a.m.

From: melanie.stone@coloradoarts.org

To: twinkiefilmfan@urmail.com

Dear Ms. Mehra,

We found a clip of the movie your friend Preston "Skid" Matthews uploaded to YouTube. The Colorado Arts Organization was very impressed by the care and substance you poured into the film, and we wondered if you'd be interested in coming on our radio station to talk to our viewers. We think they'd be particularly interested in what your journey as a young female filmmaker has been like so far.

Of course, we will compensate you for your time. Please have your agent or representative contact us at the information below.

Sincerely,

Melanie Stone

New Artists Division

Colorado Arts Organization

719-555-5655

June 28, 6:02 a.m.

From: richard.wells@wkbr.com

To: mehra1@ppcharter.org

Dear Twinkle Mehra,

Your movie caught our attention here at WKBR Colorado Springs. We would like to invite you to our show to talk to our audience about what led you to make this movie, and the message you were trying to convey.

If you're interested, please e-mail us back or call us at your earliest convenience.

Thank you,

Richard Wells

WKBR Production Assistant

719-555-7889

June 28, 8:44 a.m.

From: editorjamie@justsixteenmag.com

To: mehra1@ppcharter.org

Hi, Twinkle!

It was fantastic to see your video from the festival at your school. Here at Just Sixteen magazine, we're always looking for new talent, and yours shines! We would love for you to write an article, 800–1,000 words, about what led to you taking the initiative to direct a movie for the festival. We'd love something personal and fun!

If you're interested, please e-mail us back. Compensation will be about $1/word. We hope to be working with you soon!

Sincerely,

Jamie Auburn

Arts Editor

Just Sixteen magazine

212-555-4321

Twenty-Five

Sunday, June 28
My room

Dear Twinkle Mehra of the future,

Hold on to this moment. You'll want to remember how you feel. You'll want to remember every tiny detail.

Right now you have eighty-eight e-mails in your in-box, all from people congratulating you on a job well done or people wanting to have you on to their shows or magazines or papers—people who want to hear what you have to say. People who think your thoughts are worthwhile. Your YouTube subscriber count is at three hundred and sixteen, and growing. Only a very small percentage are porn bots, and Dadi has promised she did not make any more accounts.

Just when you were still reeling from all the admiring words and gushing praise, unable to believe they were all for *you*, for your *art*, which you've worked at so tirelessly for so long, the doorbell rang. It was Sahil, who grinned gleefully and had you call your parents and Dadi into the living room.

When everyone was assembled, he handed you an e-mail he'd printed out, which is stapled below.

June 28, 1:32 a.m.

From: rachana.deshpande@myfc.org

To: ajit.roy@urmail.com

Dear Dr. Ajit Roy,

Your colleague, Dr. Faizal Ahmed, passed on the video directed by Twinkle Mehra. We here at the Mumbai Young Filmmakers Council are all in agreement that Miss Mehra possesses the unique ability to truly transform her characters on-screen in such a way as to spellbind her audience. Her mastery of camera angles and lighting, too, is rare in an individual of her age.

Due to her supreme skill in the arena of filmmaking, it is our honor to extend an invitation to Miss Mehra. We would love it if she could come to our facility here in Mumbai and give a talk on her experiences being a young Indian-American filmmaker in the States. We feel this would be of great value to the members of our institution, and Miss Mehra might benefit from meeting other young filmmakers as well.

Dr. Ahmed has informed us of her family situation, and therefore, we would like to also invite her parents and grandmother to be part of this event. All travel and accommodation expenses will be covered by us if the Mehra family can get their visas in order.

Thank you very much for bringing Miss Mehra and

her work to our attention.

Sincerely,

Rachana Deshpande, Director of Events

The Mumbai Young Filmmakers Council

Future Twinkle, your hands shook as you finished reading the e-mail. And then you looked up at Sahil, who was beaming at you like he was filled with a thousand stars or maybe like he was the moon.

"What . . . ? You did this?" you asked, your voice husky.

He nodded. "But I couldn't have done it if you hadn't blown everyone away with that movie."

"*Arey, yeh sab kya hai?*" Dadi said, brandishing her rolling pin around at you and Sahil.

You handed her the letter and then said, "What's happening, Dadi, is we're going to Mumbai. We're going to Mumbai, Mummy. You'll get to go home again."

There was utter chaos for a full minute as everyone talked over everyone else, and information was exchanged.

Mumbai.

Airplane fare covered.

Mumbai.

Yes, we're going.

Yes, all of us.

Mummy stepped forward and hugged you, her grip so tight it

left bruises on your shoulders. But you didn't care. Because when she pulled back, her eyes were swimming in tears. "Thank you, *beta*," she whispered, her hands on your cheeks. "Thank you."

She didn't say much else, but she didn't need to. You heard it all anyway.

Papa clapped and hugged you, while Dadi—well, Dadi began prancing around the living room until you were afraid she would break a hip. But she only laughed when you told her that. "I knew it, Twinkle!" she crowed, holding her rolling pin above her head in a victory dance. "I knew it! Chandrashekhar told me there would be travel in our future and that you would be the catalyst!" And then she swept you up and danced with you up and down the living room.

When Sahil had been properly thanked (by being fed an obscene amount of food, of course) and said he had to go back home, you stepped outside with him on the front porch.

It was raining, hard, thunder snarling and rumbling and ripping through the sky.

You looked up at his face, so full of love and joy. "You did this," you said, shaking your head, wondering how you would ever, ever repay him. Spoiler alert: You can't. "You did this because of what I told you once, in your car. The Did You Hear game."

He rubbed the back of his neck. "I did this because I love you," he said simply. "And because you deserve it."

As you watched him run to his car, the rain soaking him to the bone, you wondered how you'd ever gotten so lucky. How one girl could ever deserve so much.

I don't know if you'll ever answer that question. But I do know you'll work your entire life to be worthy of all that kismet has given you.

So remember this day. Remember this moment. And go explore the universes. They're waiting.

From Twinkle,

With Love

Acknowledgments

I cannot believe I'm writing the acknowledgments section for yet another book. The first time it happened—my book in an actual bookstore, available to readers!—felt like a fluke. This feels like . . . *chamatkaar*. Or kismet.

This book could never have happened without my dedicated, hardworking agent, Thao Le, who is always, always on my side. A million thank-yous is never enough.

My editor, Jen Ung, is not just a genius word fairy, she's also secretly a phone therapist. I could not have made it through without all of our very calming (and hilarious and petty) conversations. Thank you!

Thank you to the entire Simon Pulse team for their tireless support of and confidence in me and my work. I couldn't have asked for a better publishing home.

If you fell in love with the three dogs who made an appearance in this book—Oso, Maggie, and Roux—you should definitely thank newsletter subscribers Pinar, Jessica, and Rachael. They won the chance to insert a minor character or prop into the story, and all three chose their dogs. People after my own heart!

To the amazing YA reader community, so many of whom I've loved getting to know on Twitter, Instagram, and at festivals and events—Vanshika, Kav, Mish, Mana, Kevin, Mary, Ash, Jill, Aditi, Maddie, Christy, Nancy, Stacee, Sasha, Nick, and so many others—thank you so incredibly much for your support and love. This book is for you.

Some of my favorite people in the book world are indie booksellers. A big shout-out to the staff at Tattered Cover, Old Firehouse Books, One More Page Books, Hicklebee's, Parnassus, Ripped Bodice, Strand, Changing Hands, Oblong Books, Odyssey Books, Quail Ridge Books, Red Balloon Bookshop, Lemuria Bookstore, The Book Stall, Village Books, Book People, Once Upon a Time, and all the other amazing indies out there. You're really bookish fairy godparents in disguise, and I am so grateful to you.

A special thank-you to Aila, who designed the spectacular artwork for the pre-order campaign. I am in awe of your talent, and cannot wait to see where you go from here!

Thank you, as always, to my ever-patient, ever-loving husband, Tim. If our children inherit the writing gene, please accept my humblest apologies (and bribes in the form of gummy bears).

Last, but far from least, this book is especially for you, Resolute Reader. You, who stumble but refuse to fall. You, who refuse to dim your shine. The world desperately needs your voice, your courage, your heart. Twinkle on.